GLITTER BOMB

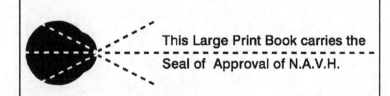

A SCRAPBOOKING MYSTERY

GLITTER BOMB

LAURA CHILDS
WITH TERRIE FARLEY MORAN

KENNEBEC LARGE PRINT

A part of Gale, a Cengage Company

GALE
A Cengage Company

Farmington Hills, Mich • San Francisco • New York • Waterville, Maine
Meriden, Conn • Mason, Ohio • Chicago

GALE
A Cengage Company

LIBRARY OF CONGRESS CIP DATA ON FILE.
CATALOGUING IN PUBLICATION FOR THIS BOOK
IS AVAILABLE FROM THE LIBRARY OF CONGRESS

ISBN-13: 978-1-4328-5489-8 (softcover)

Published in 2019 by arrangement with Berkley, an imprint of Penguin Publishing Group, a division of Random Penguin House, LLC

Printed in Mexico
1 2 3 4 5 6 7 23 22 21 20 19

ACKNOWLEDGMENTS

Heartfelt thanks to Terrie Farley Moran, who contributed her energy, humor, and writing to this book. And to the usual suspects — Sam, Tom, Bob, Jennie, Dan, and all the fine folks at Berkley who do extraordinary design, publicity, copywriting, bookstore sales, and gift sales. An extra special thank-you to all the scrapbook shop owners, bookstore folks, librarians, reviewers, magazine writers, websites, radio stations, bloggers, scrappers, and crafters who have enjoyed the adventures of the Memory Mine gang and who help me keep it all going.

And to you, dear readers, I promise continuing adventures featuring Carmela, Ava, Gabby, Tandy, Baby, Boo, Poobah, Babcock, and the rest of my crazy New Orleans cast. As well as many more surprises!

CHAPTER 1

"Lookit!" Ava cried. "There's your butthead of an ex-husband riding up there on the King Neptune float."

Carmela Bertrand stood on tiptoes and turned ice chip–blue eyes toward the enormous, glittering Mardi Gras float that was steam-rolling toward them, lit up like a Christmas tree against the dark façades of historic French Quarter buildings. And sure enough, there he was, grinning from ear to ear as he and two dozen krewe members tossed strands of golden beads into the hands of a screaming, frenzied crowd.

"Shamus," Carmela said, his name dripping from her lips like honeyed poison. Any follow-up comment was completely drowned out as fifty brass horns blared a collective note and lithe dancers twirling flaming candelabras high-stepped their way down Royal Street. It was Tuesday night, a full week before Fat Tuesday, and most of

New Orleans was already caught in the manic grip of Mardi Gras. The city was cranked up, ready to rock, and Carmela Bertrand and her BFF Ava Gruiex were smack-dab in the center of the maelstrom. Dressed for action in tight jeans, tighter T-shirts, and multiple strands of colored beads looped around their necks, they clutched geaux cups frothing with Abita Beer.

"Wouldn't you know it, Shamus hitched a ride on the very first float in the Pluvius parade," Carmela shouted to Ava above the raucous noise of the crowd. She tipped her head and pushed back loose strands of her shaggy blond bob as she took in the spectacle. A dozen marching bands had already tromped past them, along with clanking knights on horseback, a clown contingent, and a flotilla of exotic convertibles that carried smiling, waving Pluvius krewe royalty wearing gaudy, bedazzled crowns and capes of white faux fur. Enough white faux fur to decorate a Santa's village for decades to come.

"Gotta get some of those gold beads," Ava said as she grabbed Carmela's arm and pulled her closer to the curb, closer to the action. "Throw me somethin', mister!" she shouted out. Ava was tall and stacked, with a saturnine face and masses of dark curly hair. Men either loved Ava or were frightened to death by her. She was vivacious bordering on brash and oozed raw sex appeal.

Carmela would've scoffed at the notion that she was sexy, too. But her appeal was in her quiet, contained, almost mischievous persona. She was smart as a whip, driven to be a successful businesswoman (though her craft shop was small and humble by most standards), and she could hold her own with men. Carmela wasn't averse to tossing back a bourbon and branch while hashing out politics and smoking an occasional cigar.

"What's the parade theme this year?" Ava asked.

"Spirits of the Sea," Carmela said. "The theme's always supposed to be a deep dark secret until they start rolling, but you know Shamus . . . can't keep a secret."

Shamus, Carmela's ex, was an indolent Southern boy who, when he wasn't out drinking or chasing younger women, worked at his family's Crescent City Bank. *Work* being a very loose and haphazard description for what Shamus actually accomplished.

"Spirits," Ava said. "I guess that explains why King Neptune is hoisting that ginormous jug of wine."

The float was built to represent an ancient seagoing galleon, complete with billowing sails, three decks piled one on top of the other, and a carved, barely decent mermaid figure on the prow. Pluvius krewe members hung off every railing and crossbeam, tossing beads and waving at the crowd. Fifty-one weeks of the year, these men were business moguls and staid society leaders. Their walk-in closets probably held a pair of Berluti shoes to match every one of their Zegna, Burberry, and Armani suits. Tonight, however, they were all robed in white satin and wore white, expressionless masks.

On the very top deck of the float, a rotund King Neptune figure was firmly ensconced on his golden throne. His gigantic motorized head lolled back and forth, his mouth gaped open, and his eyes fluttered and blazed yellow. Every few seconds, a surge of golden glitter pumped out of his trident and shot high into the dark night sky.

"What's old King Neptune made out of?" Ava asked Carmela. "You're the crafty one. Does it look like papier-mâché?"

"I think Jekyl repurposed an old King Arthur figure from three years ago," Carmela said. "Reworked the face, added the trident, and draped that necklace of fish and shells around him." Jekyl Hardy was a well-known float builder and one of Carmela's dearest friends.

"Whatever he did, it's impressive," Ava said as the float rolled ever closer to them. "It even looks as if Neptune's tipping that big jug forward to offer us a nice splash of vino." She suddenly pinched Carmela's arm. "Wait, is something wrong? It almost looks like the jug — and the float — is tipping *over*."

Carmela blinked as the enormous float shuddered and then slowly listed to one side. An obnoxious screeching sound, like steel wheels grinding against hot coals, rose up to pierce the air. Startled krewe members grasped for handholds on their now-unsteady perch as the float began to shimmy and shake even more.

Did the float blow a tire? Or worse? Carmela decided it had to be worse because the float was suddenly pogoing up and down, jouncing and bouncing its krewe like mad. Then the entire float began to tremble from stem to stern, its tall mast and billowing sails shaking violently.

"Dear Lord," Ava said as people all around them began to cry out in alarm.

A mounted police officer tried to make his way toward the malfunctioning float, his horse's hooves clattering harshly against pavement. But the horse, sensing imminent danger, snorted and reared up in protest, pawing wildly in the air. The officer leaned forward, tugging on the reins, trying to get his horse under control as the float continued to sway from side to side, each motion more drastic and violent than the last.

"That float's about to crash and burn!" Carmela yelled as the crowd began to back away. She glanced at the front of the float, where Shamus and a few other krewe members were hanging on for dear life. And no wonder. The float seemed to have lost all control over its direction. It was headed right into a throng of onlookers, rolling like some deadly Trojan horse as it listed badly, a ruptured ocean liner about to sink.

"Get back, get back!" a policeman yelped. And the frightened crowd did jump back. Sort of.

But not all the way. Because watching the big float pitch and quake was strangely and dangerously hypnotic. Like watching a train wreck. And how often did you see a big-assed Mardi Gras float completely out of control? Well . . . never.

But the show had just begun.

Just as the prow of the Neptune float hit the curb and bounced hard, an ominous rumble sounded from deep within, some horrible monster was about to an appearance.

"That thing's going to blow," Carr shouted as she tried desperately to pu hypnotized Ava out of harm's way.

The sound built in terrifying waves, r ing across the crowd, almost taking peopl breath away as it rattled shop windows an neon bar signs with all the ferocity of an F tornado. When the explosion finally came, i was enormous. A deafening blast that was enough to call out the dead.

Carmela felt her jaw literally drop as she stared at the very top of the float. King Neptune's head was spinning violently, like a child's top. Then, with a *whomp* that resonated deep within the pit of her stomach, Neptune's head blew off and a shimmering fountain of glitter spewed forth into the velvety dark night sky. It flew up, up, up, until the sky was ablaze with what looked like a million points of light. When the glitter had reached its ultimate trajectory, it began to sift downward, landing softly on the heads of the crowd.

The float let loose a final gut-wrenching belch and shiver, so violent it catapulted krewe members off their perches. Some somersaulted down harmlessly to lower w were tossed off the float — *splat* — on the pavement!

call 911!" Carmela cried out.

en were injured and in desper- help.

called," a man behind her yelled.

ace is on its way."

amus . . . ?" Carmela's eyes searched t for him. Had he been shaken off, he felt her stomach wobble as she at the men lying in the street. *Oh dear, are they hurt badly? Please don't let one be dead,* she prayed.

But wait. Men were slowly picking them-elves up. They were groaning, but they were alive. Thank goodness.

Then a pile of white satin stirred and Carmela recognized Shamus. Without thinking, she rushed over and threw her arms around him.

"Are you all right?" Carmela cried. Ava was right there next to her, helping pull Shamus to his feet.

"Whuh hoppen?" Shamus stammered. He had a wonky look on his face and his eyes didn't quite focus.

"Your float crashed," Ava told him.

"No," Shamus said in a loud pronouncement, as if he'd just been told the earth was flat. Then, "It crashed, really?" His left eye

14

wandered to the far left, hesitated, then seemed to snap back.

"Are you okay?" Carmela asked. "Anything broken?"

"You don't look so good, buddy," Ava said. "Your eyes have gone all googly."

Shamus took one step on wobbly legs and said, "I don't feel so good."

"Well, don't toss your cookies on me," Carmela said. She glanced around, deciding they'd all been incredibly lucky. Yes, the float was ruined, but it could have been so much worse. Nobody in the crowd appeared to be hurt . . .

Then she saw one man, still crumpled on the ground, who wasn't moving a muscle. "Oh no," Carmela said, her voice catching in her throat. "We need to . . ."

Shamus limped over to the man who was still laying on the pavement, looking like a fallen ghost in his bunched-up white robes, his body twisted in a most unnatural way. "Hey," Shamus said, kneeling down, putting a hand on the man's shoulder. "Hey, guy."

"Maybe you shouldn't try to move him," Carmela said. Now she and Ava had gathered around the fallen man as well. "Maybe we should wait for the EMTs to arrive. Let them bring in a backboard or something."

"The least we could do is wipe that gold glitter off the back of his head," Ava said, trying to be helpful.

Carmela bent closer and stared at the man as the screams of multiple sirens rose above the din of the crowd. Something didn't look right to her. And as Shamus gently brushed glitter from the man, his features slowly came into focus.

"That's not the back of his head," Carmela cried out. "The glitter's smeared all over his face! Quick, we have to clear his airway before he's smothered to death!"

16

CHAPTER 2

With gold glitter still covering every square inch of the man's face, Carmela thought he looked as if he were wearing a solid gold mask, like some kind of ancient Persian king.

"Is he even breathing?" she asked Shamus, who was kneeling down, still trying to scrub away glitter.

Ava shook her mane of dark hair, prompting another miniature waterfall of glitter. "Not if he inhaled a nose-full of this stuff," she drawled.

Authoritative voices called out from far back in the crowd of onlookers that had surged forward and created a tight wall of fear and interest. "Clear a path," someone commanded. "Come on, let us through!"

Carmela was flooded with blessed relief. The police and EMTs would surely get this situation under control in a matter of minutes. She glanced around, looking for them. But where were they? Instead, all she saw was another krewe member staggering toward them. Then that man leaned forward and put a hand on Shamus's shoulder.

"This is awful," the man choked out. "How could this happen? Was it terrorists?"

Still woozy and dazed, Shamus glanced up at the new arrival. "Who are you?" he asked.

The man pulled off his white mask. "It's me, Sam . . . Sam Spears," the man stammered. He looked like he was suffering from battle shock.

"Holy Christmas, were you on the float that just exploded?" Carmela asked.

Sam shook his head. "No, the one right behind it. The dolphin float. We crashed, too. Just couldn't put the brakes on in time. Ran right into King Neptune." He was hyperventilating as sweat poured off his forehead in rivulets.

"You don't look so good," Ava told him.

"I . . . yeah," Sam said, his confusion readily apparent. He leaned in, almost losing his balance. "Who is this, do we know? Is he still breathing?"

Shamus continued to ineffectually clear glitter from the man's face and chest. "I don't know!" He glanced around at other krewe members who were staggering around, looking dazed and groggy. "Hey, we could use some help here!"

"I know you get distracted by sparkly things, Shamus," Carmela said. "But please try to focus."

"I am, I am!" Shamus screamed. He was jangled and scared, just this side of hysterical.

Carmela jumped up and looked around frantically. "Where are the EMTs?" Her voice rose sharply. "We need to bag this guy, get him some O's!"

"Do you recognize him?" Ava asked Shamus as he brushed away the final bits of glitter from the man's face. "Oh, it's . . ." Ava shook her head in frustration. "I don't know *who* it is, but he sure has turned a weird shade of blue."

Shamus's well-meaning rescue turned to sudden recognition. "Oh no, it's Hughes Wilder," he said in a quavering voice. "Our krewe captain. I don't think he's breathing!"

"Now that you mention it," Ava said, "he looks a little crispy, too."

Sam was down on the ground now, howling in fear and frustration as the cadre of shrieking sirens drew closer. "Oh man, Pluvius krewe captains don't die like this," he yelped. "Not during Mardi Gras. Not on a street in the French Quarter."

"At least try some chest compressions," Carmela urged. "I mean, are you sure he's *dead*?"

Dead. That was the magic word that rang the bells and spun the cherries. Within a split second they were surrounded by an entire corps of emergency personnel. Cops, EMTs, and a rescue unit from the New Orleans Fire Department were finally there, looking calm and efficient, immediately pitching in to help.

A tall African American man with a shaved head and neatly trimmed beard knelt quickly and, with a practiced hand, slipped a breathing tube down Hughes Wilder's throat. With his other hand he rhythmically squeezed a ventilator bag. His partner, a small dark-haired woman, touched her stethoscope to Wilder's chest. She listened, grimaced, and then dug into her mobile kit and pulled out a large syringe.

"What's that for?" Ava asked.

"Probably gonna give him a shot of epinephrine," Carmela said. "Try to reboot his heart." As she, Ava, Shamus, and Sam watched the EMTs labor over Wilder's body, the police formed a tight cordon and pushed back the anxious crowd, creating a shaky ten-foot perimeter around the victim.

But the appearance of at least a dozen rescue workers was all for naught. Because five minutes later it was all over for Hughes Wilder. He was declared clinically dead.

The crowd, however, was still very much alive. They jostled and shouted out questions, their phone cameras strobing so rapidly it looked like a U2 concert.

"This is a complete mess," Carmela said, glancing around from her spot in the inner circle. People were hanging off second-story wrought-iron balconies trying to get a better view. The crowd was surging forward, threatening to close in again. And the Neptune float, though completely trashed, was still smoking and belching glitter. Two other floats had been run up onto the sidewalk, tilting precariously, as if they'd been put in dry dock.

A chubby police sergeant, whose name tag read *REYES,* grabbed Shamus and Sam for questioning. After jotting notes in a small notebook, he moved over to Carmela and Ava.

"And you, ladies," Reyes said, "were you riding on the float as well?"

Ava shook her head, showering the sergeant with glitter. "No, but we witnessed the explosion." She hooked a thumb in Carmela's direction. "And my friend here was married to one of the victims."

Sergeant Reyes's eyes darted toward the body of Hughes Wilder. Wilder was now partially covered with a sheet and guarded by two uniformed officers. "I'm sorry for your loss, ma'am."

"No, not the dead guy," Ava said. "The deadhead you were just talking to. The sad sack who looks like somebody just stole his lollypop."

"Mr. Meechum?" Sergeant Reyes said, consulting his notes. "Shamus Meechum?"

Ava nodded. "That's the dude. He got blown clean off the float, too."

Reyes focused on Carmela. "I have a few questions, and then you can go over and join your husband."

Carmela gave an exasperated look. "No, no, he's my *ex*-husband. And I really don't care to join him. Not now or at any other time in the history of the universe."

"Been there, done that," Ava said. "Say, when are you guys gonna haul that poor exploded body out of here anyway?"

"As soon as we get the ME and an investigator on scene," Reyes said. He looked to his left, gave a short nod, and said, "Ah, I see one of our detectives is here now."

"Oh no," Carmela said, and for a brief moment she couldn't quite catch her breath.

Striding directly toward her was Detective First Grade Edgar B. Babcock. A glint of strobe light caught his ginger-colored hair, sharply chiseled features, and strong jaw. Then, when he pulled off a pair of aviator sunglasses, his deep blue eyes met Carmela's and caused a frisson of happiness deep within her.

Reyes gave Carmela a sharp glance. "You know him?"

Carmela nodded. "Yes."

"They're involved," Ava said. "Romantically, I mean. Engaged."

"Technically we're *not* engaged," Carmela said. "Since I don't have a ring yet."

Reyes suddenly decided he was needed elsewhere. Or maybe he just needed a break from Ava's wisecracks. "I'll let you ladies take that up with Detective Babcock," he said, pulling away.

"Um . . . are there any other investigators available?" Carmela asked. "That we could give our eyewitness accounts to?" She didn't really want to get pulled into Babcock's investigation. Because . . . well, just because.

But Reyes had already disappeared into a scrum of law enforcement.

Carmela focused on Babcock, who was consulting with a man wearing a leather bomber jacket over a pair of blue scrubs.

She figured he was one of the medical examiners, called here in a hurry. Babcock, on the other hand, was dressed to perfection. The narrow lapels and high-cut sleeves of his gray pinstriped suit did little to hide his broad shoulders and tapered waist. The button-down collar of his crisp white Thom Browne shirt fit snugly around his neck, and he wore a blue silk Hermes tie with a tasteful geometric print that either looked like chains or little hearts.

Carmela sighed. There was a reason they'd been dating hot and heavy for a couple of years. Which usually made her feel like one of the luckiest women in the world.

But this was not one of those times. Because Shamus was suddenly lurching directly toward her, his feet clump-clumping hard against the pavement like the Frankenstein monster. Or maybe he'd just gotten his Jockey shorts in a twist.

"What do you want, Shamus?" Carmela asked as he lunged in front of her.

Shamus's eyes darted from Carmela to Babcock and a dark, angry look crossed his face. He tossed off the silver blanket one of the EMT guys had given him, threw back his shoulders, and adopted what he probably hoped was a power pose. Though he looked more like a cross between a pro wrestler and the scarecrow from *The Wizard of Oz.*

"I was worried about you," Shamus said.

"I'm not the one who was scrabbling around on the ground mewling and puling," Carmela said. "Holy buckets, Shamus, would it have killed you to give your friend chest compressions?"

"Or mouth-to-mouth resuscitation?" Ava asked.

"Do I look like some kind of doctor?" Shamus huffed.

"Maybe Dr. Dolittle," Ava said. "Because you were doin' very little."

"Nothing I could do," Shamus said, hunching his shoulders forward. "I'm just not qualified."

"You could say that again," Carmela muttered.

Ten feet away, Babcock's head periscoped up and zeroed in on their bickering threesome. Then he turned and walked toward them.

"What's the trouble here?" Babcock asked in a purposeful, law enforcement tone of voice.

"No trouble," Shamus said. "We're just trying to get our stories straight."

"What!" Babcock cried. "No. Each of you needs to be interviewed separately for our incident reports. There's to be no corroborating of stories."

Now Sam Spears, Shamus's buddy from the second float, hobbled over to join them. He looked a little more pulled together now, and with his dark hair, warm brown eyes, and olive skin, he was really quite handsome. "What a mess," Sam sighed.

"In more ways than one," Babcock said.

"Huh?" Shamus said.

Carmela decided that Shamus was either playing dumb or he'd seriously had his bell rung. Whatever.

As Babcock and Shamus stared at each other, Sam Spears's phone began to ring. It didn't help matters that his ringtone was Beyoncé's "Single Ladies." The catchy refrain tinkled loudly: *If you liked it, then you should have put a ring on it.*

Ava snorted. Shamus turned red as a cooked lobster and an evil grin swept across Babcock's face. He *was* gonna put a ring on it.

"What will happen to the Neptune float?" Carmela asked in an attempt to head off the two raging bulls.

"We've got the fire inspector and a city engineer looking at it now," Babcock said. He turned and watched as Wilder's body was lifted into a black plastic body bag and then placed on top of a metal gurney. "As far as the victim goes . . ."

"Who was that poor guy again?" Ava asked.

"Krewe captain Hughes Wilder," Babcock said.

"The CEO of Pontchartrain Capital Management," Spears added.

Babcock suddenly looked interested. "Which is . . . what?"

"A local hedge fund," Spears said.

"Hedge fund," Carmela said. "Aren't those things always coming under fire from the Securities and Exchange Commission?"

"Are they?" Ava said. "Wow. So maybe this bombing was, like, some kind of weird warning?"

"Could have been terrorists," Shamus said.

"Doubtful," Babcock said. He frowned at Shamus and said, "Did every one of your krewe members have an assigned seat on the Neptune float?"

Shamus pursed his lips. "Well, yeah. You don't think we just sat willy-nilly wherever we wanted, do you? We're a tightly run unit, for crying out loud. We're *organized.*"

"You're a bunch of screwups," Carmela said.

Carmela could see the wheels turning as

Babcock thought for a moment. Then he glanced over at the wrecked float and held up a warning finger. "Don't anybody leave. I need to see a man about a float."

Carmela and Ava drifted away from Shamus and his friend Sam Spears.

"They're going to have to bring in a dozen tow trucks to move all these bunged-up floats," Ava said.

"It'll be a mess," Carmela agreed as they edged toward the damaged Neptune float. "In fact, it's already a mess." Krewe members wandered everywhere, along with a few sightseers who'd broken through police lines. She could see three TV vans, all with satellite dishes on their roofs. And a wily street vendor had edged his cart into the fray and was selling bags of hot roasted peanuts.

Carmela wondered if the float would be towed to the police impound lot or back to the float den. Then, when she saw the half-dozen crime scene techs crawling all over the Neptune float like a bunch of bark beetles, she knew her question was answered. Something was wrong. Really wrong.

"Looks like they're going over that float with a fine-tooth comb," Carmela said to Ava.

"I wonder why."

"Maybe because there was some type of explosive device planted there?"

Ava's mouth dropped open. "I thought when the float blew up it was just a bad accident. That a fan belt slipped or some motor went cattywampus."

"I'm guessing it might be more sinister than that."

"Yeah?"

The closer they snuck to the Neptune float, the better they could hear what was going on. One man in a white Tyvek suit stood in the street right next to the float. He wore a headset and was clearly communicating with the techs that had clambered aboard the float.

"Anything yet?" Tyvek Suit asked.

There was a burst of static, and then a tinny disembodied voice came back to him. "Fragments."

"Can you ascertain what type of material?"

More static. Then, "Could have been a pipe. Maybe packed full of plastic explosives. We'll gather up what we can. It looks like the charge was fairly rudimentary."

"But enough to get the job done," Tyvek Suit said. "Along with creating lots of noise and gluts of smoke."

"Probably remotely detonated," came the staticky voice. "And meant to explode upward. I'm guessing your vic was directly in front of or right above the trajectory. Postmortem should tell you for sure."

"Thanks, Al, that's a help. I got a detective who's waiting to hear all this."

More static, and then the guy up on the float said, "We got some singed plastic here. Like, maybe . . . well, it could be a credit card that was dropped and got wedged in."

"Nice going," Tyvek Suit responded. "Give my guys a few more minutes, see what else we come up with."

Carmela grabbed Ava and pulled her away from the float, back toward the circle of ambulances and police cruisers. "Did you hear that?" she asked. "It sounds to me like the explosion was deliberate."

"And that means what exactly?" Ava asked, scratching her head, still trying to get glitter out of her hair.

"If an explosion was *deliberate,* it points to a homicide."

"You think somebody wanted to kill that guy, Wilder?"

"That would be my first guess," Carmela said.

"Holy guacamole, Carmela. That's terrible."

"Tell me about it."

They picked up the pace now, moving away from the float.

Ava glanced around. "I guess we better get out of here before Babcock accuses us of snooping."

Carmela threw Ava a mischievous look. "Good heavens, we'd never do that!"

CHAPTER 3

Memory Mine, Carmela's cozy little scrap-booking and graphic design studio in the French Quarter, was generally an oasis of calm. Floor-to-ceiling bins held all manner of kraft papers, albums, rubber stamps, paints, ephemera, and ribbons. Samples of invitations, brochures, and posters were pinned to a corkboard. The walls of the shop were a soft, buff-colored brick, the wooden floors creaked companionably, and there was a lovely bay window in front where crafts, scrapbook albums, and design pieces were displayed.

Originally a scrapbook shop, Memory Mine had expanded into crafts and design as customers got more and more creative, and local businesses began to ask for design help.

But this Wednesday morning, as Carmela tried to explain the bizarre details of last night's explosion, her assistant, Gabby

Mercer-Morris, wasn't feeling any of their normal calm.

"Wait a minute." Gabby, a proper Southern girl, tucked strands of blondish-brown hair behind an ear that sparkled with a tasteful diamond stud, and said in a slightly quavering voice, "It sounds like you were right there."

"Smack dab in the middle of it," Carmela admitted. *Smack dab in the middle of what was probably murder.*

"And you say Shamus was there, too?"

"He was one of the first guys to jump off the float. To try to, you know . . . see how badly Hughes Wilder was injured."

Gabby pulled the sweater of her peach-colored twin set closer around her as if to insulate herself from the terrible news.

"Except Wilder was too blown up, too far gone to save," Carmela said.

Now Gabby's face crumpled and her shoulders hunched forward in an outright cringe.

Poor dear, Carmela thought. Gabby was smart, adorable, and always bubbling with creativity. But she possessed a very sensitive nature. Sick puppies, sad chick flicks, dead ladybugs, and bloody blue murder all upset her with equal ferocity.

Standing behind the front counter,

Gabby's hands fluttered and fussed over a display of colorful beads, buttons, and charms. "So . . . do the police know what kind of an explosion it was?" she asked. "Was it a faulty engine in the float or something in the electrical system?" She paused. "Wait a minute, did Babcock show up?"

"He turned up right on cue, like the proverbial bad penny. So did the crime scene techs. Those guys sniffed around and decided the whole disaster might have been triggered by some sort of plastic explosive."

"You mean like terrorists use?" Gabby asked.

"Well, I wouldn't go *that* far." Carmela was suddenly aware that she was scaring poor Gabby to death.

"But Hughes Wilder *died.* One of the announcers on the radio this morning speculated that it might have been murder."

"I suppose that's possible." Carmela decided she'd better ease off and downplay last night's crime. After all, they had a busy day coming up — a busy week, really — and it did no good to have Gabby living in a state of hyped-up anxiety.

"You can't get involved in this," Gabby said.

"Absolutely not," Carmela said. "Farthest

thing from my mind."

Suddenly, the front door flew open with a calamitous *whack* and Shamus stumbled in. Dark circles ringed his eyes as if he were a demented raccoon and his hair stuck out like he'd plugged his finger into a light socket. He clutched a cup of Café du Monde coffee in his hand.

"Carmela," Shamus gasped as coffee sloshed everywhere.

"Oh dear." Gabby backed up a step. Then, glancing at Carmela, said, "Why do I get the feeling you're already involved?"

Carmela held up a hand to hopefully calm Gabby's nerves and indicate to Shamus that he should back off. "Nobody's getting involved here."

Shamus took a step closer to Carmela. "Can we talk? We really need to talk." With each rapid-fire word, his head jiggled like a bobblehead doll you'd get as a freebie at the baseball park. Carmela realized that Shamus was trying to point to her office. He wanted to talk in private.

"We can talk," Carmela told Shamus. "But that's all we're going to do." She led him into her tiny office at the back of the shop and flopped down in her purple leather swivel chair. "Sit," she said, shoving a director's chair toward him with her foot.

Shamus sat down like an obedient golden retriever.

"What's the problem?" Carmela asked. "Did Wilder's death put a dent in your partying?" Shamus was a notorious party animal and generally ditched work for an entire week during Mardi Gras. There were just too many parades, parties, masked balls, and other drinking opportunities to take advantage of.

Shamus shook his head. "This is serious, Carmela. I need your help."

Carmela put a slightly sardonic smile on her face. Here was a man who had unceremoniously dumped her — who had slipped into his boogie shoes just a few months after their heartfelt "I do's" and a custom six-layer buttercream cake. And now he was asking her for help? Hah. Double hah.

"I'm serious," Shamus said. "You're, like, the only smart person I know." He took a quick gulp of coffee. "The only person with a grain of intelligence."

"That doesn't surprise me. Though it doesn't say much about your colleagues at the bank."

Shamus looked wounded. "Whatever."

"Shamus, why are you here? What exactly are you babbling about?"

"Hughes Wilder was murdered."

"Got it," Carmela said. "I was there, remember? I saw his body catapult into space and then land — splat — like a bug on the pavement. It wasn't pretty, but it was a sight to behold. Especially with all that glitter. He looked like Tinker Bell making a crash landing. And you, well, I guess if you had a role to play, you'd be Peter Pan, the boy who never grew up. The boy who never took *anything* seriously."

Shamus glowered. "Now you're making fun of me. You're poking at me."

"I wouldn't do that," Carmela said in a slightly gleeful tone. *Of course I would. Any chance I get.*

"You were much nicer to me last night, when you thought I was injured."

"Well, you're clearly not. So what is it you want?"

"I want you to please hear me out."

"Okeydokey." Carmela glanced at her watch. "You've got exactly five minutes to make whatever lame pitch you came here to make. After that you're getting the bum's rush. This shop's going to be wonderfully, horrifically busy today and I have a lot of work to do. A class to prepare for."

Shamus leaned forward and pulled his face into an earnest expression. "I want you to figure out who killed Hughes Wilder."

"No."

"Why not?"

"Just no," Carmela said. "The answer is no."

"Carmela, you're good at this stuff. In fact, you're absolutely brilliant."

"Flattery will get you nowhere."

"Come on, you witnessed the entire explosion and its messy aftermath last night. Plus, you have an *in* with law enforcement." Shamus's voice had gone from pleading to an annoying wheedle.

"Uh-uh, no way." Carmela shook her head. "Babcock would kill me if I got involved."

"You're already involved," Shamus said. Then he gazed at her, eyes narrowed, as if he had a trump card stuck up his sleeve, ready to play. He let a few beats go by, then slapped that trump card down. "The problem is, *I'm* one of the suspects."

"I don't believe it," Carmela said, trying to hide her surprise. "You were trying to *help* Hughes Wilder last night. There were a gazillion witnesses who saw you."

"Then why did Babcock grill me for two hours? A hard two hours."

Carmela lifted an eyebrow. "He questioned you for two hours?"

Shamus blew out a glut of air. "Babcock

can be a real bully, you know that? And he's nasty, he enjoys pushing people around."

"He's a cop," Carmela said. "A detective first grade. That's his professional persona, it's not him."

Shamus shook his head and this time he looked genuinely nervous. "Babcock made no bones about the fact that I was one of his prime suspects."

"That's ridiculous." Carmela wasn't buying it. "Why would you be a suspect? What makes you so special? You're just a dopey banker."

Shamus held up an index finger. "That's exactly why I'm a suspect."

"You're talking in riddles, Shamus. And your five minutes are just about done. Now can we please wrap up this conversation?"

"Only if you agree to help."

"Shamus." Carmela was getting both frustrated and steamed. "*Why* would you need my help? *Why* would Babcock consider you a suspect? Give me one solid reason."

"Because I made a bad investment."

"Excuse me?"

"And because Hughes Wilder, aka the dead guy, is the CEO of Pontchartrain Capital Management."

"So I've heard," Carmela said slowly. She'd seen several mentions of Pontchartrain Capital Management in the business section of the *Times-Picayune,* but had never paid much attention.

"They're a hedge fund," Shamus said.

"So what?"

"I put money into their hedge fund and it turned out to be a bad investment."

Shamus had her attention now.

"How bad?" Carmela asked.

Shamus sucked in his breath and screwed his otherwise handsome face into a grimace of pain. "Really bad."

"Give me a number."

"Sixteen million."

Carmela was gobsmacked by the number. The sum was so stratospheric that it was hard to contemplate. *Is Shamus that foolish and gullible?* she asked herself. The answer came ricocheting right back at her. *Yeah, he is.*

"Shamus, are we talking about your personal money or the bank's money?" Carmela didn't think Shamus's bank account was quite that fat. Or was it? Had she been royally screwed in their divorce settlement?

"Of course it was the bank's money," Shamus said. He shook his head as if a hive of angry bees were buzzing around him. "Do you really think I'd risk my *own* money in a hedge fund? Those things are like freaking Las Vegas on steroids."

So why did you risk the bank's money? Carmela wanted to ask. But instead she said, "Good gravy, Shamus. Does Glory know about this? Does she know that you lost — possibly squandered — that much of the bank's money?" Glory Meechum was Shamus's older sister. She was mean as cat pee, parsimonious as hell, and served as chairman on the bank's board of directors. In other words, Glory controlled the purse strings at Crescent City Bank. It was also family owned. Which meant she had Shamus by the short hairs.

Shamus reared back in alarm. "Of course Glory doesn't know."

"When she finds out you lost the bank's money she's going to skin you alive."

"Don't I know it." Shamus lifted a hand and shook a warning finger at Carmela. "And don't you dare tell her."

"I try to avoid any and all communication with Glory," Carmela said. On their wedding day, once upon a time in a galaxy far, far away, Glory had referred to Carmela as *a hot mess.* From that point on, any and all dealings between the two of them had been as frosty as a box of frozen fish sticks.

"So as you can see," Shamus said. "I'm in big trouble. On two fronts."

"Can you somehow get the money back?" Carmela asked.

"There's that nasty little clause, printed in two-point mouse-type at the bottom of every contract and prospectus, and it says, 'Past performance is not an indication of future earnings.'"

"So Babcock thinks you might have killed Wilder in retaliation for your losses," Carmela said. She could see that it was a predicament of sorts.

"Bingo. Give that lady a plush pink panda." Shamus reached inside his jacket pocket and pulled out a sheet of paper. "I made a list of all the guys who were riding in the Pluvius parade last night. I thought it might help you figure things out. Do you know that the *Times-Picayune* even cooked up a name for the killer? The Neptune Bomber!"

"Wait a minute. Are you telling me that other guys in the Pluvius krewe also lost money with this hedge fund? That they might've had a beef with Hughes Wilder, too?"

"Uh . . . yeah." Shamus shrugged. "That's the money angle so far, along with a couple of other things."

"What are the 'couple of other things'?" Carmela asked.

42

"Maybe . . . Danny Labat. You know, he's the guy who owns that fancy car dealership?" Now Shamus let loose a small chuckle. "The thing about old Danny is that he was sweet on Hughes Wilder's wife."

Carmela's antenna perked right up again. "How sweet?"

"Danny and Maribel . . . did you know she used to be Miss Baton Rouge?" Shamus bobbed his head and gave a foolish grin as if he'd suddenly drifted off into a dreamy reverie. "Yeah, Maribel looked mighty fine in her sparkly crown and silver hot pants."

Carmela knew there had to be something going on here. More than just a hint of a relationship. She snapped her fingers in front of Shamus's face to get his attention. "Keep talking. What about Danny Labat and Maribel Wilder? Spit it out."

"Labat's been having an affair with Maribel for a good six months."

"Holy cats, Shamus, that's as good a reason as any for Danny Labat to detonate some kind of bomb and kill Wilder."

"Kind of like Babcock would like to do to me?" Shamus asked.

"He doesn't want to kill you," Carmela said.

"Then what does he want?"

"If somebody stuffed your body in a

43

gunnysack, roped it to a cinder block, and dropped it in the Barataria bayou, I think that'd be just fine with him."

"Be serious," Shamus said.

"I am." Carmela held up a hand. "Wait a minute. Was Danny Labat riding on the float last night? When it exploded?"

"Imploded."

"Whatever."

"Yeah, he was. But I don't think . . ."

"That's the problem with you, Shamus, you never think. You get tangled up in all sorts of wacky messes and then you roll your sad, brown, puppy dog eyes and hope someone will rush in to save your fat butt."

"My butt's not fat." Shamus looked wounded. "I'm still at my fighting weight of one-eighty. Same as when I played football at Tulane."

"Never mind that you were third string and sat on the bench like a lump. That's another story."

"Whatever," Shamus said. "But the big question is . . . Will you help me?"

Carmela thought for a minute. She'd be insane to let herself get pulled into a sticky situation like this. It had *La Brea Tar Pits* written all over it. After all, Shamus was her ex, and Babcock was her future. Well, her sort-of future, because they weren't exactly, formally, traditionally engaged yet. But they'd made promises to each other. And *talked* about an engagement ring.

"I'll have to think about it," Carmela said.

"Think about helping me or think about who the killer is?"

"Both," Carmela said in an almost-whisper.

"That's my girl," Shamus said, turning on his megawatt, pick-up-a-babe-in-a-bar smile.

"Shut up, Shamus. Get out of here."

Carmela sat at her desk, thinking, staring at the walls where she'd tacked up dozens of design ideas for scrapbook pages and related crafts. She had to figure out how to work this shadow investigation of hers — if that's what she was going to do. If that's what she wanted to do. She knew she could probably cajole *some* information out of Babcock. Such as, could the bomb have been deto-nated by someone in the crowd? And who exactly were his other key suspects? But she couldn't be too obvious, too blatant. She'd have to ply Babcock with shrimp jambalaya and maybe even an étouffée. Then, when he was sated with rich food and wine, she'd casually drop a few more questions.

Yes, it could be done. Carefully, gingerly,

oh so discreetly.

"Carmela?" Gabby was standing in her doorway. "Mmn?"

Carmela swiveled in her chair to face Gabby.

"The workmen just called about the chicken wire. They're planning to be here after lunch."

"Excellent." Every year, Carmela reinforced her front windows with plywood and chicken wire so they wouldn't break. The crush of crowds, their wild enthusiasm and carelessly flung beer bottles, claimed several French Quarter storefront windows every Mardi Gras season.

"Well," Gabby asked. "Are you going to help Shamus?"

"I'm still thinking."

"I see that look on your face," Gabby said. "That mischievous, foxy look. You're going to help him, aren't you?"

"It's an interesting, um, situation."

"Don't try to defang last night's explosion by downgrading it to a situation. This is a case of murder, pure and simple. And I get the distinct feeling that you're about to dive in headfirst."

"I'll be careful. I'm always careful."

"That's what you always say," Gabby said. "For me, I'm going to stop by that new

Saints and Sinners shop on my lunch hour and buy myself a couple of extra holy medals."

"You think they'll help?"

"Couldn't hurt."

"Then maybe get one for me, too. Just in case."

There was a loud *da-ding* as the front door opened. Then Gabby leaned backward to take a look and said, "Hang on to your hat, we've got customers. Six of 'em."

"Be out in a jiffy," Carmela said.

But first she grabbed her phone and called her friend Jekyl Hardy, float designer extraordinaire. Rail-thin and sleek, he dressed in dapper black velvet jackets and silk slacks just like the vampire Lestat in Anne Rice's novels. Jekyl was also a denizen of the French Quarter and famously regarded for his over-the-top champagne parties (which he referred to as "twirls") and his prodigious nose for ferreting out the latest, juiciest gossip.

Carmela knew that if there were any wild rumors floating around in the troposphere, Jekyl would already be privy to them.

"Jekyl," Carmela said, when he answered. "Do you have time for lunch today?"

"This is about last night," Jekyl said. It was a statement, not a question. "The explosion during the parade and the so-called Neptune Bomber."

"That's exactly right," Carmela said. "Which is why I need to talk to somebody on the inside."

"Then I imagine that would be me," Jekyl said. Jekyl designed and supervised the building of floats for the Pluvius, Nepthys, and Rex krewes, the three top krewes in New Orleans. He knew all the dirt, gossip, scandals, and salacious goop on everyone in the French Quarter, the Garden District, Faubourg Marigny, and the CBD. "Shall we say twelve o'clock sharp at Brennan's?"

"Works for me."

"Tootles, girlfriend."

CHAPTER 4

Tomato cream sauce. That was the color of paint used on Brennan's iconic stucco façade. Located on Royal Street, mere blocks from last night's parade fiasco, Brennan's Restaurant was a French Quarter fixture. Eight elegant dining rooms, perfect for any type of assignation, along with out-of-this-world Creole cuisine and an outdoor veranda complete with turtle pond. What wasn't to love?

The hostess led Carmela into the Havana Room, where Jekyl was casually sprawled at a table, sipping a Sazerac cocktail and practically holding court, like some kind of New Orleans–style Dorothy Parker.

"Jekyl," Carmela said.

Made even more slim by his severely tailored black suit, Jekyl popped up from his chair and immediately swept Carmela into an embrace. Then, in the manner of a French count executing a *faire la bise,* he planted a gentle air-kiss on each of her cheeks. "Sit down," Jekyl instructed, pulling out a chair. "Have a drink. Shall we order a bottle of wine to go with lunch? I'm particularly fond of the Louis Michel Montmains Chablis Premier Cru."

Carmela shook her head as he sat down beside her. "No thanks. Just a Diet Coke. I need to keep a clear head right now."

Jekyl leaned forward and focused on her intently. "Let me guess." His dark eyes bored into her. "Your ex came crawling to you asking for help."

"How did you know?"

Jekyl sighed and steepled his fingers together. "Maybe because Shamus is a needy, callous jerk who's probably under investigation?"

"He's also a two-timing rat," Carmela said.

"Of course he is. But you still love him."

"Oh no, I'd never go that far."

Jekyl peered at her. "But you still having feelings for him?"

"Yes, but probably not the good kind."

"Then why do you suddenly want to lend a hand?"

Carmela glanced around the Havana Room and sighed. Lovely pineapple-patterned wallpaper and pineapple chandeliers met her eyes, but no succinct answers materialized.

"I don't know," she said finally. "Maybe because Shamus shares custody with Boo and Poobah?" Boo and Poobah were Carmela's dogs, Boo being a cuddly Shar-Pei and Poobah a black-and-white mongrel that Shamus had rescued from the streets. "Or maybe because . . . Shamus needs taking care of?" She hadn't meant to make it a question.

"So does my pet goldfish," Jekyl said. "But you don't see me busting my hump to dig up fresh grub worms for him."

"When did you hear about the float exploding?" Carmela asked.

"About two minutes after it happened," Jekyl said. "I was still at the Pluvius float den over in the CBD. You have no idea how difficult it is to get all those floats lined up and ready to roll. To say nothing of loading up drunken krewe members. Like herding cats. And then, of course, there's the technical aspect — all those lights, the giant figures, the little servomotors that control motion for the animated characters . . ."

"The bomb stuck on board."

"I am not taking responsibility for *that*," Jekyl snapped. "Is it *my* fault some looney tune wanted to waste some rich fool? No, of

51

course it isn't."

"You sound like you've already spoken with the police."

"They came sniffing around immediately," Jekyl said. "That cute, muscle beach–type detective who works with your boyfriend . . . I believe his name is Bobby something."

"Bobby Gallant."

Jekyl aimed a finger at her. "That's the one. Gallant asked me a ton of questions. Some of them about Shamus, some about other members of the krewe."

"Really," Carmela said. So being a suspect wasn't just some wacky idea in Shamus's head. This was for real.

"They asked me about the explosion, too," Jekyl continued. "What I thought might have caused it. Which I said was completely removed from my wheelhouse. I mean, what would I know about plastic and detonators when my role is purely float concept and design!"

"Would you care to place your order?" a voice at Jekyl's elbow suddenly asked. The server had snuck up behind them.

"Our order," Jekyl snapped, a little too loudly. Then, more smoothly, "Why yes, we would." He pulled his brows into sharp arcs. "Carmela dear?"

Carmela ended up ordering the Creole-spiced shrimp salad and a Diet Coke, while Jekyl did what Carmela always thought of as "The Hollywood Order." Which was Jekyl basically saying, "Here's what I feel like — a pecan-crusted redfish, but broiled, not panfried like you usually do. And can you add a side of dirty rice?"

Jekyl also opted to stick with his Sazerac.

"How well did you know Hughes Wilder?" Carmela asked. "Our illustrious victim."

" 'Victim,' " Jekyl said. "Don't care for that word."

"But that's what he was."

"Wilder and I weren't exactly bosom buddies," Jekyl replied.

"You didn't get on with him?"

Jekyl lifted a thin shoulder in a dismissive gesture. "Hughes Wilder was a complete stiff."

"In what way?"

"Oh . . . Wilder was one of those self-important executives who acts friendly enough, but you can tell it's just for show, because what he's really doing is grubbing around for business."

"You're saying Wilder was superficial," Carmela said.

"He was as shallow as one of my aunt Espath's bone china saucers. The other thing that frosted my Wheaties . . . Wilder considered himself to be 'highly creative.' " Jekyl motioned a set of quotation marks with his hands. "He was always trying to micromanage float design. If I sketched a dolphin head, Wilder would propose a starfish." Jekyl pursed his mouth. "Which would have been totally absurd."

Carmela didn't see how a dolphin or starfish would matter on a big, gaudy Mardi Gras float with a bulbous King Neptune head, but she nodded in agreement to appease Jekyl. After all, this was a fishing trip, no pun intended.

"What else?" Carmela asked. "What about his business?"

"You mean the fact that he headed up Pontchartrain Capital Management?" Jekyl asked. "Not that there was a whole lot to head up."

Carmela reached over and put a hand on Jekyl's arm. "What exactly do you mean by that?"

Jekyl glanced around, as if he were about to impart a deep, dark secret, and then said, "Hughes Wilder talked a big game with his hoity-toity hedge fund. Blah, blah, start-up this, blah, blah, tech company that. But, from what I heard through the grapevine, which is probably the most reliable form of communication next to Twitter, he probably wasn't the savviest financial guy in town."

Carmela was fascinated. This certainly jibed with what Shamus had told her about Wilder's hedge fund losing his sixteen million dollars. But still . . . Wilder did have a very public reputation for being a big-time mover and shaker. For being a very wealthy man.

"The impression I always got was that Wilder was fantastically rich," Carmela said. "His picture was always in the paper for something, a ribbon cutting or a fancy charity event." Carmela recalled that Wilder had even donated money to help expand the New Orleans Zoo. Something about a new duck pond?

Jekyl's eyes blazed. This was the kind of gossip he *lived* for. "Actually," he said, "Wilder's wife, Maribel, is the one who comes from money. Big money, as in oil and gas exploration over near Lake Charles. They hold a lot of oil leases and I believe they actually had some gushers. Black gold." Jekyl paused. "But all the oil wells in the state aren't going to help keep Wilder's hedge fund afloat."

"What do you mean?"

Now Jekyl got even more confidential. "I can tell you for a fact that Pontchartrain Capital Management was not a whopping success story. Several . . . and I do mean several . . . members of the Pluvius krewe, as well as investors in some of the other krewes, lost a devastating amount of money."

" 'Devastating'?" Carmela said. Here, indeed, was motive.

Jekyl nodded. "I know there were lawsuits being drawn up. And a good deal of angry mumbling about . . . well, let's just call it drastic measures."

"Are you telling me that some of the guys who sustained financial losses wanted Wilder *dead*?" Carmela asked, almost in a whisper.

"Probably they wanted to turn him upside down and slit his throat. Or, as you witnessed last night, blow him to bits." Jekyl looked almost happy. "Which someone finally did."

"A lot of people talk tough, but never do anything," Carmela said. She hated to think that someone in Shamus's krewe was a stone-cold killer. "They never act on their impulses."

"Someone surely did last night."

Carmela paused, holding her glass in midair. "But who?"

"That, my cute little button, is for *you* to figure out. You and your hunky detective-cum-fiancé."

"Babcock's not going to let me anywhere near his investigation."

"Then you'll just have to worm your way in. Or trick him."

Carmela knew that Babcock was not easily tricked. She took a sip of Diet Coke and thought for a minute. "What do you know about Maribel Wilder and Danny Labat?"

"Ah, I see you've been hearkening to the local gossip."

"Shamus mentioned them. Is there any truth to the rumor?"

"I was just getting around to that decadent duo," Jekyl said as their food arrived.

The waiter placed their entrées in front of them, poured out more ice water, and then quietly retreated.

"Mmn, absolutely delicious," Jekyl said, savoring his first bite of his redfish. "Tender, plump, juicy . . ."

"I'm dying of curiosity here," Carmela said. "Tell me about Maribel and Danny Labat."

"Let me just say, as Wilder's fortunes dwindled, Maribel's amorous needs were being kindled."

"So she and Labat really were having a full-blown affair?"

"Their canoodling has been well-documented all over town. They were even seen carrying on in the Pluvius float den — which I find nearly sacrilegious."

"Did you hear any rumblings of a divorce?" Carmela asked.

"To my knowledge, she never asked for one."

"I don't think women ask for divorces anymore," Carmela said. "Now they just file papers."

Jekyl smiled. "Touché."

"Maribel's gotta be a suspect," Carmela said. "The police have to view her as a prime suspect."

"I would think so. As well as her paramour, Danny Labat."

"Another car dealer," Carmela mused. Gabby's husband, Stuart, was a car dealer as well. The self-proclaimed Toyota King of New Orleans.

"But Labat deals in high-end sports cars," Jekyl said. "You want to get your Ferrari fine-tuned or have your Aston Martin greased . . ." Jekyl gave a wicked grin. "Labat's your man."

Jekyl didn't have a lot more to offer besides a few snarky innuendos, so Carmela finished her lunch, tossed down her share of the bill, and hurried back to Memory Mine. As she swung open the front door, her mind toggling between Wilder's murder and how to create some collaged tea tins, Gabby's face poked out from behind a rack of gauze ribbon.

"Babcock's here," Gabby said by way of greeting.

That stopped Carmela dead in her tracks. "He's here now?" She looked around but didn't see him.

"Camped out in your office."

Holy crap! "What does he want?"

"Wipe that guilty look off your face and I'll tell you," Gabby said.

Carmela drew a deep breath and willed herself to remain calm. To hopefully look *uninvolved.*

"Babcock just wanted to have a quick lunch with you because he adores you, Carmela. You're his sweet little kumquat. And I happen to know that, to prove it, he brought you a po-boy from Pirate's Alley Deli."

"Okay," Carmela muttered. "I . . . okay."

She rushed into her office and slid to a stop on the slippery floorboards.

"Edgar," Carmela said, hoping she didn't look as flustered as she felt. "Long time no see."

CHAPTER 5

Babcock was sitting at her desk, handsome as always, working on the last of his sandwich. It looked like a meatball po-boy. Yes, it was a meatball po-boy. Carmela could see drips of marinara sauce staining the cover of her sketch pad.

"Hey, you're back." Babcock grinned at her between mouthfuls. "I brought you a sandwich." He shoved a paper-wrapped sandwich across the desk. Carmela saw that it was already leaking grease. Must've been something yummy and fried.

"Thank you," Carmela said. Babcock hadn't seemed to register her surprise. Or was it apprehension that was making her jittery and giving her jimmy legs?

"It's your favorite," Babcock continued. "A fried oyster po-boy. But then, when I found out you weren't around, I decided to hang out here and eat mine." He swallowed hard. "Where the heck did you run off to, cutie?"

Carmela crossed her fingers as a way of neutralizing the little white lie she was about to tell. "Just running errands. Nothing important." If Carmela told Babcock that she ate lunch with Jekyl, he'd immediately suspect that she'd been snooping. And he'd be right.

"I had a whopping twenty minutes to spare so I figured we could get cozy and have lunch together." Babcock was wiping his hands on a paper napkin, still smiling. "I'm sorry we weren't able to connect."

"Me, too. But why don't you let me make up for it? Maybe you could drop by my place for dinner tonight?" *So I can grill you on a few choice questions.* "I could whip up a shrimp jambalaya. Make it hot and spicy, just the way you like it."

"Mmn, you mean hot and spicy like you." Babcock flashed another grin at her, looked as if he was about to say yes, and then hesitated. "But I'm afraid I'll have to take a pass. Since this bombing case was dumped in my lap I'm juggling a ton of —"

"Wait a minute," Carmela said. "You're handling the bombing? You're lead detective on it now?"

Babcock's brows pinched together. "Yeah.

Remember I was there last night?"

"Lots of first responders were there. I figured pretty much everyone got the call-out."

But Babcock wasn't really listening. He was glancing at his watch, frowning, running a quick calculation. "Okay . . . now I really do have to scram. I'm due in a meeting with the chief in less than ten minutes."

Carmela pounced on him. "Have you learned anything more about the explosive?"

"Not really. The techs are still working on the fragments that were found. They think it was probably a secondary explosive." He balled up the paper from his sandwich and tossed it at the wastepaper basket. Managed a decent rim shot.

"What does that mean? Secondary?" Carmela asked.

"That it was probably some sort of plastic explosive, something that can be molded and pressed into place, and then set off with a detonator by someone on the float or maybe even in the crowd." Babcock stood up, brushed a bit of shredded lettuce off his Joseph Abboud shirt, and said, "Why do you want to know?"

"Because it's interesting, that's all."

Babcock wasn't fooled. "Oh no you don't," he said, giving her a stern, knowing look. "No investigating for you. Not on this case, not on *my* case. That's an order, Carmela."

Gulp. Haven't I already dipped a toe in the water?

"Whoever set off this bomb wasn't fooling around," Babcock warned. "This guy was a real pro, he knew exactly what he was doing. And if he did it once, he could do it again. Which scares me to death, since we've got an entire *week* of Mardi Gras stretching ahead of us." Now he stared at her with his law enforcement jaw firmly stuck out. "Do you realize we've got an estimated one-point-two million out-of-town visitors invading our fair city? And they are all bound and determined to drink themselves silly, ingest too much rich food, and maybe even contribute to our skyrocketing crime rate by venturing out at three o'clock in the morning and getting themselves mugged? Do you know what a challenge that is? And now we've got the media stirring the pot with lurid tales of the Neptune Bomber!"

As Carmela walked Babcock to the door, she was only half listening as he continued his worried rant. Thoughts were swirling inside her brain. A real pro? Someone who knew what he was doing? Who on earth could that be? And then, recalling Jekyl's conversation about Maribel Wilder, thought, *Was it Maribel? The former Miss Baton Rouge?*

Jekyl had said that Maribel's money came from oil and gas exploration. Didn't that industry use major explosives? Blasting caps and dynamite? Nitroglycerin? Sure they did. Of course they did. And Maribel could have wanted her husband dead if she was hot and heavy in an affair with someone — that someone being Danny Labat. If Maribel had wanted to clear the decks, she could have easily hired some shady oil field roust-about to kill her husband in a most spectacular manner.

"What about Wilder's wife?" Carmela suddenly blurted out. "What's her name again?" Carmela knew darn well what her name was.

"Maribel Wilder," Babcock said.

"Don't you always take a good hard look at the spouse? Isn't that the first person you look at in a case like this?"

"Not always. But, in this case, we did run a quick check on Maribel Wilder. She's not only clean, she has an ironclad alibi. Maribel was sitting in Antoine's, having a very expensive dinner with a dozen of her closest friends, when her husband's float exploded like Krakatoa."

But Maribel still could have hired some-one, Carmela decided. Why would Maribel get her own dainty hands dirty, risk every-thing, when she was rich and powerful enough to pay some poor fool to do the deed for her?

And then there was Danny Labat. Car-mela wanted to find out a little more about him . . .

At the door, Babcock bent and gave Carmela a little kiss. He grinned to himself when he felt her let loose a little shiver.

But it wasn't the kiss that had thrilled Carmela — it was the thought of murder and the possibility of investigating any number of suspects.

At one thirty, the workers arrived to put up the chicken wire. They'd also come with several sheets of plywood in hand.

"Plywood?" Gabby protested. "You want to wall in the entire window like 'The Cask of Amontillado'? That window's about the only natural light we get in here."

The worker in charge, a tough-looking fireplug of a man named Vince, said, "No caskets, ma'am, just boards."

"But the light . . ."

"You want us to skip the plywood, just say the word. But we ain't taking no responsibility if your window gets busted in by some crazy, drunken jackhole."

Carmela was hastily consulted.

"What if we just put plywood on half the window?" Carmela said.

That worked for Gabby.

But Vince squinted one eye shut. "Which half are you thinking?"

"The bottom half," Carmela said. *Duh.* "That's the part the drunks and crazies are more apt to knock up against."

Vince nodded. "That's pretty sound thinking." He gestured to his silent partner and they both trooped outside, tool belts jangling, to survey the job site.

"Everything okay with Babcock?" Gabby asked Carmela.

"Oh, you know, same old, same old. I asked him about the explosion last night and he warned me to stay out of his investigation."

"So will you? Stay out of it, I mean?"

"What do you think?"

Gabby allowed herself a faint smile. "I think you're probably in it up to your eyeballs."

"I wasn't going to let myself get pulled in," Carmela said. "Mostly because Shamus wanted me to get involved. But after talking with Jekyl, there's something really rotten going on. It sounds as if Hughes Wilder was for sure a slippery character, but then someone decided to take the law into their own hands."

"And that goes against your sense of fair play?"

"A little, yeah." Carmela hesitated. "Did you ever bring in those tea tins? The ones I was going to collage? Or decoupage?"

"Right here." Gabby ducked down behind the front desk and pulled out a bright yellow shopping bag. "Here you go," she said, handing it over, happy that Carmela had changed the subject. "Three tea tins."

Carmela pulled out a medium-sized square tin and balanced it in her hand. "Earl Grey. Very nice."

"What's it going to be reincarnated as?"

"I'm thinking pages from an Italian newspaper for the first layer. Then maybe using a few of those Leonardo da Vinci rubber stamps. And then roughing up the whole thing with some dabs of blue and ochre paint. The paint would be rubbed on judiciously, of course."

"Wow," Gabby said. "You came up with an idea just like that?"

"Well, I had a couple minutes earlier to noodle around a few ideas."

"But that was the best one?"

"Um . . . do you like it?"

"No, Carmela, I love it."

Carmela had just brushed a nice, thick layer of Mod Podge onto her paper-trimmed tea tin when the door opened and a young man walked in. Since Gabby was ringing up two customers at the front desk, Carmela smiled at their guest and said, "May I help you?"

They didn't get a lot of men in the scrapbook shop, but Carmela always tried not to be judgmental. Men were just as capable of writing journals or putting together a nice photo album as women were.

"That depends," said the young man. He was in his late twenties or possibly early thirties, with dark eyes and a closely trimmed beard. His manner of dress was studied casualness. He was a hipster — dark slacks and sweater, trench coat, a scarf looped around his neck.

"We just got in a new shipment of albums," Carmela said. "Great for photos or business-oriented scrapbooks." Lots of small companies were doing scrapbooks these days to show off their products. Catering companies, floral shops, even some custom clothiers.

"No thanks." The man touched two fingers to his chest. "Do you know who I am?"

"Internal Revenue? DEA? ATF?" Carmela asked.

He looked faintly amused. "Are you skirting the law or something?"

"Just having fun with you," Carmela said. "No, I don't know who you are. Suppose you tell me."

"I'm Jake Bond. I used to be the on-air financial reporter for KBEZ-TV." There was a note of bitterness in his voice.

" 'Used to be'?" Carmela vaguely remembered seeing him on TV. Very vaguely.

"I had a plum reporting job until Hughes Wilder had me fired for doing what he thought was an unflattering story about Pontchartrain Capital Management."

Carmela leaned back in her chair. "Ah. I'm sorry you lost your job." *So what are you doing here? What do you want from me?*

As if reading Carmela's mind, Bond said, "I understand you're investigating the death of Hughes Wilder."

"Me?" Carmela let loose a slightly squeaky laugh. "No, no, somebody's been pulling your leg. I specialize in crafts. Scrapbooking, rubber stamping, graphic design for party invitations, that sort of thing."

"That's funny," Bond said. "Your husband, Shamus Meechum, told me you were involved. In an amateur way."

"He's not my husband," Carmela said. "Hasn't been for a while. In an amateur way."

"But you are investigating."

"No. Of course I'm not. Does this look like the Eighth District precinct station? Do you see detectives answering phones and running around? No, I don't think so."

Bond sat down at the craft table across from Carmela and offered her a thin smile. "You really should talk to me, you know."

"Why?" *When I want you to leave me alone.*

"Because I've gathered quite a lot of dirt on Hughes Wilder."

"Perhaps you should take whatever information you have to the police," Carmela said. "Mr. Wilder, and whatever business issues he had, seems to be their problem now."

"Wilder was a problem for a lot of investors, too," Bond said.

Carmela picked up a rubber stamp and levered it back and forth on a stamp pad. "I wouldn't know about that."

"Shamus tells me you're smart as a whip."

"Shamus runs his mouth way too much. In fact, if you're investigating financial impropriety, maybe you should take a careful look at Crescent City Bank. The bank Shamus's family owns." Carmela touched

70

the stamp to a sheet of paper, creating an image of an ornate frame.

Bond ignored her last remark. Instead, he gestured at the tin she was working on. "This is what you do?"

"Among other things." Carmela gazed at him intently. "Now, really, if I can't interest you in our new line of albums or rhapsodize about a few sheets of handmade mulberry or lokta paper . . ."

"You're asking me to leave?"

"We are awfully busy."

But much to Carmela's consternation, Bond proved to be extremely persistent. He remained glued to his seat, staring at her.

"So you don't want to hear the dirt I've gathered on Hughes Wilder?" Bond asked. "There's plenty of it." He paused. "And plenty of people who wanted to get rid of him."

Carmela couldn't help being a little bit intrigued. And like the mongoose drawn to the coiled cobra, she leaned forward in her chair and said, "Like who?"

"His wife, for one thing. Maribel Wilder."

"Interesting." *Not really.*

"And the wife's lover."

"Uh-huh." *Tell me something I don't already know.*

"There's another person," Bond said. "A

man named Tom Ratcliff."

Carmela searched her brain. The name sounded familiar, but she couldn't quite place it.

"Ratcliff is a captain of the Nepthys krewe," Bond said. "One of your husband's rival krewes."

"Ex-husband," Carmela said.

"Ratcliff is also a fairly well-known art dealer."

Carmela snapped her fingers and pointed at Bond. "That's where I've heard the name. His gallery's over on Royal Street. Ratcliff on Royal."

"Exactly," Bond said. "Tom Ratcliff's kind of a big deal on the art scene. He also just bought a very large Italianate mansion in the Garden District."

"Good for him," Carmela said. "I hope he's assessed an exorbitantly high property tax. The city needs the revenue."

"Ratcliff also hated Wilder," Bond said. "Despised the man, in fact."

Carmela held up a finger. "So you're telling me that this Tom Ratcliff guy wanted to get rid of Hughes Wilder? Or, as they say in the military, terminate him with extreme prejudice?" She was finding this new information mildly interesting. But only if it was true.

Bond nodded. "Ratcliff lost a huge amount of money in Wilder's hedge fund and had been bad-mouthing him all over town. As well as making threats about doing bodily harm."

"And you know this . . . how?"

"I make it my business to keep tabs on the financial community," Bond said. "The big guns, the brokers and financial planners, the wannabes. You get the idea."

"And you continue to work at this even though you're no longer a financial reporter?"

"I will be again," Bond said, slapping a hand down on the table, making a pair of scissors jump and clatter. "Just because Wilder got me fired from the TV station doesn't mean I won't be back on top again. Everybody better watch out."

Carmela glanced toward the front of the shop. Gabby had stepped outside, and their two remaining customers had gone with her. Probably looking at the scrapbook pages in the front window display — what they could see of it after the chicken wire was up. Now, left alone with Jake Bond, she suddenly felt unprotected and vulnerable.

"I wish you all the luck in the world," Carmela said, trying to sound blasé.

Bond finally stood up. "I want to dig deep,

get to the bottom of this murder," he said. "So I'd really appreciate it if you kept me in the loop."

"There is no loop," Carmela said. *Damn, Shamus, why did you have to tell this guy that I was investigating? And he's a reporter at that. Maybe out of a job now, but you never know what tomorrow will bring . . .*

"Sure. Right," Bond said. "You realize, I may be persona non grata at some of the news outlets in town . . ." He lifted an eyebrow. "Maybe even right here. But if I can get a handle on this murder investigation — help crack the case and write the story — I'll be back on top." He turned and stepped away from her. "Then I can write my own ticket."

"Good luck," Carmela said. She watched as Bond slipped through the front door, nodding politely to Gabby as she came back in. Carmela guessed she should feel a slight amount of sympathy for Bond. Fired from his TV job because he'd stumbled upon some information about Pontchartrain Capital Management. Information that might have even saved some investors from financial ruin.

Carmela let her brain ruminate over this new information for a few moments, thinking about Bond's accusation against Tom

Ratcliff and Bond trying to solve the murder of Hughes Wilder. Then, suddenly, she came — clunk — right up against a rather irrefutable fact.

If Wilder was the one who'd gotten Jake Bond fired from KBEZ-TV, then didn't those circumstances conspire to make Bond a plausible suspect in Wilder's murder?

The idea took her breath away.

Dear Lord. Jake Bond could very well be the killer. The Neptune Bomber. And here he was, sitting right across the table from me, polite as a preacher, trying to drag any information he could out of me. No wonder I felt uncomfortable.

Should she tell Babcock about Bond?

That might be tricky. Then Babcock would know for sure that I've been snooping. That I might be in too deep.

Carmela decided the best thing to do was to be very careful from now on. Very, very careful.

CHAPTER 6

Carmela stood at the stove in her galley kitchen sizzling onions and mushrooms in a cast-iron skillet. Babcock had recently taken her to a little Italian-Creole restaurant in Lacombe, on the other side of Lake Pontchartrain, and Carmela was trying to re-create the flavors and essence of their delicious pasta. Cooking for Ava tonight was a sort of dress rehearsal for a future evening's tête-à-tête with Babcock. She figured she could score beaucoup romance points by dazzling him with her gourmet skills.

"Whatever you're cooking, it smells fantastic," Ava said. She was lounging on a leather chaise in Carmela's living room, wrapped in a purple paisley caftan that was cinched at the waist with a studded black leather belt.

"Thank you," Carmela said. "I just hope I can get it right."

"You will, I have faith." Ava held a glass

of Sauvignon Blanc in one hand and was dispensing dog treats with the other. If Auntie Ava was too slow on delivery, Boo, Carmela's fawn-colored Shar-Pei, would gently nudge her hand with her padded muzzle. Poobah, a spotted rescue dog, was a little less aggressive and generally willing to wait her out.

"Why doesn't my apartment look this cozy?" Ava murmured to herself. Carmela's garden apartment, just across the courtyard from Ava's shop and upstairs apartment, actually looked like an adult lived there. Haunting the scratch-and-dent rooms of the French Quarter's antique shops, Carmela had discovered leather furniture, an antique dining room table with genuine cane chairs, old photos and engravings, and a slightly threadbare Aubusson carpet. Ava's apartment, on the other hand, was painted to look like the inside of a Pepto-Bismol bottle and liberally adorned with animal-print throws and pillows. She had rolling racks of exotic clothes stashed everywhere.

"How are you doing on wine?" Carmela called. "Isn't that good?"

Ava held up her glass. "*Cher,* this is fantastic wine. I hope you have another bottle stashed away because this slides down oh so smoothly."

"Be careful you don't get tipsy."

"I only have to navigate the courtyard," Ava said. "And try not to stumble into the fountain." She picked up the TV remote and clicked the green button. "What are you cooking? It smells *très* delicious."

"Shrimp and pasta in creamy paprika sauce. A new dish I'm trying." She poured a splash of cream into her pan and stirred. "*Trying* being the operative word here."

"I love being your sweet little guinea pig. It's the only time I eat really well."

"You don't always have to exist on takeout, you know. You could cook. You've got a stove."

"Which I use as my desk to write out bills and moan over credit card charges."

"Oven?" Carmela said.

"Storage for sweaters."

"Do you ever forget and turn it on?"

"Once," Ava said. "I turned a perfectly good angora turtleneck into burned wool. Or would that be boiled wool?" Ava shrugged. "Whatever. It was always a little stinky after that."

Ava scrolled through the TV channels and stopped when she came to a scene where an exotic-looking woman was creeping along in a dark, shadowy room. Ava leaned forward and watched intently as the screen flickered and scary music began to build. "Did you ever notice that serial killers only go after women who wear matching bra and panty sets?" she asked. "Victoria's Secret-type babes?"

"Exactly what are you watching?" Carmela called from the kitchen.

"Don't know. Something spooky. Ooh, sweetie, don't go down those stairs!" Ava covered her eyes. Then she opened her fingers so she could peek.

"Maybe you should turn that off before it warps your brain. Or scares you half to death."

Ava aimed the remote control at the TV and hit the power button. "Hey, guess what?"

"What?"

"I got a very interesting invitation today — actually *we* did. Lisette Galvan . . . you know, the lady who manages The Latest Wrinkle resale shop? Anyway, Lisette asked if we wanted to be models in their fashion show this Saturday."

"Models," Carmela said, as she shook a flutter of paprika into her pan. "But we're not models."

"Speak for yourself, girlfriend. Because I think this might be a golden opportunity. I mean . . . a couple of gorgeous gals like us . . . we could get discovered big-time!"

"Just who do you think would discover us?" Carmela opened her cupboard, pulled out two plates and two bowls.

"Some hotshot from a New York modeling agency, of course. And before you pooh-pooh the idea, I want you to imagine some of the possibilities." Ava's eyes took on a dazed look. "Walking the runways at New York Fashion Week, popping over to the Cannes Film Festival, hitting the shops in Milan . . ."

"We're thirty," Carmela said, grinning because it always fell to her to be the practical one, the Republican in her little cloth coat in a room full of exotic, velvet-cloaked, bejeweled bohemians. "We're not exactly super *young* anymore."

Ava's face fell. "Then I guess I'd better collect my Medicare card and make nursing home reservations. I hear Shady Valley whips up a great prune pie."

Carmela hastily amended her words. "Well, *I'm* thirty, although I do realize that you're much, much younger."

Ava wasn't any younger than Carmela, but this was the nicey-nice game friends sometimes played to keep each other happy.

"The thing is," Carmela said, "we need to be realistic, to kind of temper our expectations. Most modeling agents today are look-ing for stick-figure teenagers. The Gigis and Kendalls of the world."

Ava took a sip of wine as she considered Carmela's words. Finally she said, "Then maybe we could just do the modeling for kicks? And because Lisette said we could probably keep some of the clothes."

"Keep the clothes? Now you're talkin'."

As Carmela ladled sauce over her pasta and shrimp, Ava lit two tall tapers on the dining room table and dimmed the lights.

"It's looking nice and moody in here," Ava said. "All we need are a couple of good-looking guys who can dazzle us with amus-ing dinner conversation."

Carmela carried their dishes out on a tray. "Would you settle for just dinner?"

Ava grinned. "Would I ever." As Carmela set their steaming dishes on place mats, Ava poured out more wine. Two minutes into dinner, Ava said, "So how's your investiga-tion going?"

"What makes you think I'm involved in an investigation?"

Ava tilted her head as she spun pasta onto her fork. "Oh please."

"All right," Carmela said. "I'll admit it, Shamus did kind of suck me in."

"He probably asked for your help because

he's suspect numero uno."

"Yes, but other suspects have surfaced," Carmela said.

"Do tell."

"Well, there's Maribel Wilder, the victim's wife. And Danny Labat."

"Labat," Ava said. "The sports car guy."

"Right. Apparently the two of them are having a torrid affair and might have wanted to get Hughes Wilder out of the way."

Ava nodded eagerly. "The wronged husband is always the last one to know. Or the first one to get axed."

"There's a guy named Tom Ratcliff, too," Carmela said. "An art dealer."

"Sounds like a high-class suspect," Ava said. "How did this Ratcliff get on your list?"

"A sketchy dude by the name of Jake Bond paid me a visit today. He informed me that Ratcliff lost a shitload of money with Hughes Wilder's hedge fund."

"Badda bing," Ava said. "That's a raft full of suspects right there. You think there'll be more?"

Carmela lifted a shoulder. "Who knows? They seem to be popping up like errant mushrooms in a damp forest."

"But Babcock doesn't know how much you're into all of this?"

"No," Carmela said. "And don't you tell him."

"I'd make a zipping motion across my mouth, but then I'd have to stop stuffing my face. And I can't. Carmela, what did you *do* to this pasta?" Ava moaned.

"Added a little paprika to the cream sauce?"

"No, you've spun semolina flour into pure gold. I am seriously addicted. Any chance of seconds?"

"Of course." Carmela always made extra when Ava dropped by.

"Um, so good." Ava twirled more of the creamy pasta on her fork. "You know, it's going to be a crying shame when I'm no longer just a hop, skip, and jump away from your kitchen anymore."

Carmela frowned. "What are you talking about? You're not thinking about moving, are you?"

"Only temporarily," Ava said. "Remember that I told you I was going to house-sit for my sort-of boyfriend, Harrison?" She pointed a fork at Carmela. "Well, it's actually his parent's house."

"Wait, what?" Carmela said. "You're telling me this is happening soon? That you're moving into this house?"

Ava nodded. "Tomorrow."

"Where's Harrison in this equation? Why isn't he being the dutiful son if his parents are off gallivanting around the globe?" Harrison Harper Wilkes III was Ava's trust-fund boyfriend that Carmela liked to say was born with a silver shoe in his mouth. Also known simply as H, Harrison had cajoled Ava into house-sitting at his parents' ginormous Garden District manse.

"I told you," Ava said, "Harrison's vacationing with his family in Majorca."

"And why aren't *you* with them, all oiled up and cavorting on an exotic beach in your string bikini?"

"Good question." Ava held up an index finger. "Which will be asked. And an answer will be provided once Harrison returns. But for now the question is, will you help me move?"

"Of course. But I think this calls for another glass of wine."

"Let's pop that cork," Ava said. "You know, wine is to women what duct tape is to men. It fixes everything."

Carmela opened a second bottle and refreshed their glasses.

After a long swallow, Ava said, "You're right about Harrison. He should have invited me along, not left me here in the cold."

"It hit sixty today."

"Whatever. The sticking point is he *left* me."

"I agree," Carmela said. "You ready for seconds on that pasta?"

Ava patted her tummy. "Mmn, maybe." She peered hopefully from behind masses of curly, dark hair. "Unless there's dessert?"

"I bought a king cake at the Merci Beaucoup bakery."

"Mmn, white sugar. One of the four basic food groups."

"You got that right."

Ava helped clear dishes while Carmela sliced the king cake, which wasn't really a cake at all. It was more like a pastry, traditionally baked at Mardi Gras, and covered with purple and green frosting and sprinkles. As a kind of bonus, there was always a little plastic baby baked inside. If you found it, you were guaranteed good luck. Unless, of course, you choked to death on it.

They sat in the living room and ate their king cake, washing it down with wine.

"You really have to move tomorrow?" Carmela asked.

"I'm not in the mood to house-sit," Ava said, "but I promised . . . Say, can Boo have a teensy-weensy bite of king cake? She's wiggling her butt like crazy, just begging for a nosh."

"No, she's watching her weight," Carmela said.

"Aren't we all," Ava sighed. "Oh, you know what? I discovered this super new diet." She reached down and started to paw through the tote bag that sat next to her. She pulled out a pair of spangled pantyhose, an eye-shadow palette the size of a bread box, and a copy of *Star Whacker* magazine. "I found the diet in this magazine. It has to do with fasting on alternate days. You, like, eat five hundred calories on Monday, Wednesday, and Friday, and then gorge the rest of the week."

"It's Wednesday," Carmela said.

"So I'll eat like a pauper tomorrow," Ava said. She tapped the magazine, which featured a photo of a super skinny model on the cover. "This diet is based on actual scientific fact. It's supposed to send your metabolism rocketing into hyperdrive."

"My metabolism is humming right along, thank you very much," Carmela said. "And please, tell me why you love to read trashy magazines like that?"

"Because real literature depresses me and —"

A sharp ring of the phone cut off the rest

of Ava's words.

Carmela grabbed her phone and glanced at the caller ID. Ugh, it was Shamus. She almost let his call go to voice mail, then changed her mind at the very last minute.

"What?" Carmela said sharply.

"Hey, babe," Shamus said.

"Why would you tell Jake Bond that I was investigating Wilder's murder?" Carmela shouted at him. She felt it was best to get right to the point. Chew him out properly.

"Because you *are* investigating," Shamus said. "You promised, cross your heart and hope to die, to help get Babcock off my case."

"For all I know you did kill Hughes Wilder."

Shamus let loose a hearty chuckle and Carmela could hear people talking in the background. Along with tinny-sounding music and the clinking of glasses.

"Shamus, are you in a bar?"

"Um, yeah. Hey, do you remember my buddy Sam?"

"Sam," Carmela repeated.

"Sam Spears."

"Right. The other idiot who got bounced off a float onto his head."

"Sam's here with me at Dr. Boogie's," Shamus said. "We were wondering if you

87

could come over and join us for a drink."

"Because . . ."

"We're just tossing a few ideas around." Shamus paused.

"Concerning?"

"Possible murder suspects." There was a sudden burst of laughter in the background, and then Shamus said, "Hey, I told Sam that you were Detective Babcock's girlfriend."

"Tell her I wish she was *my* girlfriend," Sam's voice boomed through the phone.

"You hear that?" Shamus asked.

"How could I not?" Carmela said.

"C'mon," Shamus urged. "Come over here and have a drink with us. We're only a couple of blocks away."

Carmela dropped the phone and gazed at Ava. "Shamus wants me to come have a drink with him."

"Go for it," Ava said. "Me, I gotta go home and start packing for my big move tomorrow."

"One drink," Carmela said to Shamus. "I have to clean up here and then I'll see you in twenty minutes."

Dr. Boogie's was jammed for a Wednesday night. Then again, it was jammed almost every night. Carmela elbowed her way through the crowd, heading for the bar. The place smelled like spilled beer, spicy chicken wings, and desperate singles. She could hear balls being racked at a nearby pool table and a singer crooning away in an adjoining room. The bar called it their Cabaret Room, but it was usually populated by down-and-out singers working solely for tips.

"Carmela!" Shamus exclaimed when he saw her. "Babe."

Carmela finally made it to the crowded bar. Three bartenders worked frantically, mixing drinks and pouring beer. Behind them, there must have been five hundred different bottles of spirits sitting on glass shelves that were backlit with colored lights.

"You remember Sam, don't you?" Shamus said.

Sam favored Carmela with a smile and a respectful nod. "Nice to see you again," he said. "Thanks for coming."

Carmela decided that Sam Spears looked a whole lot better tonight than he did last night. He wore a sand-colored suede jacket over jeans and a sport shirt and seemed to have recovered from his case of float crash hysterics.

"Sam runs a software company," Shamus said, continuing with his introduction. "He's one of our local movers and shakers."

Sam handed Carmela his business card. "I don't know about the movin' and shakin' part, but I'm the CEO of Velocitech Software."

"Neat logo," Carmela said, brushing a finger across the card. It was yellow with bouncing black type. A ferocious-looking velociraptor was embossed just to the right of Sam's name and title. "Catchy."

"People remember it," Sam said. "The raptor's got a nice connotation for being tough and fast."

"Just like you," Shamus said, jabbing an elbow into Sam's ribs. "Hey, Carmela, what would you like to drink? We've been imbibing a little Wild Turkey ourselves."

"This looks like the beginning of an exciting Hardy Boys adventure," Carmela said. "But is there a legitimate reason for my being here?"

"We feel awful bad about our krewe captain being killed in the explosion," Sam said.

"Not just killed," Shamus said. "Murdered. Whoever placed that bomb on our float also detonated it."

"Anyway," Sam continued. "Shamus here thinks you can be of some help."

"Absolutely she can," Shamus said. "Carmela's one smart cookie. Tough, too. She knows how to handle me, ha ha."

"Not quite," Carmela said. She ignored Shamus and focused on Sam. "Shamus said you two have been knocking around a few ideas concerning suspects?"

Sam nodded. "That's right."

"And who comes to mind?" Carmela asked.

"I kind of hate to say this," Sam said. "But Danny Labat was having —"

"*Is* having," Shamus interrupted.

"Is having an affair with Wilder's wife, Maribel," Sam finished.

"Are you positive?" Carmela asked. This was exactly what she'd been hearing, but Carmela wanted to be one hundred percent sure of that relationship before she started pointing fingers.

"We're sure," Sam said.

"And then Jake Bond told you about Tom Ratcliff," Shamus said.

"James Bond?" Sam said.

"*Jake* Bond," Shamus said. "Yeah. This Ratcliff guy lost a pile of money in Wilder's hedge fund, and Jake and everybody else heard him spouting off about how angry he was. And how he wanted to get even."

"But getting even might have meant getting his money back," Carmela said. "It doesn't necessarily mean Ratcliff was out to murder him."

Shamus gave Carmela a wonky-eyed look. "There's a stone-cold killer walking our streets," he said. "And it sure ain't me, no matter what your boyfriend might think."

"Shamus is completely innocent," Sam said.

"Innocent, naïve, whatever," Carmela said. She focused on Sam because he seemed the easiest to converse with. The most sober. "So the rumor that Pontchartrain Capital Management hadn't been doing very well is true?"

"It's true that PCM wasn't giving the returns they'd promised their clients," Sam said. "But that's no reason to murder their CEO."

"So you're saying that a lot of investors have lost money," Carmela said. "Besides Shamus."

Shamus brooded over his glass of whiskey. "Wish you didn't have to bring *that* up."

"It's a darned shame investors lost money," Sam said. "But I also heard that PCM recently invested in a number of start-ups that are poised to take off."

"I heard that, too," Shamus said. "Simca Communications and Promoplex, just to name a couple."

"So maybe Pontchartrain Capital Management, what's left of it, will be able to turn things around," Sam said.

"What *is* left of it?" Carmela asked.

"Well," Sam said, "Maribel sits on the board of directors."

"Was she there before?" Carmela asked.

"No," Shamus said.

"Does she have a head for business?" Carmela asked. "Is Maribel suddenly going to turn into a Wall Street genius?"

Sam shrugged. "Who knows? Who cares?" He took a sip of his drink and looked thoughtful. "The most important thing right now is to solve Hughes Wilder's murder. It's in the best interests of Wilder's company, his wife, and especially all of us in the Pluvius krewe." Now Sam gazed meaningfully at Carmela. "That's why we're asking you for help. Shamus said you're smart beyond belief, that you're a pit bull when you sink your teeth into a tough case."

Carmela reached over and took Shamus's drink out of his hand. She helped herself to a sip of Wild Turkey as she ruminated over all the things Shamus and Sam had just told her. Then she said, "What about this reporter you sicced on me? Jake Bond?"

"Bond?" Shamus said. "He's a good guy. Completely trustworthy."

Carmela took another sip of Shamus's

drink. *Is Bond a good guy?* She'd gotten a vibe off Bond earlier today and it hadn't felt warm and fuzzy. More like cold and prickly.

CHAPTER 7

Thursday morning, the sun shone brightly outside Memory Mine. Luckily, there was still a hint of sunbeams streaming through the top half of the bay windows — the part that hadn't been nailed over with plywood and chicken wire. Anticipating that this barrier might present a problem for potential customers, Gabby had hastily placed a wooden shelf in the window and arranged a display of paper theaters on top of it. She was comforted by the fact that passersby would at least see *something* crafty peeping out of Memory Mine's front windows.

"So nobody's crashed into our windows?" Carmela asked. "No arms and legs sticking through when you got here this morning?" At her perch behind the front counter, Gabby seemed to be exuding bursts of nervous energy.

"Not enough drunks moving about yet," Gabby said, pushing back a strand of hair and looking earnest. "But just wait until this weekend, when the bars and restaurants really crank up. Then you'll see some trouble, mark my words."

"Would you call that a glass-half-empty or a glass-half-full point of view?" Carmela asked.

"Neither. It's just reality."

Carmela nodded as she grabbed a packet of purple cardstock off the front counter. Ever since Memory Mine had thrown open their front door at the stroke of nine that morning, they'd been crazy busy. Customers had flooded in, clamoring for ideas on paper, design, and printing. It seemed that everyone needed creative inspiration for the place cards, menu cards, and name cards they wanted to set out at their Mardi Gras parties. And, wouldn't you know it, that afternoon Carmela was also scheduled to teach a class that she'd fancifully titled Masks with Mojo.

"Why does everybody always wait until the last minute?" Gabby asked, lowering her voice so that the people who were frantically grabbing green and gold ribbon, stencils, and paper wouldn't overhear her.

"I don't know," Carmela said, "but they always do."

"Good thing you were able to finish the

programs for the zoo's fancy black-tie party."

"Tell me about it. I had to do a major wheedle on Harvey, our favorite printer over at Inkspot. I talked him into bumping us to the front of the line in exchange for designing their new business cards. And it's a good thing I pushed him like I did, because that zoo lady, Cynthia Ronson, called a few minutes ago. She's going to stop by this morning and pick up her order."

"Which I've got stashed right here," Gabby said, reaching down to touch a hand to a cardboard box overflowing with zebra-striped programs.

"Good. Better keep 'em under wraps until then."

Gabby gave Carmela a sideways glance. "I don't know if you want to talk about this, Carmela, but I've been wondering. How is your investigation going? Have you made any progress at all?"

Carmela tilted her head back and half closed her eyes, thinking. "I'm not exactly burning with ideas, but it's not for lack of trying. Shamus has been prodding me nonstop. I've talked to him more in the last twenty-four hours than I did in six months of marriage. And — can you believe it? — he even had me meet up with him and a friend from his krewe last night."

"What about that young man who wandered in yesterday?" Gabby's face colored slightly. "I couldn't help but overhear some —"

"You're talking about Jake Bond? The ex-reporter dude?"

Gabby nodded. "That's the one."

"Bond seemed like your typical TV guy. Bursting with ideas and schemes about trying to sandbag some guy named Tom Ratcliff. This guy Ratcliff apparently lost a ton of money in Hughes Wilder's hedge fund."

"Wait a minute, are you talking about Tom Ratcliff, the guy who owns the art gallery?"

"Yes. Ratcliff on Royal." Carmela peered expectantly at Gabby. "Do you know him?" Maybe Gabby had some background information that would come in handy.

"Only a little bit," Gabby said.

"How little?"

"Ratcliff donated some artwork to a charity gala that Stuart and I attended last fall. For their silent auction to benefit cancer research."

"Interesting," Carmela said. "Tell me, was the art that Ratcliff donated fairly decent stuff?"

"It wasn't exactly at the level of a Jasper Johns or Willem de Kooning. But it was nice. As I recall, there were two watercolors. A woman and child staring out to sea, and then two kids playing in the sand. Lots of pinks and blues. Very romantic."

"Dentist's office artwork," Carmela said.

Gabby couldn't help but laugh. "Oh, Carmela, you are such an art snob."

"Nah, it's just not my taste. You know I only like crisp, clean graphic design or faded, shabby-chic New Orleans glam." She held up a finger. "But getting back to Mr. Ratcliff, Jake Bond figured him to be a prime suspect in Wilder's murder because Ratcliff lost a pile of money, too."

"I thought Shamus was the prime suspect."

"He is and he isn't, because I know Shamus didn't do it. Shamus is a wimp who could never kill anyone. Shamus can barely kill a spider. Heck, he was going to buy one of those special mini vacuum things that suck up insects but doesn't harm them."

"As seen on late-night cable TV?" Gabby asked.

"Yeah, only Shamus ended up ordering a combination toenail clipper/compass instead."

Gabby looked shocked. "You're not serious."

"Not really, but it does give you a clear

picture of what kind of mind Shamus has. Highly flawed."

"Okay, we know Shamus didn't set off the bomb, and I'm guessing this Ratcliff guy didn't either," Gabby said. "So who are the other suspects? Wait a minute, *are* there other suspects?"

"Funny you should ask," Carmela said. "Apparently Hughes Wilder's wife was having — or *is* having — an affair with some car dealer guy. Do you know Danny Labat?"

Gabby nodded. "I was introduced to him for all of two seconds at a big multi-dealership meeting over at NOLA Motorsports Park. Then Stuart rushed me off to take a test-drive in some weird prototype car that looked like a jelly bean on wheels."

"So you don't really know Labat."

"Not really. Aside from the fact that he sells super high-end sports cars. I mean, if you're in the market for an Aston Martin or a Lotus, Labat's your guy. Your friendly, finance-your-luxury-car-with-me connection."

"Excuse me," called a slightly gravelly woman's voice. "Do you have any fleur-de-lis rubber stamps?"

Carmela turned and held up a finger. "We do and I promise I'll be right with you." She grabbed three packs of silver beads off the counter for another customer and said, "Duty calls."

"Did you know . . . ?" Gabby began.

Carmela glanced back at her. "Did I know what?"

"Maybe I shouldn't mention this, but I read in this morning's paper that they're holding a visitation for Hughes Wilder tonight."

"A visitation already?" Carmela said. "Huh, the morgue must have released his body."

Gabby stiffened and her face blanched white at the words *morgue* and *body*. "Now I wish I hadn't mentioned it at all."

"No," Carmela said. "I'm glad you did. Popping into that visitation tonight could prove to be . . . interesting."

Carmela got frantically busy then. She helped customers select paper, cardstock, gel pens, ribbons, and colored tissue paper. She showed one woman how to make fun place cards by using small vellum envelopes filled with gold and purple glitter and then writing the guests' names on them in sparkly ink.

Carmela helped another customer create a Mardi Gras party menu. She explained how to print the menu offerings out on cream and gold-tinged paper, back the printout with a second sheet of purple paper that was slightly larger in size, roll the two pages into a tube, and then secure them with a piece of gold cord.

Late morning found Carmela showing a customer how to wrap pieces of marbleized paper around pillar candles and decorate them with velvet ribbon and dangling charms. *Adorable!*

Carmela was sticking craft supplies into brown paper bags as Gabby hastily rang up customers when Cynthia Ronson, the development director for the New Orleans Zoo, walked in.

"Cynthia," Carmela said. She ducked down, grabbed the box of zoo programs, and hauled it out from behind the counter.

Cynthia saw the box in Carmela's hands and grinned. "You did it. And with a ridiculous deadline at that." Cynthia was dark-haired and petite with luminous dark eyes. She was dressed head to toe in trendy black — an architecturally constructed sweater and matching skirt — and she had a pair of red octagon-shaped glasses perched on her pert nose. She looked a bit like a trendy librarian, though Carmela guessed she was a whiz at soliciting donations from all the zoo's patrons.

"Let's take these back to the craft table," Carmela suggested as she hefted the cardboard box.

"I can't wait to see the programs you designed," Cynthia cooed, following Carmela. "It felt like kind of a gamble scheduling our big event on Fat Tuesday, but the response has been overwhelming. People really want to come! They've been RSVPing like crazy."

"Glad to hear it," Carmela said. Truth be told, Fat Tuesday had become such a wild and crazy spectacle, especially in the French Quarter, that natives of the Crescent City generally preferred to attend their own private balls and parties.

"You know, this is the first big party we've thrown for all our patrons and hardworking volunteers since the zoo expanded and a number of our exhibits were rebuilt." The New Orleans Zoo had taken a terrible hit during Hurricane Katrina. Many of the zookeepers and workers had stayed there, weathering the brunt of the storm, risking life and limb, to help keep the animals safe. Of course, some of the exhibits had sustained terrible damage or been swept away entirely. That had led to some of the animals being boarded at other zoos and facilities. In one case, all the New Orleans Zoo otters had sheltered at the Monterey Bay Aquarium for several years. Now all the creatures were safely back home, and the zoo was ready to celebrate.

Carmela handed a program to Cynthia. Gold raised letters against zebra-striped paper proclaimed, *Monkey Around for Mardi Gras*.

"I love it!" Cynthia said. When she flipped the program open, an even wider smile lit her face. "This is perfect. Absolutely gorgeous. I can't believe you were able to fit all the information about our brand-new exhibits and events onto this double spread."

"And look," Carmela said, turning the program over. "Here's a photo of the monkeys and a list of Platinum Circle Donors, just like you asked."

"Love it, I just love it."

"Phew." Carmela put a hand to her chest and gave a mock sigh. "It took some doing, but we got it done."

Cynthia closed her program and said to Carmela, "You're invited, too, you know."

"What do you mean?" Carmela asked. Then, "Oh, you mean to *this* party? Oh no, it's specifically for all your donors, your big-bucks muckity-mucks. You don't want me . . ."

"We most certainly do want you, Carmela," Cynthia said. "You were the one who designed this program pro bono and then pulled it all together at the very last minute. The production couldn't have been easy. You had to be the head honcho on all the artwork, paper stock, typography, and printing. In my book that makes you one of our major donors."

"Really," Carmela said. She was tickled by the invitation.

"Bring a date," Cynthia said. "Or bring a friend. Or whoever. But please do come, okay?"

"That's very kind of you." It was black-tie and Carmela wondered if she could sweet-talk Babcock into a tuxedo. While he enjoyed his role as the fashion plate of the NOPD, he wasn't a big fan of the tuxedo. Or maybe he just didn't like the kind of social events where a tuxedo was required?

Cynthia touched a hand to Carmela's arm. "It's the least I can do. After all the good work you did for us."

Around one o'clock, when memory mine was merely busy rather than completely inundated, Gabby ran down the block to grab some lunch while Carmela manned the front counter. When Gabby returned with crab and avocado salads for both of them, along with a gigantic bag of fresh-popped kettle corn (Gabby's rationale being: "There was a vendor with a cart, who could resist?"), Carmela grabbed her salad and retreated to her office.

Besides feeding her face, there were two things Carmela wanted to do: prepare for her Masks with Mojo class that afternoon, and do a little Internet snooping on Pontchartrain Capital Management.

But first the masks. Last week, Ava had helped her shape some thin pieces of leather into three different styles of mask: a full mask, a half mask, and what Ava called a barely there mask. Now Carmela checked the molded hunks of leather and decided they were going to be just perfect. Of course, if someone wanted to do some judicious trimming or customizing, she also had plain cardboard masks available as well.

Okay, enough with that.

Carmela forked up a few bites of salad, chewed slowly, and thought about the demise of Hughes Wilder, the head guy at PCM, Pontchartrain Capital Management.

But wait a minute, I need a little more information before I can move ahead. This company was touted as a hedge fund. So what exactly is a hedge fund?

Carmela really didn't know the precise

definition, so she fired up her computer and started clicking away. *Okay, hedge fund.* Here was a good description: a hedge fund was a type of alternative investment that used pooled funds from investors and was set up as a private-investment limited partnership.

So that means they don't let every goofball in. Just goofballs with money. Like Shamus.

Carmela also learned that hedge funds, because of their nature, were aggressively managed in hopes of generating exceptionally high returns.

Seriously? In this market?

Carmela also found out that hedge funds were generally considered to be high-risk and required investors to keep their money in for at least a year, sometimes more. They also faced far less regulation by the SEC than traditional stocks or mutual funds.

To Carmela, a hedge fund sounded like a license to make risky investments using *other* people's money. Unless, of course, a nefarious hedge fund owner planned to keep the money for himself. *Hmm. It certainly would help to know what Hughes Wilder's bank account looked like on the day he died. Maybe that was a question to ask Babcock? Maybe.*

Carmela clicked onto the website for Pontchartrain Capital Management. The splash page had a graphic of a financial chart with a bright red arrow rocketing upward. She guessed it was supposed to symbolize that the sky's the limit. *Well, good luck with that.*

Clicking on the About Us section, Carmela found lots of rah-rah prose that promised unlimited opportunities and huge returns. Underneath the text was a color photo of Hughes Wilder himself. The angle of the photo, combined with the smirk on his face and the thrust of his jaw, made him look arrogant and pugnacious. Almost like old photos she'd seen in history books of the Italian dictator Mussolini.

Carmela wondered if Wilder, embalmed and lying still in his casket, would still be wearing that trademark smirk.

Probably not.

CHAPTER 8

The front door blew open and Baby Fontaine came blasting in like the Flying Nun. Baby was one of Carmela's regulars — she attended almost every scrapping and crafting class — and was also a dear, dear friend. Today she wore a pair of light blue skinny jeans topped with a tweed Chanel jacket. Diminutive and as poised as a seventeenth-century French aristocrat, Baby didn't look anywhere near her fifty-something years, but Carmela had attended enough of Baby's lavish birthday parties to know she had come by her pixie-cut silver-blond hair honestly.

Baby glanced around Memory Mine, smiled, then focused bright blue eyes on Carmela. "Am I the first one here?" she asked. Then, taking a quick sip of air, said, "Good, I need to talk to you about something."

"And I need to talk to you," Carmela said.

She wanted to ask Baby about Tom Ratcliff, who was supposedly one of her new neighbors in the Garden District.

But first . . .

SLAM. BANG.

The front door flew open again, and Tandy Bliss, another regular, surged on through. Skinny as a rail, with piles of hennaed red hair, Tandy exuded so much energy and enthusiasm she was a party all by herself.

"Here," Tandy said, thrusting a round blue tin at Carmela. "Treats for everyone."

"Thank you," Carmela said. Tandy was a baker *par excellence* and always brought cookies or bars along with her to class.

"But don't be fooled by the can," Tandy warned. "Those are *homemade* brownies in there. You know I don't hold with store-bought."

"I'll keep that in mind," Carmela said.

"Good," Tandy said. Although she was soft-hearted when it came to friends and family, she wasn't known for her soft voice. Tandy never held back when it came to expressing her opinion about politics, religion, books, movies, city services (or lack thereof), and local rumors. And she shared her thoughts often and with great gusto.

Gabby slid out from behind the front desk

to join them. "If you'd like to take a seat at the craft table, ladies . . ."

But Tandy was focused squarely on Baby. "Where do you want to sit, chickadee? I intend to copy every square inch of whatever mask you create, so Del won't know who's who at your party on Saturday night." Del was Baby's husband, a well-known and wealthy New Orleans attorney, and Tandy took great pleasure in ribbing him mercilessly.

As Baby and Tandy settled in at the craft table in the back of the shop, three more women came rushing in. One of them, Mary Jo Carver — a statuesque brunette — was a transplant from East Texas who still spoke with a distinctive twang.

"Y'all didn't start without me, did you?" Mary Jo asked. Her diamond-stud earrings were as big as dimes and flashed like disco balls.

"Not to worry," Carmela told everyone as they took their seats around the table. "In fact, we haven't even had a chance to pass Tandy's brownies around yet."

"Yippee!" said Mary Jo, as if she'd just tamed an angry bronc.

The brownies went around the table, followed by a nervous Gabby passing out paper napkins and worrying about crumbs.

Carmela wasn't worried about crumbs or even coffee spills and splotches. She figured that once the ladies were hot and heavy into decorating their masks, it would all meld together beautifully. The best sort of creativity was the messy kind.

When Carmela took her place at the head of the table, all eyes turned toward her. "Masks with Mojo," she began. "Just in time for Mardi Gras."

"Love it," Tandy snapped out.

"Yee ha," said Mary Jo.

Carmela held up her three mask templates. "I figured the easiest way to begin would be to jump-start you with premade templates. So you've got your choice. A full mask, a half mask, and a small mask called the barely there mask that really just covers the eyes."

"Like the Lone Ranger," Mary Jo said.

"Which mask are you going to decorate?" Tandy asked Baby.

Baby considered all the masks. "I think maybe the half mask."

"Then that's what I want, too."

Two of the other ladies chose the half masks as well, while Mary Jo vacillated between the three, then finally opted for the full mask.

"The thing is," Carmela said, "before you

start decorating, it's important to have your colors and theme in mind."

"What exactly do you mean by that?" Tandy asked.

"Let me show you," Carmela said. She held up a barely there mask that was completely covered in feathers. "This one obviously has a bird theme. I glued small pink and blue feathers all over the mask and then added a couple of peacock feathers that curl upward." She chuckled. "Kind of like antennas."

"It's gorgeous," Baby said. "Like an opera diva might wear."

"Here's another one," Carmela said, holding up a full mask. "This has more of a Venetian feel. I painted the leather gold, then glued sequins around the eye holes and the mask's outer edges. Then I painted sexy, full lips around the mouth."

"And I love the row of crystals across the top," Tandy said.

"Right," said Carmela. "Now this one . . ." She held up a half mask. "This one's kind of coquettish. It's painted pink, has a large clump of purple feathers on one side, a squiggly line of beads along the top, and then gold and purple ribbons that stream down from each side."

"They're all so different," one of the

women commented.

"That's the beauty of a mask-making class," Carmela said. "You get to make it all your own."

"Not like the ready-made masks you see in the T-shirt shops or over in the French Market," Tandy said. She nodded. "Yup, I like it."

"Still going to copy what I do?" Baby asked.

"I'm thinking, I'm thinking," Tandy said.

"Okay," Carmela said. "Keep this in mind as well. You're probably better off if you start by painting your mask with a base color, then take off from there. Add feathers, beads, ribbons, lace edging, tassels, or fringe. Or you can decoupage your entire mask and then add a few embellishments. Crystals, brads, anything you want. Just have fun and do whatever your creative juices tell you to do."

Everyone got busy then, painting their masks, shopping the store for the perfect decorations to add.

Carmela sat down and worked on a mask, too. She painted a half mask using pinky peach paint, then decoupaged bits of paper onto it, placing a quotation right in the center of the forehead: *All that we see or seem is but a dream within a dream."*

"Catchy," Tandy said. "Something you came up with?"

"I have to give credit to Edgar Allan Poe."

"Ooh. I like that, honey. It's spooky," Tandy said. "What else are you gonna do with it?"

"Probably add a dozen or so strings of beads, almost like a beard," Carmela said. Now she had Baby's full attention, too. "And what else?" Baby asked.

"Lots of feathers on top, which I'm going to anchor with a vintage brooch."

"Well, la de da," Tandy said. "I'd say you got us all beat to heck."

"I don't think so," Carmela said, looking around. "I see some very creative work being done here."

Twenty minutes later, Carmela was helping Baby select a few pieces of metallic ribbon.

"What was it you wanted to talk to me about?" Carmela asked.

"Del was at the courthouse yesterday afternoon," Baby said. "And apparently there are all these wild rumors flying around."

"About the exploding Pluvius float?" Carmela asked.

Baby nodded. "And about Shamus, too."

"The police consider him a suspect for

the time being. He foolishly lost a good deal of money in Hughes Wilder's hedge fund, so they just assumed . . ."

"But there have to be other suspects, too," Baby said. "I don't mean to sound unkind, because you were once married to him, but Shamus does seem to be more of a player than a killer."

"You said a mouthful," Carmela agreed. "And there *are* other suspects. One's even a member of the Pluvius krewe. Um, Danny Labat. Unfortunately, the other suspect is Wilder's wife."

Baby stared at her. "Not Maribel!"

"You know her?" This was an interesting twist.

Baby nodded. "Maribel and I have served on a couple of boards together. She also owns a home in the Garden District."

"She's also rumored to be having a torrid affair," Carmela said. "Which could be one of the rumors Del heard."

Baby shook her head. "Such a nasty, lurid business."

"There's been another name bandied about, too," Carmela said. "Tom Ratcliff. Do you know him?"

"The art dealer?" Baby said. "I think he lives fairly close to me, too."

"That's the guy," Carmela said. "What do

you know about him?"

"Practically nothing. Except that Ratcliff recently moved into the neighborhood and drives a rather ostentatious-looking silver Bentley. Of course, Del thinks it's gorgeous and wants to get one for himself." Baby gave a *What can you do?* sigh.

Carmela glanced over at the craft table where everyone was working away — painting, gluing, glamming up their masks. "I wish I could figure out a way to meet Ratcliff," she said. "Talk to him."

"If I were you, I'd just do what I always do."

"And what is that?" Carmela asked.

"Grab the bull by the horns and pop into his gallery. Give Ratcliff a big song and dance about how you're a dedicated art lover."

"Well, I am."

Baby smiled. "There you go."

"Good-bye," Gabby said. "Thanks for coming. Enjoy your masks."

The mask-makers had finished and packed up, and were slowly filing out the door. Everyone seemed delighted with their masks and held them up for Gabby to see.

"Oh my gosh," Gabby exclaimed. "Like the Phantom of the Opera!" She pointed at

Mary Jo's mask. "And that one looks like a bejeweled Bluebeard. I love it."

Only Baby lingered at the craft table.

"I want you to be careful, Carmela," she said.

"Yes, mom."

"Now don't get smart with me, young lady. I mean it. You go poking your nose into a murder case, you could get hurt."

"Babcock's already given me the standard lecture."

"And you didn't pay a bit of attention to him, did you?"

"Well . . ."

Baby leaned forward and gave Carmela a kiss on the cheek. "Just promise me you won't take any foolish chances. Don't rush in where angels fear to tread."

"I won't," Carmela said. "I'll be careful."

Baby was barely out the door when the bell once again *da-ding*'ed noisily.

"Oh dear," Gabby moaned. "Should I tell them we're . . . ?"

"Closed," Carmela said. "I think that's the prudent thing . . ." She stopped mid-sentence when she finally focused on who their late caller actually was. It was Glory Meechum. Shamus's big sister. And she didn't look happy. Correction: Glory's face resembled a thundercloud about to burst.

"Carmela," Glory said. Her voice was low and sibilant, like the hiss of a pit viper.

"Glory," Carmela replied. *Oh jeez. Long day. I sure don't need this.*

Glory had a red-faced, raw-boned look to her. She had the face of a woman who cared little for skin creams, makeup, or even the occasional facial. Today, Glory was dressed in her trademark shapeless brown suit and had her gray hair lacquered into a helmet that looked like something a Soviet Army soldier would wear — in the Second World War.

Glory didn't mince words. She stuck a fat finger in Carmela's face and said, "You're to blame for all this trouble."

"*I* am?" Carmela responded. "What did I do?"

"That detective fiancé of yours. He's been grilling Shamus, questioning him about the death of Hughes Wilder."

"Perhaps it might be best if you spoke to Detective Babcock directly?" *Wouldn't he just love that?*

"I'm here, talking to *you*," Glory seethed, almost spitting her words. "Because you of all people should know that Shamus is completely innocent."

Carmela sighed. "Glory, I know and you know that Shamus didn't plant that bomb.

And, probably, the police will come to their senses in a few hours and arrive at that exact same conclusion. So until Shamus is carted off to prison wearing leg-irons, I don't think you should have a brain fart about it. So please stop worrying."

"Worry," Glory shot back. "That's all I do these days!"

"Then maybe you should try yoga. Or Pilates. Or if all else fails, electric shock treatments." Honestly, Carmela thought, Glory was like a rabid wolverine.

"Don't sass me, Carmela, I'm not in the mood."

Carmela shrugged. Whatever.

"Since you are *engaged* to this overzealous Detective Babcock, I put it on your capable shoulders to rein him in. To talk some sense into him. Get him to investigate alternative suspects."

"I'm sure he's doing exactly that."

"Let me be perfectly clear," Glory said. "This isn't a request, I'm *ordering* you."

"You don't have a thing on me, Glory," Carmela said. "Shamus and I are divorced, the settlement is settled, and we remain on speaking terms only because we share two dogs." Carmela paused and drew a cleansing breath. "Now, I appreciate your concern and I *will* speak to Babcock. But only because it's in everyone's best interest that this tragedy — this apparent murder — is solved."

Carmela gave a sharp nod to Gabby, who immediately sprang to attention like the doorman at the Four Seasons. She pulled open the front door and waited as Glory harrumphed, spun on her orthopedic shoes, and left the shop.

As Glory trundled away in her shapeless suit, Carmela wondered if Glory knew about the missing sixteen million dollars — the money Shamus had invested in Hughes Wilder's hedge fund. Glory hadn't mentioned it, but Carmela knew that money — cold hard cash — was the one thing that was near and dear to Glory's hard little heart.

And if Glory *did* know about the sixteen million dollars, and was royally upset about it, was it possible that *she* had something to do with Hughes Wilder's untimely death? Could Glory have been seeking revenge without Shamus's knowledge?

The thought chilled Carmela to the bone. Because of all the people Carmela knew, Glory was the one person who was crazy enough to go out and hire herself a Craigslist killer.

CHAPTER 9

Carmela hustled along Royal Street, heading for Juju Voodoo. Ava's shop, a funky little hideaway with unlimited appeal, would be a welcome respite from being harangued by Glory Meechum. Carmela decided she might even pick up a voodoo doll (complete with stick pins!) to help get Glory off her back.

It was late afternoon and a few clouds had started to roll in. The atmosphere in New Orleans, always a little damp to begin with, now felt positively soggy. Off in the distance, Carmela could hear a few mournful toots from tugboats cruising the Mississippi River.

But as Carmela approached Juju Voodoo's shiny red door with the bouncing black type, her mood immediately lifted. Here was a French Quarter shop that, like Lafitte's Blacksmith Shop and the Old Absinthe House, was much-loved and much-photographed. An exterior of weathered wood was topped by an old-fashioned shake roof, giving it the appearance of a witch's cottage. A neon sign of an open palm glowed red and blue. Bottles, charms, incense, and amulets were on display behind the antique wavering glass of the small front windows.

Carmela opened the door to a chorus of moans that sounded like a visit from *The Walking Dead*. When she closed the door, the moaning immediately ceased. Definitely a twist on the traditional door buzzer.

The interior of the shop was dusky but not gloomy, thanks to the dozens of votive candles that flickered everywhere. They issued just enough light to show off a family of skeletons that hung from the rafters. The skeletons — led by their patriarch, Señor Muerte — clicked and clacked softly each time a door opened or closed, or someone breezed past below them. Sometimes bony feet got tangled in an unsuspecting customer's hair!

"You're just in time, *cher*." Ava stood behind her retail counter, dressed in a red silk blouse that was soft as liquid and tucked into a pair of her trademark black leather slacks. Her eye makeup was lush and exotic, her mouth enhanced with lip liner, and her dark hair cascaded down to her shoulders in soft masses of curls.

"In time for what?" Carmela asked. She moved to the counter, where a dozen saint candles blazed: Saint Peregrine, Saint Lazarus, and the rest of the holy crew. Crowded inside the display case was an arrangement of small bottles that Carmela had never seen before. There were purple bottles that looked like they might contain poison, square green bottles with carved cork stoppers, and cute round bottles with small atomizers.

"I just got in a new shipment of perfume." Ava picked up a pink bottle with an atomizer, aimed it at herself, and gave her abundant cleavage a quick spritz.

Carmela wrinkled her nose. "What is that?" Even though the scent of sandalwood incense permeated the shop, the perfume managed to hold its own. It was strong bordering on overpowering.

"This is a special love perfume," Ava said. "An intoxicating hint of roses mixed with vanilla, strawberry, and patchouli oil."

Carmela took another sniff. She decided the scent was somewhere between a noxious weed and a hippie colony.

"Guaranteed to drive a man crazy in under sixty seconds," Ava boasted.

"My record's better than that," Carmela

said. "I seem to be driving Babcock crazy on a routine basis."

Ava handed Carmela the bottle. "Take it. It's a gift. You're probably going to need it."

Carmela stared at the little bottle. It looked like something a hookah-smoking caterpillar would bestow upon her.

"Things might be copasetic between you two lovebirds right now," Ava continued in a philosophical tone. "But your messing around in this murder case could lead to catastrophic consequences. Especially since Shamus is involved."

"That's the crazy thing," Carmela said. "Shamus *isn't* involved."

"The police think he is."

"The police are wrong."

"Ooh," Ava said. "Double-o-seven Carmela with a license to . . . what is it you do again? Investigate?"

"You were there when the float exploded," Carmela said. "It was wild . . . horrific. But it was also intriguing. After witnessing that much chaos, wouldn't you like to get to the bottom of things?"

"I'm not attracted to chaos the same way you are. Especially when Babcock specifically told you *not* to investigate."

Ava's words gave Carmela pause. What exactly was she doing and why was she doing it? Because Shamus had begged her? Or because she wanted to ferret this murder mystery out on her own? She knew that she'd already moved way past Babcock's tolerance level into dangerous territory, from orange alert into red. But what he didn't know wouldn't hurt him, right?

"Take the perfume," Ava said, pushing it into Carmela's hand. "All Babcock has to hear is a whisper about you diving in to help Shamus. When that happens, his poor brain will explode like a faulty nuclear reactor and steam will shoot out his ears."

"The thing is," Carmela said slowly, "I'm sort of humoring Shamus. He really believes Babcock is all over him for Hughes Wilder's murder."

"Because he probably is."

"But there are other suspects besides Shamus."

"Yeah, but Shamus is the one you were married to. Which makes Babcock see red. You should know that by now. This isn't about Shamus as a murder suspect, it's a turf war. A grudge match."

Carmela reached a hand up and scrubbed at the top of her head. "Oh jeez."

"And, Carmela, trust me on this. You do not want to lose Babcock." Ava peered at her. "Do you?"

"Of course not."

"And you are engaged."

"We are in a promissory way, but not technically."

Ava placed a hand on one shapely hip. "When *are* the two of you going to shop for rings?"

Carmela reached over and pulled a white fabric voodoo doll out of a small wicker basket. "I dunno." She stared at the blank doll. It had only cross-stitched eyes.

"You dunno. That's just peachy. One of the sexiest men alive has asked you to marry him and you dunno."

"I thought Dwayne Johnson was the sexiest man alive. Or David Beckham or Chris Hemsworth."

"Those beefcakes are in the *People* magazine category," Ava said. "We're talking reality here."

"Okay, you're right, I'll set a date."

"For the rings *and* for the wedding." Ava fluttered her eyelashes as she arranged small colorful bags of gris-gris. "And I assume I'll be the maid of honor."

But Carmela's mind wasn't on wedding plans. It was on Shamus's predicament — which had somehow become her predicament.

"What do you think I should do?" Carmela asked. "Just walk away from all this? Do you think Babcock knows about Maribel and Danny Labat? Or about Tom Ratcliff? I mean, who's going to tell him?"

"Not you," Ava said.

"You want me to call in an anonymous tip?"

"That does sound tacky. But . . . maybe we could figure something out."

"How?"

"Madame Blavatsky's in back. Let's go ask her to do a tarot card reading."

Carmela stared at her friend. "You think the answer's in the cards?"

"You never know. At least it'll pull you out of your brain fog."

"You're right," Carmela said. "A tarot card reading is no more ridiculous than my promising to help Shamus the rat."

"You scoot on back there and I'll bring us some hot tea," Ava said.

"As long as it's not rose and patchouli."

The tea Ava served was actually a lovely autumn blend from Harney & Sons.

"A blend of Chinese black tea with flavors of peppermint and chocolate," Ava said. She placed three steaming mugs on the reading table in the small, octagon-shaped reading room and smiled at Madame Blavatsky.

"Did Carmela tell you what we are up to?"

Madame Blavatsky, who in real life was Ellie Black, nodded. "She did. And I think she could benefit from a little guidance." Madame Blavatsky took a sip of her tea. "It feels to me as if Carmela is being pulled by unseen forces."

"You think her soul is in a tug-of-war with good and evil?" Ava asked.

"Nothing quite that sinister," Madame Blavatsky assured her.

"Maybe my panty hose are too tight," Carmela said. "Maybe that's where the tugging comes in."

Madame Blavatsky, who looked very celestial with her red paisley shawl, purple skirt, and long dark hair, shook her head. "No, but there are forces at work that could possibly conspire against you."

"That sounds terrible," Ava said. "So what do we do? How do we counteract this ominous force field?"

"We ask the cards for guidance and say a prayer," Madame Blavatsky said. She smiled at Carmela and added, "If you wouldn't mind . . . kindly shuffle the cards?"

Carmela reached out, picked up the deck of tarot cards, and shuffled them, just as she'd been instructed. She set them down. Now Madam Blavatsky rubbed her hands together, almost as though she was washing them in the gentle currents of air that blew through the room.

Air currents. Carmela realized she was shivering slightly. Was it just cool weather moving in, or was something else going on here? She gazed at the heavy green draperies that hung on the walls, at the stained glass window that had been rescued from an old church. The window depicted an angel holding a small white lamb. Very peaceful and serene. Then she focused on what Madame Blavatsky was doing.

Madame Blavatsky was bent over the cards and making a soft humming sound, like a friendly, focused bee. Then she snapped four cards out of the deck and laid them, faceup, in a cross pattern on the table. Top, bottom, left, and right.

"These indicate the four directions," she said in a hushed tone. "North, south, east, west. They also correspond with the four elements: earth, air, fire, and water."

Carmela noted that all of the cards she'd been dealt were major face cards of the tarot deck. Was that good? She didn't know.

But Ava obviously thought so. "Now we're gettin' somewhere," she whispered.

"You face challenges, Carmela, but the cards are also indicating great opportunity,"

Madame Blavatsky said.

"Gulp," Carmela said. She didn't really believe in tarot, the I Ching, or Ouija boards. Then again . . .

Madame Blavatsky placed a fifth card directly in the center of the layout.

"This represents your position in the universe at this very point in time," she said.

Carmela peered at the card. It was the Moon card, a rather lovely card all colored in soft blues and greens. The moon was shining down on two baying wolves. A crawfish was crawling out of a pond. What could it mean? Did the wolves indicate Shamus and Babcock facing off against each other? And the crawfish? Did that foretell terrible danger or just a tasty étouffée?

Now Madame Blavatsky made direct eye contact with Carmela and said, "As lovely as this card looks, it can also indicate struggle."

That's for sure, Carmela thought.

"The Moon card can also mean deception or hidden enemies. So whatever you do, wherever you go, please be extremely careful."

"I will," Carmela said. *This is freaky. It's the second time today that someone has warned me to be super careful. Perhaps I should actually start listening?*

Carmela picked up her cup of tea with both hands and put it to her lips — only to find it had gone stone-cold.

Back out in Ava's shop, Carmela wandered about, pondering Madame Blavatsky's words, half-heartedly looking at jewelry.

"This is something you might like, *cher*," Ava said. She pulled an amulet off a display rack and passed it to Carmela. "For good luck."

Carmela fingered the silver disk, which was emblazoned with a horseshoe, a heart, a four-leaf clover, and an elephant with his trunk raised up. "It's cute. But do you really think I need it?"

"Couldn't hurt," Ava said.

She sounds like Gabby with her holy medals.

"What are these?" Carmela asked, fingering a different pendant. "Is this a real tooth?" It was a silver wolf's head set on top of a long, curved tooth.

"The wolf's head is crafted in sterling silver," Ava said. "The wolf fang is made out of resin."

"I guess there just aren't enough real wolf teeth to go around," Carmela said. "Not enough wolves having root canals."

Ava nodded. "That's probably it."

"You know," Carmela said, "there's a

visitation for Hughes Wilder tonight. Since the man died right in front of us, the least we could do is go and pay our respects to his widow."

"Hah," Ava said. "From what you've told me about the philandering Maribel, she must be a very merry widow."

"Still, the visitation could be interesting."

Ava considered Carmela's words for a few moments. "So they put Wilder back together again, huh? Just like Humpty-Dumpty."

"I guess. Though I'm pretty sure it's going to be a closed casket."

"So no mangled dead guy to look at. Okay, that's a definite plus. I guess I could tag along with you. What have I got to lose? But you're still going to help me move my junk afterward, aren't you? Over to Harrison's parent's house?"

"Of course I will. Um . . . exactly how much stuff do you have?"

"Not too much," Ava said. "My clothes, a couple of shopping bags full of makeup, jewelry, a few wigs. Oh, and don't forget my kitty. And her carrier. I was thinking that if we put the top down on your car, we could probably squeeze everything in. And then, just to be safe, I could kind of spread-eagle myself on top and hold everything down."

"Sounds like a plan," Carmela said, even

though it had disaster written all over it.

Ava nodded. "Yup, if we're lucky we might just make it."

CHAPTER 10

Carmela pulled her snappy red Mercedes — a long-ago, pre-divorce gift from Shamus — over to the curb and shut off the engine.

"We just passed Prytania Street, so according to the directions in the online obituary, the funeral home should be right at the next corner," Carmela said. "Besides, this seems to be the only parking spot on the block."

They both got out and looked around. Carmela was dressed in a pair of black jeans and sedate black suede blazer. Ava was also in basic black, which for her meant a black leather miniskirt topped with a black and purple satin bustier with lace trim. She'd pinned an extra Dynel fall in her hair so now she looked like some kind of exotic dark angel.

"Spooky around here," Ava said. It was a solidly residential area. A few very large homes interspersed with a few medium-sized Caribbean-style bungalows.

"And we're not even near any dead bodies yet," Carmela joked as somewhere a dog barked.

They tiptoed down a narrow brick sidewalk, brushing past stands of banana trees, ducking under Spanish moss that hung down in thick strands from large oak trees.

"Watch out for bugs," Carmela warned. Clouds had rolled in unabated now, shutting off any chance of moonlight.

Their destination, the Chamberlain and Beale Funeral Home, turned out to be a brick antebellum mansion set on a well-manicured lawn and surrounded by a tall, wrought-iron fence. It looked, Carmela thought, like a foreign embassy or maybe even the capitol building for some tiny principality. The entry was marked by an arched trellis abundant with green leaves and what were undoubtedly purple flowers, although the blooms were puckered up tightly for the night.

"Morning glories at a funeral home," Ava observed. "How appropriate, since they die every night."

"But they'll resurrect themselves in the morning," Carmela said. "Unlike poor Hughes Wilder."

They followed the sidewalk to a spacious

front veranda that was supported by massive stone colonnades. Before it had been turned into a funeral home, Carmela imagined socialites in frilly frocks had sat there, sipping lemonade, languidly fanning themselves, reading Tennessee Williams aloud to one another.

Mahogany double doors at least ten feet high were decorated by ornately carved scenes that looked like illustrations right out of Dante's "The Divine Comedy." To the right of the doors, an engraved brass plate told visitors they'd arrived at the Chamberlain and Beale Funeral Home.

Stepping inside, Carmela and Ava gazed around in awe at what could only be called funereal glamour. In the foyer, a table with marble pedestals held an enormous chinoiserie vase filled with white lilies and roses. Deeper into the lobby, cream-colored chairs and settees, all trimmed in gold brocade, were arranged in four different seating areas. Purple velvet draperies swagged the tall windows, and winged gold cherubs fluttered overhead on a background of rose-colored wallpaper.

"It's awfully showy," Ava said. "What would you call this type of décor? The last dregs of the Austro-Hungarian Empire?"

"Either that or Madame de Pompadour's

boudoir," Carmela said.

An incredibly well-groomed young man in a black cutaway coat and gray-striped trousers stepped forward to greet them. "May I be of assistance to you, ladies?" He looked barely old enough to drive.

"We're here for the Hughes Wilder visitation," Carmela said.

The young man feigned a solemn look and a grieving sigh. "We have placed Mr. Hughes in our Emperor's Room," he said.

"Sounds so tasteful," Carmela said. "And where would that be . . . ?"

"Right this way, ma'am."

"Argh," Ava grunted as they entered the enormous, wood-paneled Emperor's Room. "Did you get a load of that kid? We got ma'amed. A hit-and-run ma'aming."

"Sucks, doesn't it?" Carmela said.

"And I don't look a day over eighteen."

They stood together, surveying the huge crowd that was milling about.

"Popular guy," Ava said.

"Or maybe these are all the investors that were bilked by Wilder," Carmela said. "Do they look angry?"

"Mostly they just look mellow. Everyone seems to be holding a drink."

"Probably because there's a bar set up over on the far wall," Carmela said. "So I guess this would be your basic cocktail-hour visitation."

"Sounds right to me," Ava said. "Nothing beats an *après*-work drinky-poo."

Carmela glanced in the direction of the casket. "And over there, standing just to the left of the casket, is, I believe, our newly minted widow."

"Where?" Ava squinted, searching for Maribel. "Oh wait, I see her." Now Ava's brows pulled together in a disapproving frown. "Yes I do. Hmm."

A svelte, well-coiffed blonde in a body-con black cashmere dress stood a few feet away from an enormous bronze casket.

"Maribel Wilder," Carmela breathed.

Maribel looked as if she spent all her free time taking spin classes, doing Pilates, and getting seaweed wraps. She was as sleek and exotic-looking as a Siamese cat and knew it. At least six men hovered about Maribel — good-looking, country club–type men. Her face was animated as she spoke to each of them, her fingers flashing with diamonds.

"That's some fancied-up widow lady," Ava said. "I thought she'd be heavily tranquilized, but now I see she's just heavily made-up."

"You think a woman like that could give

the order to have her own husband murdered?"

"She looks awfully predatory," Ava said. "Not only that, she's wearing this season's Manolo Blahnik boots. I'd kill to get my hands on those."

"You're sure they're Manolos?"

"Yeah, they've got that kinky, studded look."

"We should get in line and talk to her," Carmela said. She was anxious to meet Maribel face-to-face — curious to question her about the future of Pontchartrain Capital Management.

But nothing ever comes easy. Because first they had to get in the line that snaked past Hughes Wilder's casket.

"This is awful," Ava complained as they shuffled along. "Like being in a school lunch line."

"Worse," Carmela said. "Because there's no pepperoni pizza or chocolate brownie waiting for us at the end."

Finally, the line brought them to within spitting distance of the guest of honor. Resting on a shoulder-high, mahogany bier, Hughes Wilder's oversized burnished copper casket gleamed like a shiny penny. It was closed, probably because he'd sustained some pretty nasty head wounds. Or maybe his bereaved wife just didn't feel like looking at him anymore. Tall pillar candles blazed at both ends of the casket, and floral baskets were parked everywhere.

Ava pulled out her cell phone. "What do you think? Want to take a selfie? Us standing next to the casket? You could create a lovely death-becomes-her scrapbook for Maribel."

"No thanks," Carmela said. "But look at all these flowers. It's like they emptied out every floral shop within fifty miles. Was Wilder that well-liked?"

"I'm guessing that's a rhetorical question," Ava said as they gazed at the multitude of baskets and sprays. There was even an over-the-top horseshoe-shaped arrangement. "Look at that, like Hughes Wilder just won the Kentucky Derby."

"Get a load of the floral spray on top of his casket," Carmela said. It was a swirl of white mums and blue delphiniums encircling a large King Neptune head that had been created entirely out of flowers, like a miniature Rose Parade float.

"Tasteful bunch of guys, that Pluvius krewe."

Carmela wondered if, inside that casket, Wilder still had glitter in his hair. But no — the funeral director, or the mortician who prepared him, would have washed it all out by now. She gripped the edge of the casket to steady herself, thinking about Wilder's body splayed out on a metal table, the spraying of water, the drumming of sinks, the gurgling of pipes. Awful.

"You okay?" Ava asked. She'd just slipped a quarter into a slot and lit a vigil candle.

"Let's go talk to that widow," Carmela said.

Carmela stuck out a hand. "I'm Carmela Bertrand. Please accept my sympathies, I'm so very sorry for your loss."

"Ditto that," Ava said.

Maribel Wilder grasped Carmela's hand in hers and squeezed. Her eyes turned misty as she struggled to work up a single tear. She gave it her best shot, but no dice. Carmela figured it was just as well. Maribel wouldn't want to ruin her professionally done makeup.

Maribel's response, however, sounded almost genuine.

"I just don't know what I'm going to do," she purred in a whispery little voice. "How I'll survive without Hughes at my side."

"I'm sure you'll muster up the courage," Carmela said. *Seeing as you already have Danny Labat buzzing around you.*

142

Maribel gave a sad smile. "I hope so."

"Some of us — actually, a lot of us — have been wondering," Carmela continued. "Will you be able to keep your husband's hedge fund up and running?"

"Excuse me?" Maribel said. A wary look shone in her eyes.

"The hedge fund?" Ava prompted. "Aren't you on the board of directors?"

Maribel shook her head and gave a hopeless, hapless shrug. "I — I have no idea about that. It's way too early and far too complicated to contemplate what might happen with my husband's business. But thank you for your concern. And thank you for being here tonight."

"We wouldn't have missed it for the world," Ava said.

Now Maribel pulled herself together and launched into a pat speech probably intended to drum up interest for tomorrow's funeral. "I just hope you'll be able to attend my dear husband's funeral tomorrow morning. We're having a small interring ceremony at the family crypt in Lafayette Cemetery."

"We'll be there with bells on," Carmela said.

Now Ava stepped forward. "I don't know if you realize this, but Carmela's fiancé, Detective Babcock, is the investigator in charge of your husband's murder case."

Maribel stifled a gasp and refocused on Carmela, staring at her with eyes that had suddenly turned hard and appraising. "Indeed," she said, as the temperature in the room suddenly plummeted twenty degrees. Then Maribel hastily reached past them to greet her next visitor.

"She couldn't wait to get rid of us," Ava said.

"It sure felt that way, didn't it," Carmela said. "Especially when you mentioned Babcock."

"Maribel was like the Wicked Witch of the West when Dorothy doused her with a pail of water. And, really, do you think she always talks like that? In that annoying faux-sweet little girl voice?"

"Either that or she's got a bug stuck in her craw," Carmela said.

"She struck me as a woman whose ego is as large as her pores."

"And who is supposedly having a torrid affair with Danny Labat," Carmela said.

Ava narrowed her eyes and looked around the room. "Yeah. Labat. Which one is he anyway? Is he here?"

"I have no idea, I've never met the man."

"Then we have to look for the guy who's

pretending not to be interested in Maribel."

"That's funny," Carmela said. "Because I meet guys like that all the time. Only they're not pretending."

"*Cher,* you do not! You get hooted at and catcalled by some of the best dudes in town. Why, only last week, that guy over on Dupre Street, working the jackhammer . . ."

"The one wearing the *Shotgun Billy's Gentleman's Club* T-shirt? Please don't remind me."

"Uh-oh, here comes somebody we know."

Carmela turned to find Shamus striding toward them, looking confident and smug, smiling, nodding occasionally at people he knew.

"Shamus," Carmela said, her lip curling slightly.

"You came," Shamus said, favoring her with a huge smile. "That means you're still investigating. That you *believe* in me."

"Don't push it, Shamus," Carmela said. "The poor man died on the street in front of us. Paying our respects is the least we could do."

Shamus gave her a sly wink. "You don't fool me, I know you're ravenously curious. You love a good murder mystery. You even get worked up over Colonel Mustard in the library with a candlestick."

"Carmela inherited the curiosity gene," Ava said.

"Did you meet Maribel?" Shamus asked. "What did you think of her? Does she look like she's guilty as sin?"

"Maribel struck me as somewhat strange," Carmela said. "As well as being a fairly skillful actress."

"She could probably do dinner theater," Ava said.

"You don't think Maribel's really in mourning?" Shamus asked. "Good." He did a fist pump. "Neither do I. I think that woman is as phony as a three dollar bill."

"What about this guy Labat that Maribel's been seeing on the sly? Is he here tonight?" Carmela asked.

"Yes he is," Shamus said. "Danny Labat showed up just like I figured he would. I'll introduce you guys, but for gosh sakes don't mention anything about the affair. Maribel and Danny think it's a well-kept secret, and we don't want to tip them off that we're investigating." Shamus winked. "This has gotta stay hush-hush."

"Mum's the word," Ava said.

Carmela and Ava followed Shamus as he elbowed his way through the crowd.

"Danny," Shamus said, stopping in front of a good-looking man in a dark gray Armani suit. "I'd like you to meet my ex-wife, Carmela, and her bestie, Ava."

Danny Labat had tousled dark hair, a perpetual suntan, and the whitest teeth Carmela had ever seen. If she didn't know for a fact that Labat sold luxury cars here in New Orleans, she would have pegged him for a Miami Beach gigolo.

"Carmela." Labat executed a small bow and Carmela could just imagine his heels clicking together. "And Ava."

Ava extended a languid hand, and Labat, with slightly lowered eyelids, bent to kiss it.

"Ooh," Ava giggled. "A real gentleman." Carmela rolled her eyes.

"Honey," Labat said, still holding on to Ava's hand, "you are hotter than fish grease."

"Player," Carmela muttered under her breath.

"Tell me," Labat said to Ava, "do you have an affinity for fine motorcars?"

"Who doesn't?" Ava said, enthralled.

"I don't mean to brag, but I own Labat Luxury Sports Cars. Perhaps you've heard of us?"

"Perhaps," Ava tittered.

"We specialize in the highest of the high-end sports cars. Porsche, Maserati, Lotus. Stop by some time and I'll take you for a test-drive."

"Now there's an offer I can hardly refuse," Ava said.

Labat turned toward Shamus. "You know, I'm still looking for an upscale sponsor or two to drive in our Mardi Gras Road Rally this Monday."

"You don't want me as a driver," Shamus said with a laugh. "You want Carmela. She's the local speed demon."

"You like fast cars?" Labat asked Carmela.

"I've been known to redline a sports car or two," Carmela said. She'd also wrecked a couple cars, but figured Labat didn't need to hear about that.

"Would you be willing to sponsor her, Shamus?" Labat asked.

"I guess," Shamus said. "If the sponsorship isn't too expensive."

Labat turned an appraising eye to Carmela. "Can you drive stick?"

"Of course. Best way to get mega speed."

Labat smiled. "Know how to double-clutch?"

"I can ace an Alfa Romeo, but it takes me a little longer to get the hang of a Porsche 911 Carrera."

"Oh yeah," Labat said. "You have to drive in our road rally. Absolutely have to. Besides, we don't get many women drivers, so

I'm thrilled to add you to our roster."

Carmela decided to play hard to get. "Thanks for asking, but maybe some other time. Right now I'm up to my eyeballs . . ."

"Cher," Ava implored, "you can outdrive any guy in town. Give it a shot, this is a chance to strut your stuff."

"Please," Labat pleaded, putting his hands together in mock-appeal. "Pleeeeease?"

"Oh all right," Carmela said. "Sign me up."

"Attagirl," Shamus said. He smiled knowingly, pleased that Carmela had wormed her way in with Danny Labat. After all, in his mind, Labat was a prime suspect!

Carmela and Ava wandered over to the appetizer table. Ava was still bubbling with excitement about Carmela driving in the road rally.

"I'll be your pit crew," Ava said. "And I know just what to wear. Tight white jeans and a black-and-white-checked blouse. You know, like the checkered flag they wave at the finish of a race."

Carmela was only half listening. She was eyeing the bountiful spread of crawfish beignets, boiled shrimp, and mini beef-kabobs.

"Carmela?" said a friendly voice at her elbow.

Carmela turned to find Sam Spears smiling at her.

"It's a pleasure to see you again," Sam said. "Even though this is a rather sad occasion."

Carmela cocked a finger at him. "The raptor guy from Dr. Boogie's. Nice to see you again, too. Ava, do you remember Sam Spears?"

Ava gave Sam a curious look. She was thinking hard, obviously trying to place him.

"The ill-fated Pluvius parade?" Sam said, giving her a whopping hint. "I was part of the sorry aftermath."

Ava's mouth flew open and she pointed at him. "You're one of the guys who got bounced off the second float."

"That's me," Sam said. "Unfortunately, I landed with very little dignity intact."

"So why did Carmela call you 'the raptor guy'?"

"Because Sam owns Velocitech Software," Carmela explained. "And he uses a velociraptor as his logo."

"Oh, fun."

"I see you ladies don't have a drink yet," Sam said. "May I bring you a glass of wine from the bar?"

"That would be lovely," Ava said. "Chardonnay?"

"Same," Carmela said. "Thank you."

"Nice guy," Ava said when Sam retreated. "He seems like a perfect gentleman."

"As opposed to Shamus?"

"Oh, forget about Shamus, he's a stupid putz. Let's grab something to eat. Are you hungry?"

"Not very."

"What's wrong, *cher*?"

"Somehow I thought if we came here tonight the answers might fall neatly into place," Carmela said. "If I talked to Maribel or Labat, stared right into their eyes, then I'd somehow *know*. Except now . . . now I'm not sure what to think."

"Just too many suspects?" Ava asked.

"I guess. I mean . . . could Maribel really have killed her own husband? Or did Danny Labat do it for her?"

"He does seem awfully nice," Ava said.

"Don't get any cute ideas about Mr. Motorhead," Carmela warned. "Besides being spoken for, he's a murder suspect."

"The good ones often are," Ava said.

"And I still have the oddest feeling about Jake Bond, that ex-reporter."

"The one Shamus sicced on you?"

"Exactly. Maybe . . . maybe I should to

talk to Shamus again. See if there's anything else I can pry out of his pea brain. You head off Sam and grab our wine, okay?"

"Will do," Ava said.

Carmela found Shamus perched on a folding chair, shoveling shrimp and crackers into his mouth.

"Hey, cutie," Shamus said when he saw her.

"Don't *cutie* me," Carmela said. "I need to talk to you."

"Shoot."

"It's about Jake Bond, the ex-reporter that slithered into my shop yesterday."

"Whuh about 'im?" Shamus said, still chewing like crazy.

Carmela made a face. Talking with food in his mouth was one of the annoying habits she didn't miss about Shamus.

"Bond accused Hughes Wilder of getting him fired, right?" she said.

"Yeah."

"And now Bond is throwing shade on Tom Ratcliff, the art dealer who's also a member of the Nepthys krewe."

"Is there a point to all this, Carmela?"

"What if Bond is the one carrying the grudge against Wilder? What if Bond is the killer?"

"Holy smokes," Shamus exclaimed, practically spitting cracker crumbs all over her. "I never thought of it *that* way."

"Interesting permutation, don't you think? Bond accuses Ratcliff, when Bond's the one who secretly got even by killing the man who took away his meal ticket."

"That is good, smart, linear thinking, Carmela."

"Except for one fly in the ointment."

"What's that?"

"Apparently Tom Ratcliff, this art dealer, also lost a pile of money investing with Hughes Wilder."

"Are you kidding me?" Shamus said.

"I'm dead serious." Carmela looked around. "Well, not the Hughes Wilder kind of dead. But I am certain about the information."

"So there's an off chance that Tom Ratcliff could be the killer," Shamus said in a loud whisper. "Wow, you're really doing a bang-up job here. There are a lot of possibilities. Aside from me, of course. Carmela, darlin', you know *I* didn't do it."

"Shh, keep your voice down."

"You've got to investigate these guys, Carmela."

"Which one?"

"All of them!"

Carmela sat down on the folding chair next to Shamus and let loose a sigh. Too many suspects, too much confusion. It was hard to figure out what to do next. Should she just let the chips fall where they may and hope that Babcock dropped Shamus from his suspect list? Or should she —

"Uh-oh," Shamus muttered.

"What's wrong?"

"Don't look now, but your stud muffin *du jour* just walked in."

"*What* did you say?"

"Babcock."

Carmela glanced toward the doorway and saw Babcock standing there. He was flanked by his assistant, Bobby Gallant, and trailed by a young guy in a tweed suit and horn-rimmed glasses. They looked like the opening scene of *The Untouchables*.

Babcock pulled himself to his full height and studied the room with cool, law enforcement eyes. When those eyes finally skimmed over to her, Carmela gave a friendly little wave. But under her breath she muttered, "Rats."

CHAPTER 11

Like a heat-seeking missile, Babcock headed in Carmela's direction. When Shamus saw Babcock coming, a hint of fire in Babcock's eyes, Shamus immediately jumped up and took off. Melted into the crowd.

Deserter, Carmela thought.

"What. Are. You. Doing. Here." Babcock stood in front of her, his hands on his hips. His eyes blazed; his jaw was clenched so tight Carmela was afraid he'd pop a filling.

"Excuse me," Carmela said. "Have you seen my handsome, sweet-talking fiancé? I thought for sure I caught a glimpse of him earlier, but now he seems to have left the building."

Babcock plopped down next to Carmela and sighed. Then he picked up her hand and massaged it gently with his thumb. "Okay, message received, loud and clear. I'll take it down a notch. However, my question still stands. What's going on? Whatever possessed you to show up at a visitation that is barely one step away from a crime scene?" When Carmela remained silent, he said, "I know why. You're investigating."

Carmela could hardly deny that fact. And since she'd pretty much exhausted all of her smoke screens, she decided to come clean. "What if I am?"

"I specifically told you not to."

"No, you *asked* me not to. That's a different thing altogether."

"You're splitting hairs."

"I don't know what that phrase means," Carmela said.

Babcock opened his mouth, started to say something, and then seemed to change his mind. "I guess I'm not entirely clear on what it means either."

"See?" Carmela said. "I knew we could agree on something."

"This is all about Shamus, isn't it?" Babcock asked.

"Not really."

"I think it is. I think you still feel some kind of misplaced loyalty to him."

"Well, the dogs do seem to love him."

Babcock tightened his grip on her hand. "But do you?"

His question rocked Carmela to the core. "Me? No!" she cried. "Of course not! I love

156

you."

Babcock leaned closer to her. "You mean everything to me, Carmela. I don't want to lose you."

Despite the grim setting — and the casket — Carmela threw her arms around Babcock's neck. "You mean everything to *me*," she said, hot tears suddenly oozing from her eyes.

They stayed like that for a minute or so, until people started giving them quizzical looks. Carmela pulled away. She accepted Babcock's hanky, dabbed at her eyes, and sat back primly.

"You're investigating because Shamus asked you to," Babcock said.

Carmela sniffed and nodded. "Kind of."

Babcock let loose another deep sigh and said, "He's no longer a suspect."

Carmela perked up. "Really? You're not just saying that to make me feel better, are you? Or to get me to stop looking into things?"

"No. I'd like to stop you, but I'm not making things up."

"So you trust me," Carmela said.

"We have to trust each other, sweetheart."

"Yes, we do."

They sat in companionable silence for a while, and then Carmela said, "Quite a few suspects have popped up, you know."

Babcock's eyes searched her face for a moment. "Why don't you bring me up to date?"

"Why do I think you're humoring me?" Carmela asked.

"I'm not. Cross my heart."

"Okay then." It took Carmela all of three minutes to tick off her list of suspects: Maribel, Danny Labat, Tom Ratcliff, Jake Bond. Along with the whos went the whys — her rationale for finding each of them so suspicious.

Jake Bond was the one person Babcock didn't know about. That one surprised him.

"He was fired from his job as a financial reporter?" Babcock asked.

"That's exactly what Bond told me. Right before he pointed his sneaky little finger at Tom Ratcliff."

"I don't like the fact that Bond came into your shop. Promise me you'll keep the door locked from now on. At least until I check him out. Better yet, until this entire case is resolved."

"I can't do that. I have customers coming into my shop all day long."

"Can't you have them knock or something? Ring a buzzer, like at those high-end jewelry and antique shops?"

"I'll see what I can work out," Carmela said, knowing she wasn't going to change a thing. "Are you going to say anything to Shamus? About his not being a suspect anymore?"

"I wasn't planning to," Babcock said. "Why? Do you think I should?"

"It would be the polite thing to do. He's pretty upset."

"I have to *absolve* him and be polite? To your ex-husband?"

"Face it, you both have me in common."

"Argh." Babcock stood up. "This is gonna leave a bad taste in my mouth."

"So gargle," Carmela said. "Or chew a stick of gum." Babcock shouldered his way into the crowd.

"Car-*mela*," Ava cried. She wiggled her way past two men who turned to give her backside an appreciative look. Then she sat down next to Carmela. Right where Babcock had been. "Here. Your wine." She handed Carmela a goblet. "Sorry I took so long." She fanned her face with a hand. "There are *so* many delicious-looking men here tonight. I had no idea a funeral visitation could be so scintillating. Better than clicking my way through Tinder or Match.com."

"I think a lot of them are men who lost

money," Carmela said.

Ava looked dismayed. "So no American Express black cards?"

"I get the feeling a lot of people are sniffing around, waiting to see what happens."

"What *is* going to happen?"

"No idea. I don't know if Pontchartrain Capital Management is fully insured, if they had key person insurance in case of Wilder's untimely death, if they'll seek new management, or if they're just going to fold up their tent and declare bankruptcy." She paused. "Or insolvency, whatever the proper term is."

"That all sounds so dang complicated," Ava said. "Very C corp, as opposed to my simple little LLC. I just buy stuff wholesale and sell it retail. But this investment business sounds brutal."

"So is solving Hughes Wilder's murder."

"Yeah, I saw you talking to Babcock. First he looked real mad, and then I saw that you had turned on the waterworks. That was smart thinking. A girl starts to cry, men collapse like a cheap card table. Never fails."

But for Carmela, it hadn't been an act. She really didn't want to lose Babcock or cause him any undue pain.

Carmela took a sip of wine as she searched the crowd. She was wondering if Jake Bond might have turned up tonight. But she didn't see him. And what about Tom Ratcliff, the art dealer? She didn't know him, and she didn't know what he looked like, so there was no chance of making contact.

"Carmela." Bobby Gallant was suddenly standing directly in front of her.

"Bobby," Carmela said, popping up from her chair. "Hello."

Ava didn't just stand up — she slinked out of her chair, unfolding her jiggly parts, all the while looking very come-hither. "Hey there, sweet cheeks," she said.

"That's how you talk to an officer of the law?" Gallant asked. You could tell he was pleased. Gallant had always had a thing for Ava but never acted on it.

"Are you guys here to talk to Maribel?" Carmela asked.

"No, not tonight," Gallant said. "We've already interviewed her twice already. We're just here to observe."

Carmela figured *observe* was code for hoping to make an arrest.

"And who's the little guy that wandered in with you?" Ava asked. "The intense fellow wearing the Harry Potter glasses?"

"That's Peter Jarreau, our media liaison," Gallant said.

Ava walked two fingers up the front of

Gallant's jacket, causing his face to go a bright shade of crimson. "And what exactly does that mean?" she asked.

"He writes press releases for the NOPD," Gallant said. "Distributes them to the media. Liaises with TV and newspapers."

Carmela gazed across the room at Babcock, who, at half a head taller than most of the other men, was easy to spot. Peter Jarreau was right there next to him — a thorn in his side, as Babcock had recently joked.

"How's Jarreau working out?" Carmela asked. She knew he was fairly new to the job.

"Oh, you know," Gallant said. "Jarreau always tries to put a positive spin on things."

"Not always easy to do when you're writing about murder," Carmela said.

"Especially in this case," Gallant said. "A high-profile victim, a questionable hedge fund —"

"Is it questionable?" Carmela asked.

Gallant smiled. "It is because we're asking questions."

Carmela leaned in. "What have you learned?" Maybe she could pick up a few tasty bits of information.

But Gallant was no fool. He wasn't about to spill a can of beans to Carmela.

"Sorry," Gallant said. "That's privileged

information."

"Carmela will find out," Ava said, glancing sideways at him and smiling. "She always does."

Out in the vestibule, her mission pretty much concluded, Carmela decided to sign the guest book. It was huge and showy, with an oxblood leather cover and gold edging on the pages.

"Why?" Ava asked.

"To send Maribel a message. Let her know we were here, that we're watching her."

"You really think Maribel's guilty, don't you?"

"I think a lot of people *look* guilty," Carmela said. "But that doesn't mean they are. The trick is ferreting out the genuinely guilty party."

"The killer," Ava said. She watched as Carmela signed her name. "That guest book is something else. It's ginormous." She reached over and touched one of the pages. "And the paper feels handmade. Like something Gutenberg might have used."

"It's just run-of-the-mill parchment paper," Carmela said. "No big deal."

"Huh," Ava said. "Maybe Maribel had to cut corners somewhere."

Outside the funeral home, the night was dark and chilly.

"Maybe we shouldn't have stayed so long," Ava said as they hurried down the sidewalk to Carmela's car. "We still have a lot to do."

"But you're all packed up?"

"That's right. I stuffed everything into —"

"Shh," Carmela said, interrupting her. She grabbed Ava's arm and pulled her to a stop.

Ava's eyes were as big as saucers. "What's wrong?" she whispered.

"I thought I heard footsteps."

"Somebody's following us?"

"Maybe." Carmela listened again, carefully. Trying to filter out the night sounds — the rustle of leaves, the flow of traffic two streets over — from the scrape against sidewalk bricks that she *thought* she'd heard. "Or maybe not."

"Who could it be?"

"Don't know."

"On my count," Ava said. "We run for your car. Go on three."

"Okay."

"One . . ."

Carmela and Ava bolted like a pair of greyhounds out of a starting gate, running full tilt down the street. Once they'd pulled open the car doors, they flung themselves inside.

BAM!

The door locks were slammed into place.

Carmela hunched forward and peered anxiously into the dark. Neither of them made a sound — they were trying to catch their breath, calm their overwrought nerves.

"Do you see anybody?" Ava finally asked.

Carmela shook her head. "No."

"But that doesn't mean there isn't somebody out there."

"But who?" Carmela asked.

"I don't know." Ava shivered. "Maniac? Guy with a chain saw? Guy with a hook on his hand?"

"Those are crazy stories that kids tell around campfires."

"Honey, those are the stories that play in this girl's head nonstop."

Twenty minutes later they bumped down the back alley of their apartment complex. Carmela nosed her car onto the edge of the brick courtyard as far as she dared, and then they both ran upstairs to Ava's studio apartment.

When Ava opened the door, Carmela was relieved to see there were only two gold lamé suitcases sitting side by side. Wonderful. She knew they'd fit into her car without any problem at all.

Then she took another step into the apartment, and the scene completely shifted. Several cardboard boxes and assorted plastic bags, all stuffed to bursting, were piled haphazardly against the wall. Next to them was a rolling rack of clothes.

Ava seemed oblivious to Carmela's concern that everything fit. She picked up two boxes and a plastic bag and said, "If you could just grab those suitcases . . ."

Their first trip downstairs nearly filled Carmela's car. The second trip brought it to overflowing.

"I don't know if we can make it all the way to the Garden District with this kind of load," Carmela said. Would the springs hold? Would a tire suddenly blow out? "Are you sure all this stuff is necessary? That it's vital to your well-being?"

"Oh, definitely. And we dare not forget Isis in her cat carrier."

"What about that rolling rack of clothes?" Carmela asked.

"Maybe I'll just grab a few key pieces from it."

Carmela put down the convertible top to give Ava's belongings every last square inch of space. Then the three of them — Carmela, Ava, and Isis the cat — hurtled down St. Charles Avenue.

"All we need is a mattress piled on top and we'd look like a bunch of Okies," Carmela grunted. It was embarrassing. People in other cars were staring at them. Honking even.

"Don't mind them," Ava said. "They have no empathy for people in my situation."

"You mean ladies with too many bags full of trashy lingerie?" Carmela asked.

At one point, a streetcar rattled past them, and two teenaged boys waved and shouted out a window, "Eviction special! Whoohoo!"

As they crossed Josephine Street, which probably hadn't had its potholes filled since Huey Long was in office, two of Ava's plastic bags shot up into the air, spun around, and bounced off the rear fender. Ava made a valiant grab, but missed them by inches.

"My red thigh-high boots!" Ava cried. "And the bag with my longline bras. Stop the car. Oh no, now the cat carrier is sliding. Pull over. Quick."

Carmela hit the brakes and glanced around. "Work fast, before we get mugged."

Ava jumped out, rooted around in the gutter for a few seconds, then tossed the bags back into the car and squeezed back in herself.

Finally, Carmela hung a left on Washington, then made a right on Chestnut Street. They were in the heart of the Garden District now, surrounded by an architecturally unique neighborhood that featured immense homes built in the Greek Revival, Gothic, Italianate, and Georgian styles. Here were homes festooned with twisting turrets, cast-iron balconies, colonnades, and gingerbread trim. Authors, poets, movie stars, and people so rich you didn't even know their names lived here, surrounded by fabulous gardens and flower beds, magnolia trees, crepe myrtle, and ancient live oaks.

"Here, turn here!" Ava called out.

Carmela pulled into the driveway of a gray stone Greek Revival home with an enormous front veranda, a side porte cochere, dark green shutters, a front door with a stained glass window, and an oddly squarish fourth-story cupola on top of it all. It wasn't the classiest-looking home on the block, but it made up for it in sheer volume.

Carmela and Ava shuttled Ava's bags, suitcases, and boxes onto the veranda. When Ava picked up the cat carrier, Isis let out a long hiss.

"Somebody's all grumpy about the move,"

Ava said as she pulled a key from her purse. "Let me get this door open and put this kitty inside so she can stretch her legs."

Ava aimed the key at the lock but couldn't quite connect.

"Here," Carmela said. She pulled a tiny flashlight out of her bag and hit the button. Immediately the lock was bathed in a faint circle of light.

Ava stuck the key in, gave it a hard turn, and the door swung open with a loud, agonizing creak. Both women stuck their heads in and peered around.

The twelve-foot-high walls of the oval-shaped entryway were covered in dark oak and burgundy floral wallpaper. An ornately carved sideboard held an antique blue and white Chinese bowl along with a silver salver awaiting the next mail delivery. A few steps in, a wide, carpeted stairway led upstairs. To the right, a short hallway led to the interior of the home.

"The place seems awfully gloomy," Carmela said. And it wasn't just the lack of lighting. The place seemed to carry an air of heavy resignation.

"Let me turn on some lights," Ava said, reaching for a switch on the wall. "That'll brighten things up."

It didn't.

"Hmm," Ava said, squaring her shoulders. "Let's hope the parlor and dining room are a lot cheerier."

They weren't.

They walked down a hallway lined with oil paintings into an enormous parlor. White sheets were humped over what must've been large, impressive pieces of furniture. Dust motes twirled in the air. Ava flipped on more lights, but the bulbs in many of the wall sconces were burned out. Still, the fireplace was Italian marble and enormous; the carpets looked like hand-loomed Aubusson; and there were fine oil paintings, rich with crackle glaze, on the walls. The home had the potential to be a real showstopper if it was cleaned, properly lighted, and reimagined.

"Kind of lonely," Ava said as Isis suddenly rocketed out of her cat carrier and disappeared into the darkness.

"You sure you're going to be okay here?" Carmela asked. The place smelled like musty fabric, mothballs, and old cigar smoke — probably trapped in the drapes. "I mean, all by yourself?" The house looked like a movie set from *Young Frankenstein*.

"Don't worry about me. I'll just veg out and binge-watch some Netflix. It'll be great."

The gold candlestick phone on the spinet table suddenly jingled a brash note.

"See?" Ava said. "Things are popping already. I've only been here two minutes and somebody's calling. Probably an impromptu invitation to some ultra fancy party."

Ava picked up the phone, gave a friendly hello, and listened. "No, no," she said. "Mrs. Wilkes isn't . . ."

Wrong number, Carmela figured.

But Ava continued to listen for another few minutes, all the while trying to get a word in.

"But I don't . . ." Ava said. "At this late date?" It was obvious that she was being talked over.

Finally, Ava hung up the phone and turned to Carmela with a puzzled expression on her face.

"What was that all about?" Carmela asked. "Did you get a call from the local Welcome Wagon? Are they coming over with beignets and wine?"

Ava shook her head. "You know that Grand Candlelight Tour that happens every year during Mardi Gras?"

Carmela nodded. "Sure. The tour where a dozen or so fancy Garden District homes throw open their doors to the public. And

171

the public gets to see how the other half lives."

"That's it exactly."

"So . . . what about it?"

"It's happening here. Sunday afternoon."

Carmela frowned, trying to process this information. "Wait a minute. You mean here-here?"

"That's what Kitty Burell, the chairwoman of the Historic Homes Society, just told me. She said that the Wilkes family committed to be on the tour over a year ago, and that I should be ready for a walkthrough this Saturday." Ava's mouth pulled into a tight line. "Her committee wants to see what we've done."

Carmela looked around at the humpy-bumpy white sheets and the large gathering of dust bunnies curled under a gaming table. "But we've done nothing."

Ava glanced at her wristwatch as though an invisible stopwatch had started to tick a countdown. "Well, I've somehow got to pull this place together in the next two days." She looked around at the gloomy interior. "Make it look all cozy and elegant instead of like Miss Havisham's summer retreat."

"How on earth are you going to do that?" Even as Carmela asked the question, she sensed a group project in the making.

"Um . . ."

"Does that pregnant pause mean you want me to help?"

"Oh, Carmela, would you? Please, would you? You've got such a flair for design and color and decorating and I . . . well, I don't."

"Don't worry about it," Carmela said. "Neither does Mrs. Wilkes."

CHAPTER 12

Friday morning dawned cool and cloudy with occasional spits of rain. A perfectly moody, dank day for the funeral of Hughes Wilder.

Carmela wouldn't have missed it for the world, of course. And she'd persuaded Ava to go along with her on the promise that there'd probably be a bang-up funeral luncheon to follow. Crepes and beignets might even be involved.

So there they were, huddled together in the midst of a large and somber crowd, staring at the Wilder family's crumbling crypt in Lafayette Cemetery No. 1.

"Creepy," Ava whispered.

"Are you talking about the Wilkes house or this place?" Carmela asked.

"Both," Ava said with a yawn.

"Did you sleep all right or did something go bump in the night?"

"Honestly, *cher,* if there were ghosties and

goblins flitting about last night, I was so beat I never paid them any mind."

Standing there, Carmela glanced about at her fellow mourners, sedately attired in black. With their jacket and coat collars pulled up against the rain, she thought they looked like a clutch of vampires. Or magpies, depending on your worldview.

Carmela didn't mind the dismal quality of the day. She supposed she had a slightly dark side, one that enjoyed stormy days, relished legends of ghosts and hauntings, and held a deep fascination for this historic old cemetery. Built in the early 1800s, Lafayette Cemetery was the oldest cemetery in the city of New Orleans. Seven thousand people had been laid to rest here in the strict confines of a single city block. No wonder the cemetery was crowded wall-to-wall with ancient tilting gravestones, obelisks, ornate statuary, wall vaults (don't ask!), and run-down family crypts.

The Wilder crypt, with its chipped masonry, pockmarked stone angels, and heavy iron gate, even had a dust-coated window set into a wall, should one be so inclined to peer in at moldering caskets — a room with a view, so to speak.

As a counterpoint to all the gloom and doom, Maribel Wilder stood at the front of the pack dressed in a pastel blue Dior suit. She looked perky and a little antsy, as though she was in a hurry to get this funeral service over with so she could dry out at a nice luncheon. With a nice dry martini.

But for all her quirks, Maribel had arranged a classy affair. A string quartet sat on rickety black folding chairs gamely churning out Bach's "Sheep May Safely Graze." The notes hung in the air, clear and true for a split second, then were quickly muffled by the dampness.

Shamus and Sam Spears had shown up, along with the usual suspects.

Danny Labat stood off to one side, murmuring quietly into his cell phone. Maybe he was closing a deal on a good used Maserati while he waited for the funeral service to begin? Why not kill two birds with one stone? Or maybe he was bored with Maribel already.

Almost two dozen members of the Pluvius krewe were there, too. They were easily identified by their black armbands and the white carnations in their lapels. Carmela remembered the membership roster that Shamus had shoved into her hands a couple of days ago and wondered if she should start cranking her way through that list.

Out of the corner of her eye, Carmela also

spotted Jake Bond. The surly ex-reporter wore a weird-looking oilcloth raincoat and was scratching away on a notepad, seemingly lost in thought.

There was also a tall, good-looking man in a black leather jacket who Carmela decided might possibly be Tom Ratcliff. He looked artsy and authoritative, like someone who might own a gallery and also be high enough in the social pecking order to be a krewe captain.

Okay, Carmela thought, so the gang's all here. The question was, could she learn something? Could she watch reactions, study body language, talk to people, and somehow parse out a guilty party?

Just as she was checking out a bearded man in a tweed jacket, who she thought of as a professor type, the minister stepped in front of the coffin. With his black suit and frizzled gray hair, he looked like an old-fashioned tent revivalist. But his words were far more tempered. In a soft voice, he began to lead the mourners in The Lord's Prayer. Everyone chimed in, of course, even the heathens in the group.

Then it was time for a eulogy.

The minister, looking even more serious now, introduced a man by the name of Roger Colton. He was, interestingly enough, a vice president at Pontchartrain Capital Management.

Colton cleared his throat nervously as he stepped up to address the crowd. He spoke slowly and haltingly, sticking to a mostly platitude-filled script. He praised Hughes Wilder for his business acumen, for his outstanding leadership in the community, and, finally, for his friendship.

This was the point at which Carmela drifted off. As Colton droned on, she glanced around the group of mourners once again to see who else she knew — and to see who else was as bored as she was.

Carmela's eye immediately caught Babcock's. He must have snuck in late. She lifted a finger and gave a mini wave. He winked back. Well, good. Maybe he wasn't all that surprised to see her there? Or maybe he'd finally accepted the fact that she was involved? Naw, he was just trying to pacify her. To keep everything copasetic until he could bump her out of the way.

Carmela craned her neck to see who else was there and found herself staring at Peter Jarreau, the NOPD's media liaison. He'd struck her as kind of an ankle-biter, always jumping around, yapping his head off, and pestering Babcock for information. Then again, maybe she wasn't being fair. Maybe the kid was just trying to do his job.

Now the minister was looking out over the crowd and saying something. What was it? A final prayer? Carmela strained to hear. No, he was inviting the mourners to be Maribel Wilder's guests at a post-funeral luncheon at a restaurant over on Magazine Street. Carmela nudged Ava with an elbow and mouthed, *Luncheon — yes*? Ava nodded in agreement and did a pseudo–sign language pat of her tummy.

And then, miraculously, the service was concluded.

Carmela glanced in Babcock's direction, but didn't see him anymore. Had he already run off? Jumped in the blue BMW he'd scored in a police auction and hustled back downtown? Maybe he had a powwow with the police chief or the mayor. Whatever.

But, wait, what was this? Peter Jarreau was walking toward them, a knowing smile on his face.

Ava nudged Carmela. "Weasel alert," she said under her breath as Jarreau approached.

"Miss Carmela?" Jarreau asked. "Miss Ava?" He bobbed his head respectfully and looked like he would've tipped his hat if he had one. Unfortunately, he also arrived in a thick cloud of spicy cologne.

"Yessss?" Carmela said in a questioning tone. What was this about?

"Detective Babcock asked me to relay a message to you."

"What might that be?" Carmela asked. She subtly pinched her nose so she wouldn't have to inhale Jarreau's Drakkar Noir, or Tommy Boy, or whatever scent he was wearing.

"He said I should urge you to skip the funeral luncheon. And that I should tell you you've done enough investigating for one day."

Ava waved a hand in front of her face. "What is that, anyway?" she asked. "Vintage Aqua Velva?"

"Excuse me?" Jarreau said, frowning.

"Great, great, thanks," Carmela said. She gripped Ava's arm and pulled her back a step to escape the toxic scent cloud. "Thanks a lot. Message received."

"But I —" Jarreau protested.

Carmela and Ava already had their backs to him and were scurrying away.

"Phew!" Ava said, when they'd finally put some distance behind them. "That was awful. That boy's a regular Cologne Ranger."

"He's a walking stink bomb," Carmela said, thinking that Babcock was a sneaky snake for sending a boy to do a man's work.

Well, never mind that, because they were going to attend the luncheon anyway. Wouldn't miss it for the world.

Purgatoria on Magazine Street was a peculiar place to host a funeral luncheon. For one thing, it was a dark, cavernous restaurant done in a pseudo-religious theme. The hostess stand was a repurposed baptismal font, gargoyles peered from every nook and cranny, and the massive chandeliers all looked like they'd been ripped out of an old church.

"I've always loved this place," Ava said as they walked in. "A little bit churchy, a hint of voodoo. A lot like my personal style."

Carmela and Ava stopped at the hostess stand.

"We're here for the Wilder luncheon," Carmela said to a hostess in a slinky black dress. She was a dead ringer for Morticia Addams.

"Through the purple velvet curtains and down the hallway to our private dining room," Morticia said. "The Byzantine Room."

They walked past a mural that looked positively medieval, then past a cluster of wooden Maltese crosses that were studded with silver icons.

"Does Drew Gaspar still own this place?" Ava asked.

Carmela shook her head. "There are new owners now." She gave a crooked smile. "What? Can't you tell?"

"Very funny." Ava shook back her hair, tilted her head back, and smiled as they walked into the Byzantine Room.

The party room was larger than they'd expected. The walls were done in a warm, inviting, sepia-toned stucco, almost like you'd find on a Tuscan church or villa. Threadbare but still-elegant Oriental carpets littered the floor, and the half-dozen circular tables were each ample enough to seat at least ten people. The ceiling had a painted fresco. Something that looked like a mingling of saints, sinners, and angels.

"I wonder what the food is like," Ava said. "New Orleans is such a tough restaurant town. Lots of old-line restaurants, lots of new ones continually cropping up. It makes for a lot of competition."

"There's the buffet line," Carmela said. "Why don't we go find out how the food is?"

They were not disappointed.

"My favorite, *cher,*" Ava said. "Stuffed artichokes."

"Can't go wrong there," Carmela said.

She tipped open a silver chafing dish and took a peek. "And panko-crusted shrimp. They look delicious."

"Got some fried oysters here," Ava said.

"There's so much fried food here, I'm going to need a defibrillator."

"I still think it's a good thing I skipped breakfast."

"You always skip breakfast."

"Do I?" Ava said, acting surprised. "Maybe I'm all atwitter because I woke up in such a strange house."

"I've been meaning to talk to you about that."

"About what?"

"After we fulfill Mrs. Wilkes's obligation to the Grand Candlelight Tour, I think you should move back to your own apartment."

"No," Ava said.

"Yes," Carmela said.

"But I promised I'd house-sit."

Carmela spooned a helping of fried okra onto her plate. "They're using you."

"Harrison is?"

"And his family. Truth be known, Harrison should have never put you in that position." Ava started to protest, but Carmela continued. "I know you think you're doing everyone a favor, but it's unfair. To you." She added a croissant to her plate. "There,

I've said my piece."

Ava gazed at Carmela with a mixture of awe and respect. "You're a good friend, *cher*."

"Tell me about it. I'm even going to get us a couple glasses of champagne. Here, you take my plate, grab us a place at one of those big tables, and I'll be back with the bubbly."

"Which table?"

Carmela glanced around. "Well, not the head table. Because that's where Maribel is sitting. Holding court. Find someplace more unobtrusive."

Carmela was back with the champagne a few minutes later.

"Shamus and some of the Pluvius guys are here," were her first words to Ava. "I just ran into them."

"So is Danny Labat," Ava said. "That sports car guy."

"Yeah, I saw him at the funeral." Carmela periscoped her head up. "Where's he at?"

"He just sat down at the head table, scrunched in real tight next to Maribel."

"Holy cats," Carmela said. "They're not even putting up a pretense anymore."

"They think they're free."

"Nothing's free." Carmela glanced down

184

at her plate. "Except maybe lunch." Then she saw Shamus striding toward her. "Forget I said that."

"Carmela," Shamus cooed as he slid into the chair next to her. "What's shakin', babe?"

"Where did you slink off to last night?" Carmela asked.

"I figured you wanted to be alone with your lover boy," Shamus said.

"You just wanted me to take all the heat."

"Heat?" Shamus pretended to look confused.

"For investigating. On your behalf."

"Oh, that," Shamus said. He scrunched up his face. "Um . . . I don't know."

"He's an articulate son of a gun, isn't he?" Ava said.

"Are you poking fun at me?" Shamus asked.

"Nothing you don't deserve," Ava said.

"Go away, Shamus," Carmela said.

"How are the dogs?" Shamus asked. "Does Boo miss me? Is Poobah taking his itch pills?"

"No," said Carmela. "He gums them to death and then spits them out on my carpet. Now it's all stained green."

"He's got to take those pills," Shamus insisted. "You have to *make* him."

"I do," Carmela said. "Once he does his thing, I peel his mangled pill off the carpet, toss it in his mouth, and clamp his jaws shut until he swallows."

"Same thing she probably did to you," Ava said to Shamus.

"I'm leaving." Shamus stood up and stalked off.

"Don't get caught in the back draft," Ava called after him.

They nibbled at their food, sipped champagne, and kept a watchful eye on Maribel and Labat.

"You think she's gonna be driving in the road rally?" Ava asked.

"If she does, I'm going to take great pleasure in running her off the road," Carmela said.

"You're a good sport, Carmela."

But Carmela had suddenly caught sight of the same tall, distinguished-looking gentleman in the leather jacket who she'd seen at the cemetery. He was standing in the buffet line, helping himself to the eggs Sardou.

"Is that Tom Ratcliff?" she asked.

Ava stared at him. "No idea."

"I'm going to go talk to him and find out."

"Why?"

"Because he lost a pile of money with Pontchartrain Capital Management and could be the killer," Carmela said.

Ava gave Ratcliff an appraising look, obviously liking what she saw. "He sure doesn't *look* like a killer."

"They never do."

"Excuse me," Carmela said. "Are you Tom Ratcliff?" She didn't catch him at the eggs, but glommed on to him at the next station.

"Why yes," Ratcliff said, smiling at her as he scooped a helping of fried potatoes onto his plate. "Pardon me, but do we know each other?"

"Not really," Carmela said. "But I've been meaning to stop by your gallery and get acquainted." She touched a hand to her chest. "I'm Carmela Bertrand. I own Memory Mine, the scrapbooking shop over on Governor Nicholls Street."

"Then we're neighbors," Ratcliff said. "How lovely."

"I noticed you back at the cemetery service. It's just awful, isn't it? Hughes Wilder's murder, I mean."

"A tragedy," Ratcliff agreed.

"And the police don't seem to be close to solving it. To finding his killer."

"I'm sure justice will prevail."

"Did you know Hughes Wilder well? Perhaps he was a client?" Carmela tried to keep her tone light and breezy so it didn't sound as if she was prying. Which she was.

"No," Ratcliff said in a slow, measured voice. "Actually, I was a client of his."

"So you're an investor," Carmela said.

"I was." Now a note of wariness crept in.

"Ah," Carmela said, as if she was commiserating mightily with him. "I take it you lost money along with quite a few other investors. I guess that explains why you're here."

Ratcliff eyed her carefully. "I'm not sure I know what you mean."

"You know," Carmela said. "Follow the money." She smiled prettily at him. "Remember the movie *All the President's Men*? 'Follow the money' became Woodward and Bernstein's catchphrase. And everyone here seems to be waiting to see what will happen with Pontchartrain Capital Management. Will it fold? Will it continue? Will the money turn up?"

"You're very clever," Ratcliff said.

"Thank you."

"Are you a collector?" he asked.

Ratcliff had just pivoted the conversation one hundred and eighty degrees from where they'd been. Frustrating, but Carmela decided to go along with it.

"I have a few nice pieces," she said.

"Nineteenth-century oil paintings, some bronze sculptures, a few contemporary photographs. One by Caponigro — *Running White Deer.*"

"Sounds like you're fairly serious about your collecting."

"I try to be," Carmela said.

"You should stop by my gallery," Ratcliff said. "I'd love to show you a few choice pieces by some of our local artists."

"I'd like that. In fact, if you're going to be there this afternoon, I might even find time to pop over."

Ratcliff smiled at her. "That would be —"

CRASH! BANG!

Somewhere, a chair had toppled over.

"Get out now!" A woman's voice rose in a shrill, murderous shriek.

Carmela and Ratcliff whirled around to see who was doing all the shouting. It was Maribel. She was standing at the head table, quivering like a fish on the end of a spear, as she screamed at Jake Bond. Her teeth were bared, her hair stuck out, and her eyes blazed. Her chair was on its side, probably because she'd sprung from it like a crazed jack-in-the-box.

"I *told* you I didn't want to see your face and I meant it!" Maribel shrieked. "Not at my husband's funeral and certainly not now!"

"I'm just trying to write my story," Bond pleaded. "If you'd simply —"

"Do you not understand? There is no *story.*" Maribel seethed as her mouth pulled into a rictus of rage. Her eyes were starting to bulge, and her complexion had turned an unflattering shade of salmon pink. "So get out. Get out and leave me *alone.*" She lifted an open palm as if to give him a good whack.

"You heard the woman!" Danny Labat yelled. Now he'd joined the action, standing up, puffing out his chest, looking as if he wanted to throw a roundhouse punch at Bond.

"Dear Lord," Carmela murmured. She and everyone else at the luncheon waited with bated breath to see what would happen next.

They didn't have to wait long.

Instead of smacking Bond, Maribel snatched up her glass of champagne and hurled the liquid in Bond's face. "Go *away*! Leave me *alone*!" she screeched. That was the thing about Maribel. When she screamed, she screamed in italics.

Bond's hands clenched reflexively as he took a step toward her.

That was all the prompting Danny Labat needed. Like a guest on *The Jerry Springer Show,* he picked up his own chair, flipped it sideways, and hurled it clumsily at Bond's head.

Bond ducked as the chair went airborne, but he wasn't quick enough. One leg of the chair clipped him right in the middle of the forehead, opening a nasty gash.

"You freaking jackhole!" Bond screamed at Labat. "Are you crazy? I should have you arrested! Better yet, I'm going to sue you for everything you've got!" He grabbed a table napkin and pressed it to the mélange of champagne and blood that dripped from his wounded forehead. "You throw a chair at my head? You people are nuts! Every freaking last one of you."

With that, Bond spun around and clumped out of the Byzantine Room with as much dignity as he could muster.

"Amazing," Tom Ratcliff said, watching Bond stagger out of the room. Bond — head bleeding, tail between his legs — was still muttering angrily.

"It's not something you see every day," Carmela agreed. She turned her full attention on Maribel, who was fanning her face with a hand. Her one-act play had pretty much confirmed it: the woman had a horrible temper. When something upset her, she went from DEFCON 5 to DEFCON 1 (meaning nuclear war was imminent!) in a matter of seconds. Of course, Danny Labat was no slouch in the temper-tantrum department either. He'd looked like a maniacal banty rooster when he'd picked up that chair and tossed it.

Yes, Carmela decided, it might be a good idea to keep those two crazies under tight surveillance.

Chapter 13

Once Carmela got back to Memory Mine, Gabby quickly filled her in on the morning's sales, customer requests, and deliveries. Then, with an appropriately somber look on her face, Gabby inquired about the funeral.

"Did you ever hear the old Rodney Dangerfield joke, 'I went to a fight and a hockey game broke out'?" Carmela said.

Gabby gave a delighted giggle. Then, when she realized Carmela was dead serious, said, "Are you telling me there was an actual fight at the funeral?"

"At the luncheon afterward," Carmela said.

Gabby's mouth dropped open. "Between . . ."

"The bereaved wife, Maribel, and the reporter Jake Bond."

"An actual knock-down, drag-out fight? In front of the guests?"

"All that was missing was Don King," Carmela said.

"No."

"And it ended with Danny Labat smacking Jake Bond in the head with a chair."

"Jake Bond," Gabby said. "The reporter guy that came creeping in here?"

"That's the guy."

"These people are way too intense for something not to be going on. One of them has to be the killer."

"But which one?" Carmela shook her head. "Between the Pluvius krewe and Pontchartrain Capital Management, there are so many people involved . . . but so few clues. I keep knocking on doors but nobody's home. Just no good solid clues."

"What does Babcock say about your snooping?"

"Same old, same old. 'Don't interfere, Carmela. It's my job, Carmela, not yours.' "

Gabby straightened the strand of pearls at her throat. "And of course you're paying close attention. Since he *is* your fiancé."

Carmela shrugged. "He knew what I was all about when he asked me to marry him."

"Maybe Babcock thinks that, as the wife of one of NOPD's hotshot detectives, you'll have no choice but to stay out of his business. I mean, how do you think Stuart would feel if I was test-driving Range Rovers and Humvees all over town?"

"I think the Toyota King of New Orleans adores you so much that he'd forgive just about anything."

"You think?"

"Honey," Carmela said, "Stuart gazes at you like you're a ripe plum just waiting to be picked."

Gabby was still beaming from Carmela's words when Jake Bond lurched into Memory Mine like a drunken storm trooper.

"Hey," Bond said, bouncing off the frame of the front door, then staggering a few steps forward.

"Hold it right there," Carmela said, putting a hand up, trying to block any further progress he might attempt.

Bond scowled at her. "Did you see what happened to me this morning? Yes, of course you did. So *now* are you convinced that you should pitch in and help me? Those people, Maribel Wilder's whole crowd . . . are certifiably insane. And vicious. Just look at this!" He raised a hand and pointed to a white bandage that covered half his forehead. "I sustained a serious injury."

"Did you get a tetanus shot?" Carmela asked.

"Do you think I need one?"

Carmela shrugged. She wasn't about to offer sympathy to a man who continued to badger her.

Bond touched a hand to his bandage. "Dang thing hurts like crazy and I've got a headache that won't quit."

"Maybe you tipped Labat over the edge into a kind of psychotic state."

"I'm seriously thinking of pressing charges against him," Bond said with a snort. "Assault and battery."

"Now there's a fine idea," Carmela said. "Why don't you head over to the nearest precinct station and do exactly that." *Take it to the cops and leave us alone. Because I don't really know how innocent you are.*

"I'll get my digs in against Labat, but not until I finish chasing down this story."

"Are you telling me you have a lead in the murder?" Carmela was cautiously curious.

"Better than a lead. I have *sources.*" Bond mustered a priggish smile. "Everybody and his brother loves to feed information to reporters. And the word on the street is that Danny Labat is trying to put together a consortium to take over Pontchartrain Capital Management."

"Hard to just walk in cold and take over a company," Carmela said.

"Not so cold," Bond said. "Labat is working on Maribel to make it happen."

"And my sources say he's been working on Maribel for several months. Long before her husband was killed."

Bond surprised her by saying, "Exactly. He had to have everything lined up nice and tidy-like."

"Maybe," Carmela said, unconvinced. *And maybe you've got a new vendetta against Labat since he nailed you with that chair.* "You know, I'd be more inclined to believe you if you told me who these so-called sources are."

"Haven't you heard of the First Amendment? I'm one reporter who actually has scruples. I *protect* people who give me information."

"The last I heard you were an out-of-work reporter."

"That's all changed," Bond said. "I just started working for the *NOLA Vindicator.*"

"Never heard of it," Carmela said.

"It's what you'd call an alt-left newspaper. Still in its infancy, but going great guns."

"And let me guess," Carmela said. "You're writing a piece on the murder."

"No, I'm writing an exposé."

"You know what I think? That you should exposé yourself right out of here."

Jake Bond threw her an angry look, spun

on his heels, and disappeared out the front door, as noisily and unsteadily as he'd come in.

"What was that all about?" Gabby asked. She'd been in the back, arranging paper in wire bins.

"Jake Bond is still trying to drum up a nice, juicy story," Carmela said.

"And then what?"

"He's going to run it in some garbage tabloid that publishes, like, twice a month."

"If Bond does manage some sort of scoop, do you think he could get his old TV job back?"

"Probably," Carmela said. "As long as he's not the killer."

"Jeepers," Gabby said. "Maybe we should lock the doors."

But it was a good thing they didn't, because not two minutes later, Winnie Gilbert, one of their regulars, came in. Winnie, a poised, attractive family therapist who was in her mid-fifties and African American, was positively beaming. Her daughter, Lisbeth, was getting married.

"Congratulations," Carmela said. "To both of you."

"When's the wedding?" Gabby asked. An incurable romantic, she was known to swoon over anybody's wedding.

"In three weeks," Winnie said. "And my sole mission in life is to make it absolutely spectacular. Which is why we're having the wedding at St. Louis Cathedral and the reception at Hotel Monteleone — and we've hired Shane Dupree to be our wedding photographer."

"You'll adore Shane," Carmela said. "He's one of the best wedding and event photographers around. He's not only a fantastic shooter, he knows how to blend art with storytelling."

Winnie nodded. "I told Shane that, besides a formal album, I wanted a more . . . let's call it a casual remembrance album, for my daughter. And he suggested I visit you."

"What a great idea," Carmela said. She took Winnie by the arm and guided her back to a shelf where several dozen albums were on display.

"With everyone carrying smartphones these days," said Winnie, "I figure we'll get a flood of digital images. My idea is to have them all printed, and then arrange them in a second, less formal album, for Lisbeth and John."

"So we'll need to select an album and some paper," Carmela said. "Do you have any specific colors you want to work with?"

Winnie pulled a silk Hermès scarf from her bag. "This is Lisbeth's favorite scarf and she's been keying all her wedding colors off of it."

"Gorgeous," Carmela said, admiring the scarf. It featured a riot of pink, ivory, and silver-gray roses strewn across a pale blue background. She reached up and plucked an album off the shelf. "This album has a soft, satin cover done in dove gray. Almost identical to the gray in your daughter's scarf."

"I love it," Winnie said. "It's almost too perfect. And would it be possible to put their names and the wedding date on the cover?"

Carmela placed a square of white vellum on the album cover, then grabbed a snippet of French lace. "We could write the name and date in calligraphy and then frame it with lace. Or, if you prefer, a gauze ribbon."

"No, I like the lace," Winnie said. "What about the inside pages?"

"I'd recommend some handmade paper," Carmela said. She slid open a drawer and pulled out a couple pieces of paper. "This is an Italian marbleized paper, and this is a brushed foil with a Victorian design. Either one would make a nice counterpoint to the high-tech angle of the photos."

"The marbleized," Winnie said. "Definitely."

Even as Carmela gave Winnie a few more tips on how to personalize the album cover and inside pages, her mind kept coming back to all the different suspects. And what their motivations might possibly be.

When they were just about finished, Carmela drew a deep breath and said, "Winnie, you're a practicing psychologist. Can I ask your professional opinion on something?"

"Of course."

"My question is kind of grisly. In fact, it's in reference to the man who was killed when that Mardi Gras float exploded."

Winnie didn't blink. She just gave an encouraging nod, almost as if she were giving counsel in an office situation. "Yes, that's been all over the news."

"I guess what I'm really asking about," Carmela stammered, "is the mind of the killer."

"Go ahead."

"What do you think drives a person to actually commit murder?" Carmela asked.

Winnie considered Carmela's question for a few moments, then said, "This sounds like a police investigation."

"I'm just an interested party."

"Okay, you realize I'm not a forensic psychologist, but my general understanding is there tends to be three key motivating factors that can set a person off. Send them down a collision course of destruction."

"And what would those factors be?" Carmela asked.

"Certainly greed or money."

Carmela knew that box was checked off.

"Anger or payback is often a huge motivation," Winnie continued. "And a third factor would be political ideology."

Carmela figured that two out of three wasn't bad.

"Does that help?" Winnie asked.

"Yes, it does," Carmela said. "I feel like I should pay you for a counseling session."

Winnie smiled. "Just show me how to design that album cover and we'll call it even."

CHAPTER 14

"What were you talking to Winnie about?" Gabby asked. She was standing at the front counter unpacking a brand-new shipment of tempera paints and crackle glazes. "You two looked so serious."

"I asked her about murder," Carmela said. "About the motivating factors that might spur a potential killer into action."

Carmela's answer seemed to let some of the air out of Gabby's enthusiasm. "You brought *that* up to Winnie while you were sorting through wedding albums?"

"Well, I tried to be a little more genteel about it, but yes, I did."

"Did Winnie give you any kind of answer?"

"She was actually quite helpful. In fact, her answers sparked a couple of ideas. Kind of nudged me in a new direction."

Gabby shook her head. "I just hope you don't go out of your way to put yourself in danger, Carmela."

"I'd like to think I'm more careful than that."

"I can see why Babcock worries about you."

"He's just a worrywart," Carmela said. *Is he really? Hmm, only when it comes to me. Otherwise he's a pretty cool customer.*

"You know, Carmela, Babcock is an experienced homicide detective. He can sense when a situation or person isn't right, when there's a need to proceed with caution. He's probably honed a good gut feeling for danger."

"What do you do when you're *not* law enforcement, but you can feel those same vibrations?"

Gabby sighed. "Then I guess you do what you do. You hang it all out there and go for broke."

"Even though I'm not finding any answers?"

"I'm *glad* you're not getting anywhere," Gabby said. "And I'm still mad at Shamus for pulling you into this mess." She slipped out from behind the counter and began arranging the jars of paint and crackle. Carmela watched as Gabby aligned everything perfectly on the display shelf.

"I've got one more angle that I want to pursue," Carmela said.

"What's that?"

"I'm going to visit Tom Ratcliff at his art gallery."

"When?"

"Now. As long as you don't mind if I take off early?"

"I suppose you can't get in too much trouble at an art gallery," Gabby said.

Little did she know.

Even though it was only mid-afternoon, the French Quarter was jammed with Mardi Gras revelers who were exploring everything the bars, shops, and restaurants had to offer. The atmosphere was palpable — you could feel electricity sizzling through the Vieux Carré as folks practically counted down the seconds until the next big parade began to roll.

Horses pulling jitneys clip-clopped by, a few palm readers had set up shop on the sidewalk, and Lucky Dogs hot dog vendors haunted every corner.

Carmela turned onto Royal Street, where a crowd was clapping and dancing to a lively street band. The band was belting out a jazzy version of "West End Blues." She hummed along, forever grateful that she lived in a town that was filled with music, brimming with history, and perfect for foodies.

Royal Street, which had the highest concentration of antique shops, galleries, and jewelry shops, was one of Carmela's favorite haunts. Elegant, quaint shops sat shoulder to shoulder; pots of hot-pink bougainvillea bookmarked every doorway; and shop windows were filled with priceless heirlooms.

Carmela stopped in front of a sign that said: *WREN & RAYBURN ESTATE JEWELRY.* She looked in the window. Diamond rings, antique cameos, Tiffany bracelets, and strands of Baroque pearls glittered back at her. She thought for a minute about her diamond ring — the engagement ring she was supposed to get from Babcock. She kept putting it off, but she knew she was going to have to bite the bullet sooner or later.

Ratcliff on Royal Fine Art was the only contemporary note on a street overhung with lacy wrought-iron balconies. The front of the gallery was basically an enormous floor-to-ceiling window. Since there were no apparent reinforcements, Carmela figured Ratcliff wasn't concerned with Mardi Gras damage, or else he'd installed hurricane-proof glass. Paintings that were artful splotches of primary colors hung in the window, and a neatly lettered sign in the lower right-hand corner said: *PRESENTLY EXHIBITING LOCAL ARTISTS. WELCOME!*

Inside, the gallery was sleek and upbeat. The walls were pristine white, the perfect backdrop for the several dozen paintings that were on display. There were a few bronze sculptures, too, sitting primly on square white pedestals. Pinpoint spotlights shone down to highlight the art, and the gallery's beechwood floors were polished to a high gloss. A young man dressed all in black — obviously a sales consultant — was talking quietly to a couple that was admiring a turbulent-looking seascape. No problem. Carmela was perfectly content to wander around and take in the art. This was a new gallery, after all, and she was interested to see which local artists were being featured.

Ah, here was an artist she was familiar with. Jed Hobart. She'd seen some of his smaller works displayed in Bon Bean, a local coffee shop. But this one, a red and purple graphic, was much larger, at least six feet wide by four feet high. You'd need serious wall space for this baby.

"May I help you?" The young man in black was suddenly at Carmela's elbow. Polite and smiling.

"Is Tom Ratcliff here?" Carmela asked. "I just saw him at lunch and mentioned I might drop by."

"Who shall I tell him is here?"

"Carmela Bertrand." *Girl detective.*

"Mr. Ratcliff is on the phone right now with a client. In the meantime, may I answer any questions?"

"No thank you."

"Would you care for a bottle of imported mineral water?"

"No thanks."

He gave an elegant dip of his head. "Then I shall inform Mr. Ratcliff that you're here."

Carmela wandered through the gallery. There seemed to be a nice mix of contemporary graphics, expressionist paintings, and realist works. There was also a terrific painting — almost whimsical in nature, though it was drawn very skillfully — of a large, yellow cat posed in front of a big moon. It was titled *Cataluna.* The painting next to it consisted of swathes of blue and green paint that looked like they'd been applied with a palette knife. It was interesting and very evocative and almost felt like the artist was trying to portray a storm in a bayou. Carmela glanced at the title — *Bayou Teche.* Well, there you go. She was spot on.

"Carmela."

Carmela glanced to her right and saw Tom Ratcliff walking toward her. He wore a smile on his face, but the set of his shoulders and the rest of his body language was stiff.

Didn't expect to see me so soon?

As if reading her thoughts, Ratcliff said, "I didn't expect to see you this soon. Welcome to the gallery."

"I was running errands and found myself on Royal Street. What can I say?"

"Glad to have you," Ratcliff said. He opened his arms expansively. "As you can see, we have a lovely contemporary gallery that's featuring mostly local artists right now. I figured the influx of Mardi Gras tourists might give our local art scene a nice bump."

"Has business been good?" Carmela asked.

"It's always good," Ratcliff said. He gave a perfunctory smile and brought his palms together. "Do you see anything you like? Something you can't live without?"

Carmela decided she'd better admire something in order to keep her ruse going.

"I'm quite taken by the *Cataluna* painting," she said.

"That one's by Gerald Wesley," Ratcliff said. "Acrylic on canvas. Wesley honed his skills as a graphic artist at a small advertising agency over in Lafayette. Now he lives locally and paints full-time. Always very large canvases, the subjects usually animals." He paused. "Are you a cat lover?"

"Actually, I have two dogs," Carmela said, wondering how she could redirect the conversation back to this morning.

"Wonderful."

"That was quite a scene at Purgatoria," Carmela said, jumping in feet first.

"Indeed it was."

"I guess Hughes Wilder had a number of disgruntled investors that are making their displeasure known."

"I believe the gentleman — and I use that term loosely — who accosted Maribel Wilder during lunch was a *reporter*." He spat out the word like it was a hunk of foul-tasting gristle.

"A financial reporter," Carmela said. "Jake Bond. I know he's been nosing around, looking into possible motives for Hughes Wilder's murder."

Ratcliff snorted. "Hunting for the so-called Neptune Bomber."

"The police suspect that the bomber was an angry investor," Carmela said. "Someone who lost a significant amount of money in Hughes Wilder's hedge fund."

Ratcliff stared at her.

Carmela drew a deep breath and said, "There are rumors that *you* lost a considerable amount of money."

Ratcliff gave her a sick smile. "Do you always listen to rumors?"

"I do when they come from people I trust."

Ratcliff gazed past her, seemingly unfazed. "The *Cataluna* painting may be spoken for, but if you're interested, I can give you some literature on the artist and some color Xerox copies of his other pieces."

"That would be great," Carmela said. Ratcliff was clearly not going to acknowledge any bad investments he made or open up to her in any way. Since this little charade had proved to be a dead end, Carmela figured she'd let it play out.

"Please come this way and I'll pull together that material," Ratcliff said. He turned and hurried back to his office.

Carmela followed, albeit somewhat grudgingly. But she would accept the artist's marketing materials. After all, Wesley . . . was that the artist's name? . . . yes, it was . . . was an awfully fine painter.

"Let me give you Mr. Wesley's complete bio as well," Ratcliff said. He opened the drawer of a black file cabinet and rifled through his files.

Carmela glanced around Ratcliff's office. No paintings hanging in here — mostly just photographs. There was a photo of a ribbon-cutting, probably for the opening of the gallery. Nice. Ratcliff was standing next to the mayor, looking proud as could be. There were dozens more photos showing Ratcliff with members of his Nepthys krewe: working in their float den, having drinks on a leafy patio somewhere. There were several color photos of enormous floats rolling down St. Charles Avenue. And there was one grainy black-and-white photo of a group of dusty-looking guys in army fatigues standing in front of a Humvee.

Carmela studied the photograph. The men — a younger Tom Ratcliff was clearly one of them — looked exhausted. As if they'd been in-country or had just completed some sort of dangerous mission.

"You were in the service," Carmela said.

"Yes." Ratcliff was putting together his artist's packet.

"When did you serve?"

"Long time ago."

Carmela studied the picture. The surrounding area looked dusty and arid. "Where was this taken?"

"Iraq," he said. "Back in oh-four."

"Must have been tough."

"You have no idea."

Carmela glanced over at Ratcliff. His entire body had tensed up. As if, just for a moment, he was reliving some terrible memory.

"What did you do over there, if you don't mind my asking?"

"Tried to stay alive."

It was a flippant answer — one Carmela wasn't willing to settle for.

But Ratcliff wasn't about to offer anything better. "I've included color copies of some of Wesley's work that resides in private collections," he said. "If you're interested."

Carmela wasn't interested in color copies, but she was spectacularly interested in the army photo. Because she'd just caught sight of the hand-lettering on the door of the Humvee. It said: *BOMB RATS — Explosive Ordnance Disposal.*

Tom Ratcliff had been with a bomb disposal unit!

CHAPTER 15

When Babcock made a right turn onto Washington Avenue and parked the car a few doors down from Commander's Palace, Carmela felt a tug of delight. The celebrated teal and white building with its gingerbread frets had served New Orleans diners for half a century. Presidents and royalty had eaten here. Emeril had gotten his start here.

On the other hand, it was also a little weird that Babcock had picked the one restaurant that was kitty-corner from Lafayette Cemetery No. 1, home of the newly interred Hughes Wilder. Was this just a bizarre coincidence? Or somehow prophetic, a sign of things to come? Carmela decided she'd just have to wait and see.

"You look gorgeous tonight," Babcock whispered in her ear as they entered the restaurant. Carmela was wearing a midnight blue Herve Leger sleeveless knit dress that was shockingly short (for her) and showed off her legs to perfection. She'd borrowed a pair of teeny-tiny diamond studs from Ava that sparkled like fire in her ears.

"Thank you," Carmela whispered back as the maître d' led them to a corner table. It was adjacent to a high, wide window that framed the view of the restaurant's outdoor garden — a view made luminous by a nearly full moon. "This is so romantic," she said as she sat down. And it was romantic. Soft lights glowed from multitiered chandeliers. The starched white linens were French. Fresh flowers graced each table. And there were touches of wrought iron everywhere.

"Are we okay?" Babcock asked. He was gazing at her earnestly from across the table. "I know we've been, um, kind of at loggerheads."

"We're good," Carmela said. "We're better than good." She was determined that their evening together be romantic and brimming with possibilities.

Babcock was already studying the menu. "What about starting with a bottle of the Delas Freres? It's a grenache blend from côtes du rhône. Is that okay with you?"

"Okay? It sounds divine."

Babcock ordered the wine and then turned his full attention on Carmela. "You always seem so happy and relaxed here. Which is why I chose this place."

"It's the ambiance. The Garden Room is one of my all-time favorites, it's so warm and inviting. The moment I sit down I feel like a princess ensconced on her throne." She snuggled against the lattice-backed chair.

The wine steward returned, uncorked the bottle, and offered Babcock a taste.

"Delicious," Babcock proclaimed. "Gotta love that French terroir."

The wine steward filled their glasses and disappeared as discreetly as he'd arrived. That was another thing Carmela loved about Commander's Palace — the flawless service.

Babcock watched Carmela sip her wine, his face reflecting pleasure. "Should we look at our menus? Are you hungry?"

"Starved." Carmela studied her menu, then glanced up at Babcock. Always impeccably dressed, he wore a perfectly tailored navy Armani blazer over a blue-and-white pinstriped shirt that was undoubtedly his favorite sea island cotton. She sighed. He was definitely the handsomest man in the room. And the one with the best taste.

Taste. I'm supposed to be deciding what to order, and here I am off in dreamland about my boyfriend. Correction: fiancé.

216

As if partly reading her mind, Babcock said, "Shall I call the waiter? Are you ready to order?"

Carmela nodded.

Ordering was easy. Tuna and redfish ceviche as starters for both of them. Alligator bisque for Babcock. Then an entrée of soft-shell crab for Carmela and quail on a bed of wild rice for Babcock.

Babcock topped off Carmela's wineglass and then raised his in a toast. "Here's to us." As they clinked wineglasses, he wore a slightly sheepish grin. "Carmela, I'm feeling guilty about something."

"What?" she said. "You fell head over heels for someone else? You're quitting your job to live in the bayou and hunt alligators for a living?" She tried to make light of his words, but still felt a slight tremor of alarm.

"The thing is, I may have been somewhat out of line last night. You know, at the visitation."

So that's what was giving him a serious case of the guilts? Well, good, it showed that his behavior was improving. Slightly.

"When I saw you there I was caught entirely by surprise," said Babcock. "And my first thought was . . . well, it doesn't matter what I thought. I should have been more tactful."

"That would have been nice."

Babcock reached for her hand. "I know I jumped all over you and I'm sorry. It's just that . . . I worry when you pop up right in the middle of one of my murder cases."

"But you knew I was involved . . . you even listened to my ideas last night." Now it felt like they were moving backward.

"Please," Babcock said. "Let me finish. I'm constantly worried you'll get in over your head. I'd never forgive myself if you got hurt . . . or worse."

The honesty in his voice coupled with the sincerity in his deep blue eyes set Carmela's heart quivering. "I'm sorry that I gave you cause to worry because it was never my intent." She cleared her throat and took back her hand. "But when a man drops dead right at my feet, well, I can't help but be a little curious."

"Just let it go, Carmela. Please?" Now she detected an edge to his voice.

"Sure. Of course." *Let it go? Are you crazy? Not on your life — or my life either.*

Their waiter and his assistant arrived at their table. Like a perfectly choreographed show, the pair of them set down their appetizers, then whipped off silver covers with a flourish.

"Fantastic," Carmela said. The ceviche

looked great. Babcock still looked a little piqued.

"Enjoy," said their waiter.

As Babcock lifted his fork, Carmela said, "Edgar, thank you for being so thoughtful. For remembering I love dining here."

He blushed slightly. "I thought it would be nice to have our own private Mardi Gras party. So much has been happening lately."

"This has been a weird Mardi Gras week," Carmela said. "The Hughes Wilder murder threw a wrench into things right from the get-go."

"Mmn," Babcock agreed as he ate his ceviche.

"I was wondering," Carmela said, "if you've been able to review any of the financials for Pontchartrain Capital Management?"

Babcock waggled a finger at her. "Here we go. Only minutes after you swore off any interest in the case, you're investigating again."

"No, no, just making small talk."

"To answer your rather impertinent question, no, we haven't been able to look at the financial records. There seems to be some sort of hang-up and I had to file for a court order."

"The guy was murdered and you're the

219

detective in charge of the case. Aren't you entitled to see whatever you want?"

"Ah, the world according to Carmela. But it doesn't work like that. I can't just grab whatever I want."

Carmela persisted. "What about Maribel Wilder? If you asked her, pretty please, wouldn't she grant you access to all the financial records?"

"Hardly. It's difficult enough getting access to Mrs. Wilder. Both her attorney and her doctor are arguing that the stress of her husband's murder is adversely affecting her health. 'She needs rest, not an inquisition,' is how her attorney phrased it."

Carmela opened her mouth and closed it again. She was about to tell Babcock that, at the funeral luncheon that morning, Maribel looked more like a raving banshee than a widow in need of rest. But that would mean bringing Jake Bond into the conversation. Not the smartest idea.

"What about all the people who invested in Pontchartrain Capital Management?" Carmela asked.

"That we're working on," Babcock said. "We've been interviewing every investor in that hedge fund. Looking into their backgrounds, practically writing complete dossiers on them."

"And?"

"So far . . . nada."

They finished their appetizers, and then Babcock had his alligator soup.

"Are you sure you don't want some of this?" he asked. "Even just a taste? It's delicious."

Carmela shook her head as she nibbled one of his crackers. "No thanks, I make it a rule not to eat things that try to eat me."

Twenty minutes later, well into their second bottle of wine, Carmela decided it was time to launch a second assault on Babcock.

"What do you know about Tom Ratcliff?" she asked.

"Who?" he said.

"Tom Ratcliff, the owner of Ratcliff on Royal Fine Art. I was wondering if you could run his name through the system to check for wants and warrants."

Babcock set down his fork. "Okay, I just placed the name. Ratcliff was one of the investors. What do you think *he* did besides probably lose his shirt?"

"Just indulge me," Carmela said. "Can you trust me and do this one little thing for me?"

"No, because one little thing will lead to another. Plus, your argument has to be a lot stronger than that. I need a legitimate reason to go digging around in our system as a favor to you."

"I happen to know for a fact that Ratcliff is ex-military."

"Big deal, so am I."

"But Ratcliff was attached to a bomb disposal unit in Iraq."

"Shit," Babcock muttered softly. Then, "How do you know that?"

"Trust me, I just do."

Babcock chewed in silence for a few moments. "Okay, I'll do what you ask. But only on one condition. You're allowed one freebie in this investigation, and this happens to be it. Understood?"

"Right. Got it. Thank you."

Carmela shoved the last of her soft-shell crab across her plate, wondering how to broach yet another touchy subject. Finally, she took a fortifying gulp of wine and said, "There's something else I need to tell you about."

Babcock seemed to stiffen. "What now?"

"I'm going to drive in a road rally on Monday."

This time Babcock's eyes literally crossed. Then he coughed loudly and just about spit his bite of quail onto the white linen tablecloth.

"You know, it's funny," he said. "For some bizarre reason it sounded as if you said you'd be driving in a road rally."

"That *is* what I said."

"No, I don't think so."

"No, I said it all right. A road rally over at NOLA Motorsports Park on Monday."

"That's not what I mean."

"Wait." Carmela drew a deep breath, then exhaled in slow motion. "You're telling me *no*? As in 'don't drive in the road rally'? That kind of no?"

"I think you heard me correctly."

"But why on earth would you say that when you know how much I love sports cars? Why would you try to ruin this for me?"

Babcock leaned back in his chair. "Let me see. Is there a possible reason why you *shouldn't* indulge yourself by driving in a ridiculously high-speed race? Maybe because you could be *killed*?" His voice rose high enough that people from nearby tables looked over at them. He lowered his voice, but continued to talk through clenched teeth. "Or how about you end up in a flaming wreck? Or you flip upside down and get decapitated?"

"You certainly like to see the worst in things," Carmela said.

"That's because all day, every day, I *do* see the worst things! It's part of my job and it affects how I view life. I thought you understood that by now."

"You have to have a little faith."

"Have faith? Faith in what?"

"In me."

"Carmela . . ."

"You know I'm a good driver, that I can handle a car at high speeds. Besides, we both know that driving in a rally on a closed track is probably safer than driving the Pontchartrain Expressway during the evening rush."

"You know what I think, Carmela? I think you aren't happy unless you're trying to drive me a little crazy."

"And I think we should skip dessert and adjourn to my place for a romantic interlude."

"Is that your idea of changing the subject?"

She peered at him. "Did it work?"

Babcock grinned suddenly. "Absolutely it did." He held up a hand. "Check, please."

They were walking arm in arm to Babcock's car when his cell phone rang.

Nooo, Carmela thought. *Not now. Not tonight.*

But as soon as Babcock answered it, his voice going gruff and all law-enforcement, he was mired in business again. And Carmela knew that her best-laid plans for a romantic evening had been crushed.

Babcock talked for another thirty seconds, then clicked off the phone. "Busy night," he said. "They're calling us all in. There's been a homicide over on North Rampart."

"Can't Bobby Gallant handle it?"

"Bobby's been called in, too." Babcock opened his arms and gave Carmela an energetic but sad hug. "Sorry, sweetheart. Believe me, I'm beyond frustrated, too."

"I know," Carmela said. "Duty calls."

"Afraid so."

"What about tomorrow night? It's really important to me that you come to Baby's Mardi Gras party. Kind of show the flag."

"For her or for you?"

"For both of us," Carmela said. "Do you think you can make it?"

"I'll try," Babcock said. "You know I will."

"I need you to try super hard."

CHAPTER 16

Early morning and the phone was ringing in Carmela's ears. One, two, three earth-shattering, dream-busting *briiiings.*

Stirring slowly from beneath her down comforter, Carmela realized she was hemmed in on either side by a dog. She opened her eyes and wiggled her hips, trying to make room, pushing errant paws out of the way. Then she fumbled for her phone.

It was Babcock, sounding way too chipper for such an early morning call.

"What?" Carmela croaked.

"I really hate to admit this, but your instincts about Ratcliff were right." Babcock's voice crackled out of the phone, popping the final bits of Carmela's dream like a soap bubble.

Carmela wiped sleep crusties from her eyes as she struggled to sit up in bed and actually answer him. "What are you talking about?" As soon as Carmela was vertical, she was hit with an intense craving for a cup of strong chicory coffee.

"That art dealer Ratcliff that you asked me to look into? He served in Iraq all right, just like you said. He was in a bomb disposal unit called the Bomb Rats." Babcock paused. "Hey, don't tell me you're still in bed? It's nine o'clock in the morning."

But now Carmela was wide awake. "So that pretty much confirms it," she said. "Ratcliff would know how to —"

"Wire and detonate bombs?" Babcock said. "Yes, I'm guessing he'd be quite adept at it."

"And his gallery is right there, on Royal Street."

"Smack dab on the parade route," Babcock said. "How very convenient."

"Now what do we do?"

"*We* don't do anything. Now *you* bow out gracefully and let me do my job."

Carmela tried to think fast. "But maybe I could —"

"No," Babcock said. "I just thought you deserved to know, that's all. Because you passed along a pretty good tip. Hey, I had a great time last night. I'll talk to you later. Now wake up and get going!" The phone clicked sharply. Babcock had hung up.

Carmela laid back down in bed and

thought about Ratcliff. Could he be the one? The killer? The Neptune Bomber? Here she'd been pinning her hopes on Maribel and Danny Labat. They seemed the most logical tag team among all the suspects that had popped up. Although Jake Bond was still in the running as well. Carmela closed her eyes and let her thoughts drift for a few minutes. There were so many crazy, motivated suspects . . . .

That thought suddenly dissolved as loud pounding sounded at Carmela's front door. Boo jumped up, front paws on Carmela's expensive down pillow, and started barking — a sharp, staccato bark. *Arp, arp, arp.* Three seconds later, Poobah popped up to join the annoying chorus.

Carmela shushed them both and shooed them off the bed. Then she got up, pulled on a bathrobe, and slowly padded to the front door to peer through the peephole.

It was Ava — loaded down like some kind of pack animal with a couple of large, colorful bags. Had Ava moved back home already? Maybe. Hopefully she had. She was also carrying a pink box that Carmela knew was from the Merci Beaucoup bakery.

"What have you got there?" Carmela asked as she opened the door. "Cupcakes?" It was never too early for sugar.

Ava shook her head. "Cupcakes are so last year. I brought scones."

"To have with our tea?" Carmela was surprised that Ava had become a tea drinker.

Ava produced a tin of Chinese black tea along with a bottle of vodka. "Not regular old tea — we're going to make tea-tinis."

"We're going to start drinking? It's barely nine o'clock." To Carmela, it felt earlier — more like the crack of dawn.

"What up, girlfriend?" Ava crowed. "It's Mardi Gras. Besides, call time for our fashion show is eleven and the actual show starts at noon." Ava pushed her way in, traipsed into the dining room, and dropped her bags on the table. "Got glasses?" she asked.

"Martini glasses?"

"Anything will work. Glasses, goblets, even jelly jars."

"You want me to brew the tea?" Carmela asked. It was, after all, caffeinated. Caffeine with vodka, who knew?

"Natch. That's assuming you have a tea-kettle?"

"Somewhere." Carmela ran a hand through her hair. "Yeah, um, right-hand cupboard. No, left-hand."

"You know what? I'll do it, you still seem

a little foggy." Ava rummaged around in the kitchen and got the teakettle going. She dug around some more and produced a small floral teapot. "Perfect," she declared.

Carmela slid her feet into a pair of slippers and let the dogs outside. "Don't run away," she warned. "Boo, I'm talking to you. If you go trotting down the block and start making goo-goo eyes at that schnauzer again, you'll for sure end up with a trampy reputation." She kept a watchful eye on her dogs as they poked around, checking out the small, pattering fountain in the middle of the courtyard, sniffing at the back door to Ava's shop. She'd heard from a neighbor that a lone coyote had been spotted recently. She wondered if the coyote had found his way across the Crescent City Connection bridge from Algiers, or if he was more of a hip urban coyote — an animal that lived in parks, loped down back-alleys, and begged tourists for handouts.

When Carmela slid back into the kitchen, Ava had the tea brewing and was rinsing out a silver martini shaker. Carmela couldn't remember the last time she'd used it. Maybe never. Maybe she'd simply ripped it off from Shamus in a fit of post divorce anger.

"Tell me where the fashion show is being

held again?" Carmela asked.

"In the Fantasy Ballroom at the Marquis Hotel. Apparently it's been sold out for weeks."

"Oh." Now that the fashion show was imminent, Carmela wasn't all that excited about being part of it. The show sounded good in concept, but not when it came to actual participation in the form of modeling in front of a critical audience.

But Ava was revved to go. She opened one of her bags and dumped a huge array of makeup onto the table. "Come on, *cher*, we've got to get ourselves all glammed up."

"Won't there be makeup artists backstage at the show?"

"Nah, this is kind of a low-budget fashion show. They're going to have a couple of hair stylists, but all the models are supposed to do their own makeup."

Carmela gave a lazy smile. "But I'm not a model. Not a real one, anyway."

Ava pulled out a chair. "Doesn't matter. Put your backside in this chair and let me get to work on you."

Carmela sat down gingerly. "What exactly are you going to do?" Carmela wasn't a big believer in tons of makeup. The high-velocity humidity of New Orleans kept her skin fairly well hydrated. So all she ever needed was a touch of mascara and some lipstick. Nobody'd complained yet.

But Ava had other plans.

"First we'll do a little spackle work," she said. "Fill in a few of those fine lines and wrinkles."

Those were fighting words that sent Carmela scurrying into her bathroom to look in the mirror. Did she really have fine lines and wrinkles? God forbid. But when she studied her face in the mirror with the outrageous ten-times magnification, her pores looked like craters on the moon.

"Do I look wrinkly?" Carmela asked when she came back to the table and sat down.

"No. I'm sorry I spoke a little too harshly and gave you a scare. The spackle is really just primer. So the foundation smooths on better."

"You're sure about that?"

"Absolutely." Ava spilled a little foundation into the palm of her hand, added a dab of moisturizer, then applied it to Carmela's face using a small pointed sponge. "This looks great," she said. "Gives you a nice creamy glow."

"Now what?" Carmela asked.

"Eyes." Ava studied Carmela carefully. "I'm thinking a slightly exaggerated cat eye."

"That sounds a little *RuPaul's Drag Race.*

How about just a regular cat eye?"

"You got it."

Ava teased Carmela's brows into a wicked arch, then added some copper-colored eye shadow on her lids and overlaid that with a thin streak of blue eye shadow.

"Babcock called this morning," Carmela said as Ava worked on her.

"I kind of expected to see him here," Ava said with a grin. "Since I know he took you out for a fancy dinner last night."

"Commander's Palace. But he had to leave right after we finished eating." Carmela made a face. "We didn't even have time for dessert."

"That's a crying shame considering their sinfully rich bread pudding." Ava added dark liner above and below Carmela's eyes. "So what'd your sweetie want when he called this morning? Did he offer an apology? Ask if he could come over for a quick snuggle?"

"He called to tell me he checked up on Tom Ratcliff," Carmela said. "You know, the art gallery guy."

Ava nodded as she continued to work.

"Babcock told me that Ratcliff was in a bomb squad when he served in Iraq. Something called the Bomb Rats."

Ava stopped working and took a step

233

back. "A bomb squad? As in a bomb that would make a float go ker-pow?"

"That'd be about right."

Ava picked up a wand of black mascara and unscrewed it. "So what happens now?"

"I guess Babcock is going to pay a visit to Tom Ratcliff and ask him a few hard questions. About his financial problems with Hughes Wilder, and about his bomb-making abilities. Like has he put them to use lately."

"I'd love to be a mouse in the corner," Ava said.

"Me, too."

Ava swiped on the mascara, then smiled at her handiwork. "Lookin' good. Time to mix up those tea-tinis." She disappeared into the kitchen and poured equal shots of vodka and tea into a cocktail shaker. She added a dash of lemon juice and a bunch of ice cubes and then shook her concoction like crazy. She came out, handed a perfectly made cocktail to Carmela, and said, "If Ratcliff has taken the lead as prime murder suspect, where does that place Maribel and Danny Labat on the totem pole?"

"Oh, they're still in the running," Carmela said. "With Jake Bond not too far behind." She took a sip of her drink. "Say now, this is *good*."

"Of course it is. And Babcock approves of

you being hot and heavy into all of this? If you ask me, it doesn't sound like him. He's a sweetie, but he's also got a hair-trigger temper."

"No kidding. That's why I'm trying to tread very lightly."

"Well, be careful." Ava picked up a mirror and handed it to Carmela. "Tell me what you think?"

Carmela studied her image in the mirror. "I don't look like me anymore. I look like I'm airbrushed, like one of the Kardashians. Only without all the fake drama attached."

"You still look like you, just the new, improved you. And you come with plenty of drama." She grabbed a brush. "Here, let me finish up by dabbing on a touch of blusher."

"Don't make me look all pinky," Carmela said. "Some women, they lay on the pink blusher so hard they look like they just came from a princess party."

"You know," Ava said, "you really should bring your Mardi Gras costume along with you to the fashion show. It would save us the trouble of stopping back here." She swooped blusher onto Carmela's cheeks. "We're going to be pinched for time as it is. After the fashion show, we have to run over to my temporary mansion, get the place presentable for the Grand Candlelight Tour walk-through, and then make nice with Kitty Burell. Once we deal with all that, we have to get ourselves gussied up and hustle down the street to Baby's party."

"When I got up this morning I wasn't thinking it was going to be such a full day," Carmela said.

"Get used to it, sweetie. It's Mardi Gras!" Ava clinked glasses with her. "Is Shamus going to stop by to pick up the dogs or should we take them along with us?"

"No, no, I made arrangements to have my neighbor babysit them. You remember Mary Jane Martin, don't you?"

"Is she the nice lady who writes those funny plays for kids?"

"That's her."

"Okay then, better throw on some clothes and round up those fur babies of yours. We gotta get cracking!"

CHAPTER 17

"Thank goodness you're here! All the other models arrived *ages* ago," Lisette Galvan cried out.

Carmela and Ava had just gotten off the elevator to find Lisette, the manager of The Latest Wrinkle resale clothing store, rushing toward them. Her mouth was pulled into a worried pucker, she was taking rapid baby steps, and she looked like she was about to lose her marbles.

"We already did our makeup," Ava said, by way of apology. "Does that help?"

"Somewhat," Lisette said. She was a dumpling of a woman. She wore yellow silk crop pants and a navy blazer, and was balancing on too-high platform sandals.

"Sorry we're late," Carmela said. Maybe they'd gotten *too* relaxed drinking Ava's tea-tini concoction.

"We'll just have to make it work," Lisette said. "The important thing is that you're here now." Lisette grabbed Ava by the elbow and reached back for Carmela's hand, then pulled them through a doorway and into the fashion show staging area.

"Holy bat guano," Ava said. They had all stopped dead in their tracks to stare.

The staging area was a blur of activity. Racks of clothes clattered past, hair stylists were frantically clipping in extra pieces of hair, dozens of models were in various stages of undress, and rock music blared. Underneath all that heady excitement was a steady backbeat — the *click, click, click* of models practicing their heel-toe, heel-toe walk.

Carmela put her hands over her ears. "What a racket. How can you get anything organized in this chaos?"

Her answer came in the form of a tall, thin woman clad in a tight black leather suit. Her hair was scraped back from her forehead, the frames of her glasses were trendy brown herringbone, and she wielded a clipboard like she was an accountant with the KGB.

"It's about time," the woman snapped. "I'd almost given up." She peered at Ava. "And you are . . . ?"

"This is Ava Gruiex and Carmela Bertrand," Lisette said, stepping in to assist. To

Carmela and Ava she said, "Ladies, I'd like you to meet Elsinore Fry, our show producer extraordinaire."

"Fry with a *y* not an *i-e*," Elsinore hissed at them. With her heavily penciled eyes and bright red lips, she looked (and acted) like Cruella de Vil's younger sister.

"Got it," Carmela said. "Where do you want us? What exactly do you want us to do?"

Elsinore rapidly clicked her pen under Carmela's nose. "I want you ladies to *listen* to me carefully. You've already missed my orientation speech, so I'll run through the critical parts quickly. You'll each have three outfits to model." She held up three fingers. *"Comprende?"*

"Three," Ava said. "Comes after two, right before four."

"I'm going to forget you said that," Elsinore said. "Chalk it up to preshow jitters."

"Go on," Carmela said. "We're listening." *But we're definitely not taking you seriously.*

"Three looks," Elsinore said. "Sporty, day-wear chic, and evening. I must warn you, the show will be fast-paced, so you're not going to have a lot of time to dawdle in between changes." She peered over her glasses at them. "I hope you're not the modest types?"

"Not me," Ava said.

"Good." Elsinore pointed across the room to a young woman in jeans and a shredded T-shirt who was buttoning a jacket onto a satin hangar. "Monica over there will be your dresser. I'll give you the rest of your instructions when you're ready. Now get going!"

"Let's do it," Carmela said to Ava as they headed in Monica's direction.

They elbowed their way past a clothes rack, two semi-naked women, a photographer, and a model dressed in a short pencil skirt and beige padded bra who was screeching, "Who stole my shoes? You expect me to walk the catwalk in bare feet?"

"Frankly, I'd be more worried about going out on the runway without a top," Carmela said.

"Wouldn't bother me," Ava said as they skidded to a stop in front of Monica. "Hey, you're supposed to dress us." Ava gave her a slow wink.

But Monica was all business. "Let me guess. Carmela and Ava?"

"That's us," Carmela said.

Monica pointed at Carmela. "Tennis dress." She pointed at Ava. "Golf."

"I don't play golf," Ava said. "Never

swung a club in my life, though I did once date a caddy."

"Or maybe he was a cad," Carmela said.

Monica frowned. "Doesn't matter. You like short skirts, Ava?"

"Who doesn't?"

"Good. Put this on." Monica handed Ava a hanger draped with clothing, then shoved one at Carmela, too.

Carmela and Ava struggled into their outfits. Carmela's tennis dress fit perfectly, but Ava's clothes were about two sizes too small.

"Holy crap!" Ava exclaimed once they were dressed. "We look like a couple of country-club swells. Change my name to Muffy and hand me an American Express black card."

"You're okay with that outfit?" Carmela asked.

"Sure. Unless I'm stuck wearing sensible, old-lady shoes."

"Not to worry," Monica said. She handed each of them a pair of nude patent leather stilettos. "All models wear high heels today."

"Even with a tennis dress?" Carmela asked.

"Deal with it," Monica said. She gazed at Ava and narrowed her eyes. "Maybe you should button your shirt?"

"If I do that, how will anyone be able to see my cleavage?" Ava asked.

Monica looked like she was about to say something when Elsinore began screeching. "Sportswear models! Front and center, now!"

Monica gave them both a push. "That's you two. Get going."

Carmela and Ava joined the line of models dressed in sportswear as Elsinore herded them past the hair-styling station and into a curtained area. Somewhere — out on the runway, Carmela presumed — a woman with a very loud voice was welcoming the fashion show guests and getting them revved up to a fever pitch in anticipation of the actual show.

"This is gonna be fun," Ava whispered.

"Shhhh," Elsinore hissed. She was now wearing a headset that presumably allowed her to communicate with the lighting and sound people. "When I give you girls the signal to go, you *go*. I want to see super high energy, an upbeat attitude, but no smiles. At the end of the runway, everyone should hold for a count of three, then execute a sharp turn and walk back. Got it?"

Everybody nodded. They got it.

Now the music was blaring like crazy.

Carmela recognized the Bruno Mars song "That's What I Like." Just ahead of her, models charged onto the runway, filled with bravado and energy. Then it was her turn.

Boom! The lights, the music, and the energy grabbed Carmela and propelled her down the catwalk. She moved fast, head up, eyes straight ahead, hips swinging as she did the heel-toe maneuver, really grooving to the music.

You got it if you want it, got, got it if you want it . . .

Carmela hit the end of the runway, cocked a hip, held her pose for two beats, then three, and whirled around, only to find Ava bouncing and wiggling her way down the runway, getting ready to hit her mark, too. The audience clapped, the music blared, and Carmela suddenly realized that she was having the time of her life.

Coming back off the runway, it was business as usual. Carmela was grabbed, shoved, practically pummeled, and sent spinning back to Monica. Twenty seconds later, Ava was there, too, as if they'd been spit out of an assembly line.

"Daywear chic," Monica hectored. "Only this time, you ladies need to have your hair primped."

They stripped down to their undies and

pulled on their next outfits. Carmela wore a sleek red knit dress; Ava was in a low-cut cream-colored crochet number. Their hair was given a slight fluff by a random stylist, then it was back in line and out onto the runway.

This time Carmela felt better prepared. She was anticipating the blare of music, the blinding colored lights, and the warp-speed, almost surreal pace of the show.

What she *didn't* anticipate was seeing Maribel Wilder staring up at her as she posed at the end of the runway and snuck a glance at the crowd!

Maribel was sitting in the front row VIP section, fanning herself with the silver envelope that held her invitation. Their eyes met for a split second. But in that miniscule amount of time, Maribel seemed to register surprise, which morphed into genuine annoyance. Then Carmela spun around and walked back down the runway.

Carmela grabbed Ava the minute they were both backstage. "Did you see who was sitting in the front row?"

"Was that who I think it was?"

"Maribel Wilder," Carmela said. "That lady sure can get over a death in the family mighty fast. Maybe too fast."

Their third change of clothes was a little

more complicated. Evening gowns.

"Finally, the sexy stuff," Ava said. "Bring it on."

Monica handed Ava a long, wispy, black lace dress.

"Perfect," Ava crowed. "This is my kind of fashion."

Carmela was given a burnished satin dress that she practically had to be poured into. "This is so scratchy it's going to give me hives," she told Monica once she was zipped up.

"Deal with it," were Monica's words of wisdom yet again.

Ava, however, was in seventh heaven.

"Look at me, *cher,* my evening dress is the fashion equivalent of a mullet — business in the front, party in the back." She spun around to reveal her practically backless dress.

"Wow," Carmela said as they were led back over to the hair stylists. This time, Carmela forced herself to sit quietly, even though she could barely tolerate the teasing and spraying. "Why are we here again?" she asked Ava.

"It's a charity event," Ava said. "The Latest Wrinkle teamed up with Tisane Salon, Marva Kane Couture, and Accents Boutique."

"And the charity?"

Ava was momentarily flummoxed. "Oh . . . um . . ."

"The Youth Theatre and Read Right for Kids," the hair stylist finished for her.

"Well, those do sound worthwhile," Carmela said.

"Evening gown people!" Elsinore screamed.

"Uh-oh," Ava said. "The Wicked Witch of the West is calling."

"Gown people," Elsinore shrilled again. "Step over here for jewelry and accessories."

Carmela and Ava joined the dozen or so models who were lining up to be blinged out. And when they got to the front of the line, they were pleasantly surprised.

The lady doling out the fancy jewelry was none other than Countess Vanessa Saint-Marche, owner of Lucrezia Jewelers. It was the upscale shop located right next door to Memory Mine.

"Why am I not surprised to see you?" Carmela said, a smile lighting her face.

"Probably because I've got the best jewels and baubles in the French Quarter," the countess said. She had a jewelry box that looked like the pirate Jean Lafitte's treasure chest and was backed by an armed guard.

"Load me up," Ava said.

The countess draped two diamond necklaces on Ava, then added three pearl bracelets. "Now for Carmela," the countess said.

"You know my taste," Carmela said. "I tend to be fairly understated . . . Holy cow, is that an *emerald*? How big is that sucker?"

The countess pinned a gigantic emerald brooch to Carmela's dress. "Sixteen carats. You like?"

"I love it, but you don't have to . . . Dear Lord, are those *diamonds*?"

"Hold out your right hand, dear," the countess said.

"Wow," Carmela said as the bracelet slithered around her wrist.

"Five old mine-cut diamonds, two carats each, set in platinum," the countess said.

"That's some amazing bling."

The countess smiled at Carmela. "Speaking of bling, my dear, has that young man of yours picked out an engagement ring yet?"

"We haven't exactly gotten around to that aspect of the engagement," Carmela said. She smiled to herself. Though some aspects, also known as benefits, were humming right along.

The countess looked delighted. "By all means, send him over to my shop!"

"Gown people," Elsinore called. "Time to

line up."

The models hurried into line, all looking as if they were ready to attend a fancy Mardi Gras ball.

Ava gave an excited little twirl. "My favorite part of the Cinderella story isn't the prince," she whispered to Carmela. "It's the ball gown and jewels."

For her final strut down the runway, Carmela felt confident in spite of the itchy dress. She marked her paces, swaying her hips gently to allow her long gown to swirl about her feet. Then she stopped dead center for her three-count. As she stepped into her turn, her heel hit something slippery. Her foot shot out from under her, and she wobbled badly. Lurching forward, her hands flying out to steady herself, Carmela took one ungainly step. Then she managed to recover her balance.

What the hell?

Glancing back, she saw a slithery silver envelope lying on the runway. She blinked, looked back toward Maribel, and saw a flash of triumph in the woman's eyes.

Had she . . . ?

Of course she had. She'd put her envelope there on purpose.

Carmela seethed all the way back down the runway. Once she was backstage, she grabbed Ava. "Did you see what just happened?"

"You kind of did an oopsy-do?"

"That crappy Maribel made me trip."

"The woman's a snake." Ava touched Carmela's cheek. "But don't let her get to you, *cher*. All in all, you did great. I was behind you every step of the way, and you handled the show like a real pro."

Rock music was blaring backstage, and someone was popping corks on bottles of champagne. Models were dancing and wiggling — even the hair stylists were getting into the act.

"Come on!" Ava exclaimed. "Let's give this jewelry back to the countess, then jump into our street clothes. Join the par-*tay*!"

But just as Carmela was pulling on her favorite pair of ripped jeans, Maribel Wilder ghosted past her.

"Sheesh," Carmela muttered. Was that really Maribel? Again?

Yes, it was.

Maribel circled back and stood directly in front of Carmela, glaring. "You. You seem to be poking your nose into my business for no reason at all." Her lips curled as she spoke, her eyes filled with dark fury.

"I'm sure I don't know what you mean," Carmela said, even though she knew perfectly well what Maribel was yapping about.

"You were at my husband's visitation, you attended his funeral, and then you showed up at the luncheon. I certainly don't recall issuing you any kind of invitation."

"Actually, you did."

"No, I think you're stalking me!"

"And you purposely tripped me," Carmela cried back.

"What's the problem?" Ava asked. She crowded in, closing ranks with Carmela.

Maribel raised her thin, penciled brows and glared at Ava. "Excuse me?" she said with all the ferocity of a feral cat. "You don't really need to butt in here. Besides, you weren't invited either!"

"How soon she forgets," Carmela said.

"We came with Carmela's ex," Ava said. "We were his guests." Her words came in short, staccato bursts.

"*You're* telling *me* that it's socially acceptable for someone to drag outsiders to a private event?" Maribel gave a harsh laugh. "No, I don't think so."

"Go away, Maribel," Ava said as she pressed closer to Maribel. "Get out of here and leave us alone." She was a head taller than Maribel, and with her ratted and sprayed hair, she looked like a proud lioness.

"Stop being so dramatic," Maribel sniped.

Ava put a hand to her forehead and feigned innocence. "Dramatic? *Me?* How *dare* you say such a thing. You haven't *seen* dramatic!"

Maribel was sufficiently cowed. "And you haven't seen the last of me," she muttered as she slunk away.

"Whoa," Ava said. "I thought I was gonna have to haul off and slug that witch."

"I wish you would have," Carmela said.

"But did you see the rock on her finger?" Ava asked. "You practically needed sunglasses to look at it."

"Well, she's rich," Carmela said.

The countess was breezing past them at that exact moment. "Excuse me, but were you two ladies positively agog over Maribel's new ring?"

"It did catch our attention," Ava said.

"Of course it did — it came from my shop," the countess called over her shoulder.

Carmela and Ava stood there gazing at each other until Carmela said, "It would appear the widow has embarked on a major spending spree."

"Where do you think she got the money?"

"Hard to say, seeing as Pontchartrain Capital Management is supposedly broke."

"Perhaps her personal fortune?" Ava asked.

Carmela smiled, but it was a hard, mirthless smile. "Maybe it's time we looked into that."

CHAPTER 18

"Phew," Carmela said. "This is going to be some project."

They'd just rushed home from the fashion show and were standing in the dusty, dismal parlor at Wilkes manor, surveying the enormous job that lay ahead of them.

"Are you bummed out about Maribel?" Ava asked.

Carmela shrugged. "She's not important. You are. Let's get this done, and then we can worry about Maribel."

"You think we can pull this transformation off in time?"

Carmela glanced at her watch. "It's two thirty. What time did you say your candlelight tour lady was supposed to arrive? And who is she again?"

"Her name is Kitty Burell, and she's apparently one of the grande dames of the Hysterical Society."

"You mean Historic Homes Society,"

Carmela laughed.

Ava stared at her. "What did I say?"

"Hysterical."

"Probably because that's how I feel right now. Anyway, the great and powerful Kitty said she wanted to do her walk-through at precisely four o'clock."

"Then it's going to be tight."

"What do you suggest we do first?" Ava asked.

Carmela thought for a minute. "We can set a limit on the rooms that the public has access to?"

"For sure."

"Then let's limit the tour to this large parlor, the dining room, and the adjacent library."

"Works for me."

"First we have to pull the dustcovers off all the furniture," Carmela said. "And then . . . I guess we get busy dusting."

Carmela and Ava tore through the three rooms, pulling sheets off the furniture, balling the sheets up, and sticking them wherever they could find a spare drawer or cupboard.

"This is kind of weird stuff," Carmela said as sofas, settees, and armchairs were revealed. "It looks like it was all purchased from an ogre's garage sale."

"Because it's dark and clunky and all the feet are carved into claws?" Ava asked.

"Well, yeah."

Ava poked at one claw-foot with her toe. "Must be some kind of fancy decorating style we don't know about."

"Dracula *moderne*?" Carmela offered. "Prince of Darkness French Provincial?"

"Good one!"

But then the real work began. Carmela grabbed a dust mop; Ava wielded a feather duster. They probed and dusted lamps, mantels, and tables. It was slow, grubby work.

"There's so much dust flying around I can hardly breathe," Ava complained. "Plus, my eyes have gone bleary, and my nose is dripping like a stalactite in Carlsbad Caverns."

"Dump the feather duster and use a damp towel instead," Carmela said. "See if that cuts down on the amount of dust in the air."

It did. Sort of.

Carmela and Ava worked feverishly for half an hour. They finished dusting, then shelved books in the slightly haphazard library, straightened pictures, and arranged knickknacks. Carmela even hunted around and found a rolled-up Oriental rug on the back porch that looked perfect in the foyer. She worked with an eye to stage the home almost like a Realtor would.

When those tasks were done, they rooted around until they found a couple of vacuum cleaners. Work on the carpets and baseboards droned on for another half hour.

Finally, Carmela shut off her vacuum cleaner and breathed a sigh of relief as the annoying whine died down. "That's it. I can't take any more."

"Me neither," Ava said. She'd tied a bandana around her hair, but it had gone all cattywampus anyway. Now she looked like a crazed bandit. "I wonder when —"

DING-DONG!

The doorbell bonged and echoed throughout the old house.

"Oh holy hell," Ava said. "It's Kitty Burell. And she's early."

"Go let her in," Carmela said. "Make nice with her while I stash these vacuum cleaners somewhere."

Ava dashed to the front of the house, while Carmela pulled the vacuum cleaners behind her like she was leading a couple of surly mules. She shoved them into a closet, patted a little water on her face, and went out to greet Kitty.

Carmela heard Kitty's voice before she actually saw her.

"When was this home built?" Kitty asked in an annoying, high-pitched bray. Then, before Ava was able to come up with an answer, said, "I had no idea it was in such disrepair."

"Does that mean you want to drop it from the tour?" Ava asked hopefully.

Kitty steamrolled into the parlor, where Carmela was waiting. Kitty's entourage followed in her footsteps: a young, brittle-looking man in a too-large suit, and an older woman in a floral dress. Plus Ava trailing behind.

"No, no," Kitty said in an airy manner. "We'll just have to make do." She looked around the room, sighed, caught sight of Carmela, and said, "Who are you?"

"I'm Carm—" Carmela began, but Kitty breezed right past her and cut her off.

"Lovely to meet you," Kitty said.

Kitty was pin-thin with dark kohl-rimmed eyes and bouffant hair. She wore a yellow suit with at least a dozen long, jangling chains around her neck, and her tiny feet balanced on three-inch stilettos.

"James, what does it say on our tour program about this particular residence?" Kitty asked.

The young man, James, snapped to attention. "The text reads as follows: 'The Harris

257

Home was built by Buford Wolper in 1863. Wolper was an entrepreneur, banker, and broker, and as his fortunes grew, he added various additions to his house. Unfortunately, he was forced to sell in —"

Kitty held up a hand. "Enough."

James immediately halted his recitation.

"Which rooms will be on the tour?" Kitty asked.

"This rather lovely parlor," Ava said, waving a hand expansively, looking like a showroom model on *The Price Is Right*. "As well as the dining room and library."

"Show me," Kitty said. She was like a manic gerbil running on a wheel.

"Which room should we start in?" Ava asked.

Kitty shrugged. "Whatever."

They all trooped into the dining room and stared at the enormous oak dining table, which was the size of a deck on an aircraft carrier. There was also an elaborately carved sideboard, and a large, carved Asian screen that was arranged accordion-style in a corner of the room.

"China?" Kitty said in an imperious tone.

"I think the screen is Japanese," Ava said.

"She means *fine china*," the woman in the floral dress said. "Miss Burell would prefer it if you put out at least fourteen place set-

258

tings. Makes the room look more approachable, as if tour guests were invited to sit down for dinner."

"Sure," Ava said. "I guess we could do that."

They wandered into the library, where Kitty sniffed dismissively, then walked back into the parlor.

"Stanchions," Kitty rasped.

"Excuse me?" Ava said. "Plantains?"

But James had snapped to attention yet again. He knew exactly what Kitty wanted.

Five minutes later, James and the floral dress lady had hauled in a dozen brass stanchions with purple velvet ropes to go along with them.

"What's this supposed to be?" Carmela asked. "Studio 54?"

Kitty shook her head. "It's to help keep gawkers out of the home's private quarters. You'll thank me for this later."

Ava squirmed. "You mean the guests might try to look around on their own? Go upstairs?"

"Oh, my dear," Kitty said. "The horror stories I could tell you."

"Like what?" Ava asked.

"We had a female guest rummaging through a clothes closet one year," Kitty said.

"And another guest swiped a set of antique sterling silver English kipper forks," James added. "From the home of a very prominent family."

"We'll keep an eye on our kipper forks," Ava said. Then, as an aside to Carmela, she muttered, "What are kipper forks?"

Kitty held up a finger. "Wait one." Everyone held their breath, waiting for Kitty to speak. Finally, she did. "Something is missing." Her eyes had gone all narrow and squinty. "Where are the candles?"

Ava looked perplexed. "The what?"

"The *candles*!" Kitty shouted. "It's certainly not called the Grand Candlelight Tour for nothing! There must be candles. Dozens of them!"

"Dozens," Ava repeated as if in a daze.

Kitty made an expansive gesture with both arms. "Candlelight flickering on the walls, candles sparkling on the tables, candles on the mantel above the fireplace." Kitty snapped her fingers. "Give her the packet, James."

James handed Ava a packet. "Guidelines for the Grand Candlelight Tour," he said, and frowned, as if to underscore Kitty's words.

"Yeah, okay, I get it," Ava said.

"This will all be ready come tomorrow?"

Kitty said.

"We'll do our best," Ava said.

"Because if things aren't up to snuff, Mrs. Wilkes will certainly hear about this."

"You know what?" Carmela said, interrupting. "We can do without the bullying and the threats, okay? We'll be here, the house will be ready, candles will be blazing. From two to four o'clock, is that right?"

Kitty nodded stiffly. "Yes. Fine." She turned and led James and the floral dress lady back to the front door.

"Awright, good-bye," Carmela said as she swung the door closed on Kitty and her minions.

"I like the way you handled her, *cher,*" Ava said. "Outright disdain with a touch of sarcasm."

"Never underestimate the power of sarcasm."

"But we're going to need candles, lots of candles," Ava said.

"We can do candles. I'm sure there's a nice stash in the pantry."

But after they dug around, searching high and low and opening every cupboard, they only came up with two measly candles.

"This just ain't gonna cut it," Ava said. "All we found is one white taper and a lousy candle in a sooty red jar that looks like it

261

was stolen from a pizza parlor. Maybe I could grab some saint candles from my shop."

"Those might be a little too . . . voodoo," Carmela said. "I think we should just buy some candles tomorrow. We'll run over to Target or one of those home stores."

"What do we do now?"

"I vote we go upstairs, take a nice hot shower, and get into our costumes. Fix our makeup. It's kind of amazing, but Baby's party kicks off in less than an hour."

"How time flies when you're having fun," Ava sighed.

Upstairs in the master suite, they laid the bags containing their costumes on the bed and turned on the TV.

"Look at this," Ava said. "They've got a news story on about dogs wearing costumes. About dogs celebrating Mardi Gras."

"I tried putting a clown costume on Boo once," Carmela said. "She hated it so much she tried to bite me."

"Can't say I blame her. I wouldn't want to get saddled with a stupid clown costume either. Clowns are creepy."

"By the way, dare I ask what costume you're wearing tonight?"

"Naughty pirate girl."

"Of course you are," Carmela said.

"Got my high-heeled ankle boots, my pirate vest, a tricornered hat, and an eye patch."

"Aren't you missing something?"

"I can't imagine what," Ava said.

"So the ankle boots . . . and then I'm assuming the vest comes down over your hips?"

"Yeah."

"So . . . um . . . nothing in between?"

"Oh!" Ava laughed loudly. "You thought I wasn't wearing anything else? No, no, there's more to my costume than that."

"Thank goodness."

"I'm also wearing a pair of fishnet tights."

Carmela just rolled her eyes.

Ten minutes later, Carmela was standing in the shower, hot water pulsing against her back, when Ava suddenly let out a shriek. Leaping from the shower, Carmela grabbed a towel and rushed into the bedroom, fully expecting a masked burglar to be holding a knife to Ava's throat.

But no, Ava was bouncing up and down on the bed and grinning, pointing at the TV. "Omigosh!" she cried. "Look at this! Your sweet adorable cuddle-bear is on TV!"

"What?" Carmela pulled the towel tighter around her and sat down to watch.

Babcock was on TV, all right. He was standing in front of a jumble of microphones with the gray blockiness of City Hall in the background. He was giving a press conference and didn't look one bit happy.

"What's he saying, what's he saying?" Carmela asked. "Turn it up."

Ava juiced the volume.

"As I said before, the New Orleans Police Department is investigating a number of possible suspects," Babcock said. His mouth was pulled so tight it looked as if someone had just drilled his teeth and he was in terrible pain.

"Carmela's investigating, too," Ava said to the TV. "Doing a bang-up job. Maybe better than you."

"Hush," Carmela said. She wanted to hear what Babcock was saying.

Babcock continued: "We realize this case is of deep concern to our citizens as well as our many out-of-town visitors, and the New Orleans Police Department is making every effort to ensure the public's full safety. There should be no cause for alarm."

A female reporter shouted out, "But are you any closer to actually *catching* the Neptune Bomber?"

"It's an ongoing investigation," Babcock said. "We have a number of leads and we're doing our very best." His face assumed a quasi-sick look, and then he said, "Thank you very much, at this point I'd like to turn the press conference over to the mayor."

"Babcock doesn't look happy," Ava said.

"Like he's caught in a trap and wants to chew his foot off," Carmela said. "Dang. I wish there was something I could do for him, some way to help him."

"You *have* been helping him. You *are* helping him."

"Babcock doesn't think so."

"Just keep doing what you've been doing," Ava said. "Stay on top of those suspects. Something's bound to burst wide open."

Carmela grimaced. "Just as long as it's not another bomb."

CHAPTER 19

Wrapped in her purple Mardi Gras cape, Carmela felt vaguely overdressed compared to Ava with her naughty pirate girl costume. Seriously, were ankle boots and a vest even street legal?

But this was Mardi Gras, and Carmela knew that once she whipped off her cape to reveal her Cleopatra costume, her filmy skirt and sequined top would offer a tiny hint of risqué as well.

"Isn't this fun?" Ava giggled as they walked along. The street was lined with elegant mansions that exuded an air of luxury and indulgence. From half a block away, they could see that the gates leading to Baby's home were wide open, and colorful luminaries lit the brick sidewalk leading up to her wide veranda.

Rollicking zydeco music drifted out of an open window as Carmela and Ava followed Count Dracula up the steps. Little Red Riding Hood and the Big Bad Wolf were right behind them.

"Welcome!" Baby cried out when she caught sight of them. Dressed as the Statue of Liberty, Baby carried a shining torch and wore a long dress along with a glittering aqua-blue crown. She embraced them both with warm hugs and fussed over their costumes. "Carmela, I love your cape, but, oh my, what are you wearing underneath? Are we Cleopatra tonight? Just wait until your very own Marc Antony gets a glimpse of you."

Baby's husband, Del, a high-priced attorney by day, was Uncle Sam this evening. He tipped the brim of his red, white, and blue hat at Ava and winked. "Yo ho ho and a bottle of rum. Pirate on the premises. You're going to break a few hearts tonight."

"I certainly hope so," Ava said, flicking her dark curls over one shoulder.

Carmela gave Baby a loving squeeze. "You two are fabulous symbols of America. If Del ever decides to go into politics . . ."

"Not a chance," Del's baritone resonated. "I'd rather argue the law than write it. Now you two go on in and help yourselves to a drink or two."

Carmela and Ava stepped into the center hall and handed off their capes to an attendant in full eighteenth-century liveried regalia. Then they headed into Baby's palatial living room, where the party was in full swing. Rhett Butler and Scarlett O'Hara swept by, and so did a contingent of Venetian lords and ladies. There was also a young couple in feathery bird costumes.

Carmela smiled to herself as she gazed around. Baby was an interior decorator *par excellence,* and her home reflected her talents. Three crystal chandeliers hung from the high ceiling. At the far end of the room, a massive white marble fireplace was flanked by matching Chippendale chests. French and Dutch landscape paintings graced the walls, and a sixteen-foot S-curved sofa in dusty pink brocade ran down the center of the room. Club chairs upholstered in Chinese prints formed conversation clusters in four other areas, and right then they were all occupied.

Ava smiled at Carmela. "I hope Babcock shows up tonight. I'd hate for him to miss seeing you so sexy and gorgeous. Cleopatra has nothing on you, girlfriend. And where exactly did you get that wraparound snake bracelet? It's to die for."

"I've had it forever, I just never had anything to wear it with."

"Carmela!" a voice screeched. "And Ava!"

They turned to see Tandy Bliss scurrying toward them, arms wide open, a smile on her face. She was wearing a court jester costume, soft velvet done in a purple and gold diamond pattern.

"Are you here to make us laugh?" Ava asked. "Or will you be entertaining the entire court?"

"You know what?" Tandy said. She touched a hand to the three-pointed jester hat that sat atop her mop of red hair. "These bells are driving me crazy. For some reason I've got this perpetual ringing in my ears."

"I can take care of that," Carmela said.

Carmela swiped the hat off her head and handed it to Ava, who promptly ripped the bells off each point.

"Problem solved," Carmela said.

"But I gotta take this costume back to the rental place," Tandy said.

Carmela dropped the bells into Tandy's palm. "Oh, sorry. But you're crafty, you can just whipstitch them back on."

"And nobody will be the wiser," Ava chuckled.

"Thanks," Tandy said. "I guess." She shook her head as if to clear it. "Hey, have you ladies hit the buffet table yet?"

"No," Ava said. "We just got here. But we're starving. We're always starving."

"Then I suggest we mosey over to the food and dig in," Tandy said.

"You'll get no argument from me," Carmela said.

The sumptuous party feast began with a silver chafing dish piled high with golden-brown orbs.

"Please tell me those are oysters," Carmela said to one of the servers.

"Pecan-breaded oysters," the server said.

"Gotta go for it," Carmela said. She was an oyster lover of the first magnitude, and New Orleans chefs knew how to make the best of Gulf Coast oysters. Served raw, grilled, smothered in barbecue sauce, or submerged in vodka as oyster shooters, the little bivalves were considered a true delicacy.

The rest of the catered food wasn't bad either.

Carmela, Ava, and Tandy helped themselves to blackened catfish, crawfish and penne pasta, barbecued ribs, hush puppies, and fresh salmon topped with *beurre blanc* sauce.

They piled their plates high, grabbed glasses of champagne, and headed for a seat in Baby's solarium. It was a smaller room, not quite as grand as the rest of the house, but with elegant wicker furniture, a wood-burning fireplace, and a fabulous view of the back patio.

"The joint's really jumping," Tandy said as she daintily nibbled a rib. "There's, like, two hundred people here."

"Baby always invites *every*body," Ava said. "Friends, neighbors, people she knows from all her society events, even Del's business associates."

"Speaking of which," Carmela said to Tandy, "where's your associate tonight?" She was referring to Tandy's husband, of course.

Tandy shrugged. "Off somewhere. Eating, flirting, drinking, whatever."

"And you don't mind?" Ava asked.

"Heck no," Tandy said. "Soon's I finish this plate of goodies I'm going to get busy and do the same thing. Hey, it's Mardi Gras. Anything goes!"

By nine thirty the party was in full swing. The zydeco band was blasting out numbers like "Take My Hand" and "Hello Josephine," couples were dancing, and champagne corks continued to pop. Carmela and Ava danced, shrieked whenever they saw someone they knew, and imbibed their fair share of champagne. They ran into Gabby and Stuart and exclaimed over Gabby's adorable '20s-style flapper dress, but puzzled over Stuart's conservative black suit and lack of enthusiasm.

"What are you supposed to be?" Ava asked him after more than a few drinks. "A funeral director?"

"I'm not big on parties," Stuart mumbled. "But, you know, Gabby had her heart set on coming . . ."

"Well, butter my buns and pour on some honey," Ava said. "I'd never have guessed in a million years that you were of the conservative persuasion. I mean, Stuart, I always thought you were the original, *Animal House*–certified party guy."

Gabby leaned over and planted a kiss on Stuart's cheek. "Pay no mind to her, sweetness. You're doing just fine." As Gabby led him away, Stuart looked as though he considered having a root canal to be more fun.

Ava waggled her empty champagne glass. "Oopsy-do, time for a refill."

"Better go easy on that stuff," Carmela warned. "We've got a big day tomorrow."

"Tomorrow's a long way off for this girl." Ava plumped up her cleavage and gazed into the crowd. "I'm thinking maybe that good-looking — uh-oh."

"What?"

"Don't look now, but your ex is here."

Carmela turned and saw Shamus walking toward her. She suddenly felt like they were two planets on a collision course. To make matters worse, Glory was with Shamus, looking slightly wonky as she leaned heavily on his arm.

"Ava, come rescue me in five," Carmela said. "Wait, make that three."

Ava nodded as she dashed off. Carmela gritted her teeth, preparing for the worst.

"I figured I'd run into you here," Shamus said, giving Carmela one of his big old shit-eating grins. He looked sleepy and relaxed, which meant he was deep into his sixth or seventh bourbon. "But where, pray tell, is the hotshot detective?"

"He'll be here," Carmela said.

"Wonderful," Shamus drawled. "He can badger me some more."

"Guh druh," Glory said. She'd been drinking, too. Maybe even more than Shamus.

"Excuse me?" Shamus said, the model of politeness.

Glory held up her glass. "Drink. Get me a drink while I talk to Carmela," she finally choked out.

"That's okay," Carmela said. "I'm happy

273

to get you that drink." *Thrilled really — any excuse to make my escape.*

Glory's hand landed heavily on Carmela's arm. "No, dear, we must talk. I insist on it." She glared at Shamus, as if her fierce expression could make him disappear.

It did.

"Whatever," Shamus said as he slumped away.

"What's up?" Carmela asked. No way did she want to talk to her ex-sister-in-law. It had been a great party so far, and Glory was the worst kind of buzzkill.

"Carmela," Glory said, her voice scratchy and low, as if she'd just crawled out of a tomb.

"What?" Carmela practically shouted.

"I know about the sixteen million dollars that Shamus invested and lost."

"Glad to hear it," Carmela said. "Good to know that Shamus finally came clean."

"And I hold you directly responsible."

Carmela's mouth dropped open and her eyes bugged out. "Whuh . . . *I'm* responsible? Are you smoking dope? Yes, maybe you are, because you've clearly forgotten that I divorced your twitch of a brother years ago. And *never* have I *ever* given him one iota of advice on how to invest his money — or the bank's money."

Glory tapped a finger to her head. "Shamus isn't right in his head. He's still carrying a torch for you, he's not thinking straight."

"That's not just a joke, it's pure fabrication! Shamus manages to date a half-dozen different women per week, buys X-number of sports cars, drinks to his heart's content, lives in a luxury condo with a maid, and sits in a fancy office wearing a bespoke suit where he pretends he's a vice president when he actually does nothing at all. I'd say he's doing just fine."

Glory shook her head sadly, as if she wasn't buying it.

"And I might add," Carmela said, practically sputtering, "that Shamus has managed to wreck two of those sports cars, to say nothing of various women's reputations."

"In his mind you're still the one who got away."

"Shamus threw me away when he cheated on me," Carmela said. She was so frustrated with Glory she wanted to gag her. Put black tape over her mouth, maybe shave her head and attach electrodes . . .

Glory was staring at her with a sullen expression. "You should have stood by him!"

"No, I should have kicked Shamus out the

first time he came crawling home at four in the morning reeking of some other woman's *L'air du Temps.*"

Glory rocked back on the heels of her sensible shoes. "A good wife stands by her man. And since you weren't loyal to Shamus, the least you can do is get your detective boyfriend off his poor back!"

"Babcock's already off Shamus's back," Carmela said. "He's moved on to other suspects. *Better* suspects, I might add."

Glory peered at her, suspicion creasing her face. "I'm not sure I believe you. You'd say anything to disparage Shamus." Then, as if her brain had finally caught up to her mouth, " 'Other suspects,' you said. Like who?"

"I really shouldn't say." Carmela had a flash of instant regret. She knew she'd probably said too much already.

"Of course you should say." Now an evil smile flitted across Glory's face. "Tell me, is one of them the merry widow?"

Carmela shrugged. "It does look as if Maribel wanted to get out of her marriage."

"She's a little tart, that one. Who else?"

"Oh jeez . . ."

Glory waggled her fingers. "Come on, Carmela. Spit it out. You know you want to."

"There's a car dealer and an ex–TV reporter. Oh, and an art dealer. Really, a whole raft of suspects."

"I'd still put my money on the widow, Maribel," Glory said.

"I'm not so sure about that . . ."

"I've heard the gossip around town. Besides," Glory said in a snarky tone, "Maribel is here tonight."

Carmela was completely taken aback. "Maribel's here? At this party?" *Holy cats.*

"You didn't know?"

Carmela shook her head.

"Tsk," Glory said. Then she leaned in and said in a loud whisper, "I'm counting on you to fix things for Shamus. Get him off the hook with the police once and for all."

"Glory, whoever you count on, please don't let it be me!"

CHAPTER 20

Carmela found Ava sitting in the library, surrounded by three young men. Ava was instructing them on the finer points of false eyelashes. The men were focusing on Ava's more obvious beauty assets.

"Ava," Carmela hissed. "Come here. I need to talk to you."

Ava got up, daintily smoothed what little clothing she was wearing, and said, "Excuse me, boys."

"Are you coming back?" one of the men asked.

"Sure. Keep my chair warm." She dimpled sweetly and gave a little wiggle. Then, to Carmela, "What's got you in such a tangle?"

"Maribel is here tonight," Carmela said.

"Noooo." Ava's mouth pursed into an O. She looked around, as if Maribel might be perched on the fireplace mantel, ready to launch at them like a crazed gargoyle. "Where is she?"

"No idea, but I want you to help me find her."

"Um . . . why?"

"I want to watch her, see who she's with."

"Spy on her," Ava said.

"Well . . . yeah."

Together they shouldered their way from room to room through throngs of guests. Was Maribel in the living room? Nope. How about the dining room? Nada.

"Where is she?" Carmela asked, scanning the crowd with wary eyes.

"Maybe she came and left," Ava said.

They wandered into the solarium and looked around.

"Got her," Ava said.

"Where?"

"Outside." Ava was looking out the window, her eyes fixed on Maribel as if she was some kind of predatory bird. "She's got a plate of food and she just ducked into the gazebo."

"What are we waiting for?" Carmela said.

They pushed their way outside, walked across the patio, and dodged their way around an outdoor bar.

"Now what?" Ava asked. "I mean, we can't just walk up to her and start chatting away. Not after the way she snarled at you this afternoon."

279

"This way," Carmela said, skirting around a fire pit that was blazing away.

They stepped off the patio and into the garden, going from thousands of twinkling lights to deep darkness. They pushed their way through hibiscus and hydrangea plants; underfoot, the earth was soft and squishy.

"Yeeks," Ava whispered. "My booties."

"Shh. If we ease our way around this magnolia tree, we might be able to eavesdrop."

Carmela was quite correct. As soon as they got into position peeking through a banana tree, they pressed their ears up against the gazebo wall and heard Maribel's voice as plain as day. It wasn't just raised in anger — she was complaining bitterly.

"No one understands how difficult my life is right now," Maribel said to her unseen companion. "Everyone's offering sympathy, but the constant repetition is driving me batty."

Maribel's companion muttered something that Carmela couldn't pick up.

"I suppose they mean well," Maribel said. "But no one seems to comprehend all the problems and lawsuits I have to deal with. Hughes was so far in over his head that I'm actually relieved he's gone."

Ava opened her mouth to gasp in surprise,

but Carmela quickly muffled her. She crooked a finger for Ava to follow her, and the two of them crept out of the overgrown garden.

"That's quite an admission," Ava said once they were back on the patio amidst a swirl of guests.

"But probably not admissible in court," Carmela said. "Which means we've got nothing on her. I mean, seriously, she's not the first woman who wished her husband was dead."

"And probably not the last." Ava paused. "So what now?"

"Go back to the party?"

"I was hoping you'd say that."

Ava dashed off to find her gaggle of guys while Carmela circled back to the buffet table. And, much to her surprise, she found Babcock picking through the oysters.

"You're here," Carmela said. She was thrilled to see Babcock, to know that he'd kept his promise to drop by Baby's party. Costume or not, he still looked mighty fine in his Ralph Lauren sport coat.

"I told you I'd come," Babcock said. He picked up an oyster from his plate and smiled. "Lord, you look beautiful." He tilted the raw oyster into his mouth and let it slide down his throat. "What are you supposed to be, anyway? A harem girl?"

"Cleopatra. You know, barging down the Nile."

"Well, that costume looks fabulous on you."

"Thank you. I saw your press conference earlier today."

"Not my finest hour," Babcock said.

"So . . . are you here to stay, or do you have to run off? I'd like to talk to you about Maribel Wilder."

"What about her?" Babcock helped himself to another oyster.

"She's here, for one thing."

"Carmela, sweetheart, not now. I don't have time to talk about anything. I just stopped by to tell you that I didn't forget about you or the party. I can only stay a minute because I have a lot on my plate right now."

"Not if you keep eating like that," Carmela said.

"Very funny. I promise I'll try to make time for us tomorrow."

"Tomorrow I'm helping Ava with the Grand Candlelight Tour."

"Monday then."

"When Monday?" Carmela asked.

"I'm not sure, I'll have to get back to you."

"Could you let me know when we're going to get married, too? Or you don't have time for that either?"

Babcock set down his plate and wrapped both arms around her. "Don't be like that, Carmela. You're the one who keeps postponing things, especially our engagement. And I'm ready, I really am. Just say the word and I'll drive us over to New Iberia tonight. We can get married by a justice of the peace."

Carmela realized she might have pushed him too hard. "You'd drop everything just like that?"

"Yes, I would."

"Would we go with lights and siren?" She gave him a tiny grin, which expanded into an actual smile.

But Babcock remained dead serious. "If that's what it takes, yes. I can even alert the Highway Patrol. Tell them we'll be barreling through."

"No, that's okay. I'm sorry I've been so weird about all of our wedding stuff. Next week, when Mardi Gras is over, we'll sit down together and make some definite plans."

Babcock nodded. "That's what I want, too."

Babcock kissed her good-bye, and then Carmela watched him dash off. She was feeling a little wistful. If only she could give him a piece of information, something he could sink his teeth into . . .

"What up, girlfriend?" Ava tapped her on the shoulder.

"Babcock came. And went."

"Aw, that's crumby. So you want to blow this pop stand and hit a couple of clubs? Those guys I've been hanging out with have memberships at that new place, Bogarts, down in the CBD."

"You go and have fun," Carmela said.

"Not without you." Ava gulped down the last of her champagne. "Mmn, I'm spinning a little bit. Maybe it is time to head home."

"Let's go say our good-byes to Baby and Del."

"Cold out tonight." Ava shivered as they walked down Baby's brick sidewalk.

"Maybe if you'd worn actual clothes," said Carmela.

"Then I wouldn't have three dates all lined up," Ava said. "Bing, bang, boom."

"Isn't that kind of a slow night for you?"

Ava laughed. "I'd say about average."

Carmela looked up at the night sky. "Look at that gorgeous moon, and plenty of stars. So romantic."

"I think somebody's missing her guy."

"A little. But he really is busy."

They walked across Camp Street and turned down Washington.

Ava yawned. "Want to cut down the alley? Shave off a block?"

"Why not," Carmela said. "Those boots bothering you?"

"Killing me. Especially my right pinky toe. It's bonging away like a bass drum."

But halfway down the cobblestone alley, they suddenly realized how dark it was. With humongous mansions and old-fashioned carriage houses on either side of them, all backing up against the narrow alley, it was like walking inside a coal tunnel.

"Where are the moon and stars now?" Ava wondered.

"You're asking for the moon and stars when you already have all the eligible men?" Carmela couldn't help but laugh at her own humor.

But Ava suddenly jerked backward. "I think I . . ." She'd caught her toe in the crack of two cobblestones. She stumbled, trying to dislodge her foot, and lurched against Carmela. In the process of catching themselves, they both ended up on one side of the alley. The darker side.

"You're gonna have to twist . . ." Carmela began, just as a pair of headlights blinked on some fifty feet away. "Oh, now I can see . . ."

But the headlights didn't stay stationary. With a tremendous roar, the large car gunned its engine and surged directly at them.

"Holy guacamole!" Ava cried. She grabbed Carmela's hand, and they both jumped out of the way. In the slipstream of the passing car, Ava grumbled, "Almost feels like that guy was trying to run us down on purpose."

"It's awfully dark. He probably didn't even . . ." Carmela's words died in her throat. The car, or rather the SUV, had K-turned hastily at the end of the alley and was coming back toward them. The headlights blazed and the engine rumbled as the driver accelerated.

"Hurry up, over here!" Carmela cried. They pressed their backs against a wooden garage door as the SUV thundered past a second time.

"Who is that?" Ava cried.

"Couldn't see the driver's face," Carmela said. "The vehicle's got a tinted windshield."

Ava shook her fist at the retreating car. "If you think you're flirting with us, it's not funny." They emerged from the shelter of the garage and watched as the car reached the end of the alley.

"He's gone," Carmela said. "Good."

Then taillights flared red on the SUV as its brakes were hit, and the vehicle swung around once again.

"Holy crap," Carmela said. "He's coming back. This jerk means business."

"It's like the car from hell," Ava said. "What do we do, what do we do?" She was starting to panic.

"Follow me!" Carmela yelped. "He won't come after us if we duck into one of these backyards."

"My bootie," Ava cried. "I stepped right out of my bootie!"

Carmela reached back and grabbed Ava by the arm. "Forget it, we have to keep moving."

They scrambled up a grassy embankment into what looked to be a large backyard. From the little they could see, it was landscaped with flower beds and walking paths, with some kind of raised terrace up ahead.

"We should be okay in here, huh?" Ava asked.

"Should be." Carmela's chest was heaving with fear, exertion, adrenaline, and anger.

"Oh shit, here comes that car again," Ava said through clenched teeth.

Like some kind of malevolent, mechanized beast, the SUV came at them again. It flew down the alley, braked, and swung into a tight turn. There was a moment of hesitation, and then the SUV began to churn its way toward them, the tires kicking up huge clods of dirt and grass as the vehicle drove right into the yard.

"Dear Lord," Carmela said. She backed up against a tree and felt Spanish moss pull at her hair like soft, unseen fingers. "This is unreal."

"Tell me about it," Ava said.

"C'mon," Carmela said. "We've got to get out of here. Work our way around to the front of this house."

"Okay, but I —" Ava choked on her words as her bare foot caught in some sort of tangled vine. She stumbled and pitched forward onto a bed of green, her entire body splayed out like a rag doll that had been haplessly cast aside.

"Come on, sweetie," Carmela urged. "Get up! We have to get out of here!"

Ava lifted her head and shook it, as if she was seeing stars. "Give me a second, let me catch my breath."

The car's engine suddenly went quiet.

"Is he gone?" Ava was halfway to her feet.

There was the *click* of a car door opening, and then a spill of light.

"Holy jeepers!" Ava screamed.

For Carmela, there was just a hot surge of anger. Then everything seemed to go red, like the opening of an old William Castle movie, in which blood dripped down the screen, practically obliterating the opening credits. Trees etched against the dark sky looked red — even Ava looked red to her. A snarl rose in Carmela's throat, and her hands clenched into claws. She glanced to one side, saw a garden hoe leaning up against a tree, and grabbed it. Without thinking, she crashed through a row of banana palms, wielding the hoe like a Viking with a battle-axe.

"No!" Ava cried out.

But Carmela was too far gone, too swept up in her own rage. She smashed her way through a yucca plant and was shocked when she saw a shadow quickly slide back into the SUV. She heard the door *snick* shut. As she continued toward the SUV, its gears ground in reverse, and the vehicle backed away hurriedly. The driver negotiated a shaky turn and sped down the alley, still in reverse, going thirty, forty, then fifty miles an hour.

Carmela stood in the darkness, quivering with anger. Then she turned and headed back toward Ava.

When Ava saw Carmela's shadow stalking

toward her, she let loose a bloodcurdling scream.

That was the final straw. A yard light snapped on. A dog barked.

"You're okay, you're okay," Carmela said, tossing aside the hoe and wrapping her arms around Ava's shoulders.

Ava's teeth chattered like mad as they ran through the yard, almost falling into a swimming pool. "Holy hell!" Ava cried, catching herself just in time.

They were almost in the front yard. Ava was hopping like mad on her one bare foot, careening crazily, dipping and diving into every bit of protective shadow they could find. They knew they had to put as much distance as they could between themselves and the raging SUV driver.

Five minutes later, huffing and puffing like a couple of steam engines, they reached the Wilkes home. Ava collapsed on the front porch. "Egads," she wheezed. "I thought we were gonna die." She touched a hand to her chest. "What kind of maniac would try to run us down like that?"

Shaking with anger, Carmela sat beside her. "Maybe . . . the same maniac who killed Hughes Wilder?"

"You think?"

Carmela ran her hands through her hair.

Her scalp felt hot and damp — *she* felt hot and damp. "When I find out who was chasing us," she said, "I'm going to kill them."

CHAPTER 21

Tradition dictated that Carmela and Ava go to brunch on Sunday morning. So there they were, sitting at one of the sunny outdoor tables at Toast of the Town Bistro in the Garden District. Birds chirped in the leafy canopy overhead, then dove for stray crumbs. Folks were dressed in their Sunday best. Unfortunately, Ava was seriously hurting.

She dropped her head into her hands and said, "Even my hangover has a hangover."

"I warned you about those last couple glasses of champagne," Carmela said. After their scare last night, she'd stayed overnight with Ava and had to virtually pry her out of bed that morning.

"I should have listened to you."

"But take heart, because there is a surefire cure."

"Please," Ava moaned. "What is it? Aspirin? Midol? Oxycontin?"

Carmela shook her head. "The answer is an order of eggs Sardou and a bottle of champagne."

Ava lifted a single eyebrow until it fairly quivered. "You can't be serious."

"Hair of the dog, don't ya know?"

"Well . . . maybe." Ava picked up her menu, scanned the brunch offerings, then fanned herself. "I mean, we are in the homestretch of Mardi Gras, after all. Yeah . . . I suppose a nip of champagne might be tolerated. For medicinal purposes, of course. But I'd have to eat something, too, to help soak up the alcohol. Something real yummy. Like French toast or crepes."

"Can't go wrong ordering crepes stuffed with mascarpone and drizzled with chocolate sauce," Carmela said. She was studying the menu, too. She wasn't nursing a rotten hangover like Ava was, but she was plenty hungry. "They also have crepes with ham and Gruyère cheese, oysters Rockefeller, crabmeat-stuffed mushrooms, and shrimp remoulade."

"Stop," Ava said. "My head is starting to spin all over again."

"Hang on, girlfriend, we have to get you back into fighting shape for this afternoon." Carmela waggled a finger, got the waiter's attention, and ordered a bottle of Mumm

Cordon Rouge Brut. They ordered brunch, too — Ava requesting crepes with herbs and goat cheese, while Carmela opted for the crabmeat cheesecake, which wasn't really a cheesecake at all, but a gooey, eggy, crabby slice of heaven.

Ava slid down in her chair and said, "To tell the truth, I'm kind of nervous about this afternoon."

"You mean the Grand Candlelight Tour? Not to worry. That guy who chased us last night isn't going to turn up again."

"Hope not."

"All we have to do is stand at the door and smile pretty as people come schlepping in. From what Kitty told us, the big thing is to keep guests from going rogue, from sneaking upstairs and looking around. Or stealing things. And keep in mind, Kitty won't be there to badger us or breathe foul air down our necks."

"That is a bright point," Ava said.

The waiter brought the champagne and popped the cork.

"Ooh, so loud," Ava said, covering her ears.

But after a good long sip, she seemed to cheer up. "That was a fun party last night, huh? Baby really knows how to throw a first-class twirl."

"It was great. Except for the parts where Glory was rude to me and the car from hell tried to turn us into roadkill."

Ava frowned. "Who do you think was behind the wheel of that demon car? Could it have been Maribel? Or that art guy, Ratcliff?"

"No idea. It was so dark it was impossible to tell."

"But if it *was* one of them, it would point to them being the killer, right? The Neptune Bomber?"

"The operative word being *if*. *If* it was even either one of them."

Ava fluffed her hair and took another slug of champagne. "Are you going to tell Babcock about that car coming after us?"

"Hell no."

"Why not?"

"You know why not."

"And you want to catch this jackhole."

Carmela offered a thin, cool smile. "More than you can imagine. You know what would happen if I spilled the beans to Babcock about last night? He'd put us in complete and total lockdown. Well, maybe not you, but he'd probably assign a policeman to watch me like a hawk. Babcock would assume that the car chased us in retaliation for my covert investigating."

"Wasn't it?"

Carmela shrugged. "I don't know. Maybe. But the last thing I want is to be under house arrest. I want to keep running with this."

"I see your point," Ava said. "Ooh, thank goodness. Here come our vittles."

The waiter arrived at their table with a large silver tray and carefully placed their entrées in front of them.

"Thank you," Carmela said. "This looks great."

"Enjoy," said their waiter.

Ava dug into her crepes like a stevedore. After a few bites of food, and a second glass of champagne, she was well on her way to making a remarkable recovery.

"Do you think Maribel could have murdered her own husband?" Ava asked between bites.

"From what I know about her so far, it's definitely possible. She's not only nasty, she's evil."

"You know," Ava said, "I'd never commit a crime that stupid. If I snagged a husband who had a reasonable amount of money — like a couple million bucks — I'd stick to him like wallpaper paste."

"May I point out," Carmela said, "that you have a boyfriend with a trust fund and a rather large inheritance dangling over his head — and you're probably going to dump him. For being such a callous jerk."

"I never thought about it that way, but you're right. Harrison left me holding the bag. House-sitting Monstrosity Manor is an odious enough task, but then to get stuck doing this Grand Candlelight Tour? That's the last straw."

"Glad to hear you've come to your senses," Carmela said.

"Besides, Harrison was getting kind of boring."

"You just noticed that now?"

"His idea of a big, exciting evening was to watch Bloomberg TV and see how the market did. And he was always worrying about the Hang Seng. For the longest time I thought he was talking about Chinese takeout."

"A man who's deeply in love with his money," Carmela said. She poured herself another glass of champagne, mindful that it was going down oh so easily.

"The one good thing Harrison did was help me with my taxes. Or at least his accountant did."

"Mighty big of him," Carmela said.

"Even so, the accountant was kind of uptight and grouchy. He wouldn't let me write off my purple lace bra. He said lingerie wasn't tax deductible."

"A purple lace bra?" Carmela wasn't sure what kind of deduction that would be. Unless . . . "Was the bra used in a work-related endeavor?" she asked, fighting to keep a straight face.

Ava grinned. "Um . . . I guess you could say that."

"Then the bra seems perfectly allowable."

"That's what I thought, too," Ava said. She took another bite of crepe and looked around. "I'm glad the weather warmed up. This is nice, sitting out here on the veranda." Toast of the Town Bistro occupied the ground floor of an Italianate mansion on Coliseum Street. Inside, the décor was very formal, with loads of chandeliers, flocked wallpaper, and high-backed French chairs. But out on the veranda, casual old-fashioned wicker tables and chairs prevailed.

"Nice weather probably means we'll get lots of guests for the Grand Candlelight Tour," Carmela said.

Ava shook a finger at her. "Which reminds me, we need to pick up some more candles."

"Have you figured out where?"

"I took a look at the information packet that guy James left with us. And it turns out there's a commercial dealer over on Jackson."

"You mean like a candle store?" Carmela asked. The only candle stores she was familiar with were the ones you saw at shopping malls, with candles in glass jars in cloying scents like brown sugar and sea foam and bubble gum.

"This is a different deal," Ava said. "This place sells, like, really large candles. For churches and things. And outdoor torches, too. You know, for parties and stuff. Say you want to set up a tiki lounge in your backyard."

"Something I've always yearned to do."

"Really?" Ava asked.

"No, not really," Carmela said. She dug in her wallet, placed two twenties and a ten on the table, and said, "C'mon, let's go."

"What about my boot?" Ava asked.

Carmela glanced down. "You're wearing shoes."

"No, I mean from last night. I was hoping maybe we could retrace our steps and recover it."

"Rescue and recovery on a boot," Carmela said. "That's got to be some kind of first."

But when they drove slowly down the alley a block from Baby's house, there was Ava's ankle boot — laying on the cobblestones, looking squashed and bedraggled, as if a million cars had run haphazardly over it.

"That's my boot!" Ava cried. "Stop the car!" She jumped out, ran to the side of the alley, and picked up her lost boot. Even though it was dirty and crumpled, she cradled it to her chest.

"How's it look?" Carmela called to her. She knew it was in terrible shape, but maybe it could be repaired?

Ava climbed back into the car and showed Carmela her sad little boot. The heel was half off, the toe was ripped open, and a crosshatch of tire treads decorated the suede. "It's ruined." Ava's expression was one of total disgust. "Squashed and mangled beyond repair."

"We could *try* to take it to a shoe repair place."

"This shoe doesn't just need repair," Ava said, "it needs total resurrection."

"Sorry about that."

Ava sighed. "Maybe we'll do better at the candle store."

Lucky for them, primo candles and torches was open for business.

"What a crazy place," Carmela said as they walked into a small, old-fashioned-looking shop that was sandwiched between a hardware store and a vacuum repair shop. The candle shop smelled like hot wax and cherry cough drops, and was stocked with the largest selection of oversized candles she'd ever seen — large twisted candles, candles embedded with silver studs, and candles decorated with Celtic crosses and other religious icons.

"They must sell a lot of church candles here," Ava said.

The shop owner came out of the back room, wiping his hands on a towel. "We do sell mostly to churches," he said. "But then you've got your fancy garden parties, your voodoo shops, and your special events, too."

"So you do mostly commercial sales," Carmela said.

The owner nodded. "That's right. Our bread and butter is the altar candles, cemetery lights, and devotional candles."

"We've got a house that's on the Grand Candlelight Tour today," Ava said. "And we need to glitz it up a bit."

"Understood," the owner said. "We've had several homeowners buying candles from us precisely for that event."

"What would be a reasonable candle?" Ava asked. "Something that would really scream 'Grand Candlelight Tour'?" She was staring at an enormous white candle that had a raised relief of a white lamb appliquéd to it, along with the word *PAX*.

"Our twisted candles are extremely popular," the shop owner said. He led Ava over to a table that had a display of red-gold-and-purple-twisted candles. They were so large they looked like twisted balustrades.

"I think these might be perfect," Ava said. "Along with some pillar candles." She glanced at Carmela. "What do you think?"

"Works for me."

"Go with the red ones?"

Carmela nodded. "That'd be my choice." The Wilkes house was in desperate need of *something* to pep it up and make it look lived in.

"How many candles do you need?" the shop owner asked.

Ava counted on her fingers. "Let me think. The parlor, dining room, library. So maybe . . . ?"

"I can give you a good deal on an even dozen," the owner said.

"Make it two dozen," Ava said.

"Let me ask you something," Carmela said. She was staring at a large red candle that was mounted on a rustic wooden post. It looked almost like a Roman candle — a candle that, when lit, would explode in a glittering array of sparks. "Do you ever get involved in pyrotechnics?" She was thinking, of course, about the explosion on the float.

The shop owner squinted at her. "You mean like the fireworks they shoot off at the Dueling Barges show on the Mississippi? On Fourth of July? No, I don't do that kind of stuff."

"Nothing that explodes?" Carmela asked.

"Not me," the shop owner said. "You need a special license for that type of material. But if you're interested, there's a guy over in Slidell who handles specialty items like that. He sells aerial and structure fireworks, popping flames, and laser candles. I think maybe some cryogenics and fog as well."

"Really," Carmela said. "Do you know his name?"

The shop owner shook his head. "No, I just know that he does it as a kind of hobby business. I don't even think he's got a storefront. Maybe check on the Internet?"

"Nice try," Ava said to Carmela.

The owner rang up their purchases, wrapped each candle in tissue paper, and placed them in a large cardboard box. As he pushed the box across the counter, he said, "That fellow who sells the pyrotechnics and popping flames, I think he might own a car dealership, too."

CHAPTER 22

"A car dealership," Carmela said to Ava as they raced around the Wilkes mansion, straightening sofa pillows and blowing imaginary dust off the furniture. "A guy who handles pyrotechnics *and* owns a car dealership. Who does that sound like to you?"

"Could be your good old buddy Danny Labat," Ava said.

"Exactly my thought. And what an amazing coincidence that I'll be seeing him tomorrow." Carmela whipped out a towel and flicked at the base of a semi-nude Greek statue lamp with a shade that had been judiciously placed to conceal the critical parts.

"At the road rally," Ava said. "Are you still planning to drive in that?"

"I wouldn't miss it for the world."

"Good, then neither will I." Ava blew a strand of hair out of her face and leaned into one of the dining room's built-in china cabinets. "How many place settings did the Queen of Mean want displayed on the table?"

"Mmn . . . fourteen, I think."

"Yeah, well, that's not happening. There are a lot of dishes stacked in here, like six different sets, but so many of them have chips and dings."

"Don't you just love rich people?" Carmela said. "Most of them are really hoarders in drag."

"How do you feel about true collectors?"

"They're probably people with a shopping addiction."

"You are so *bad*. So *judgmental*," Ava laughed.

Carmela nodded. "Yeah, I know it's kind of wicked, considering I have a collection of antique children's books and a few bronze dog statues." She looked at the dishes Ava had pulled out and said, "We can make it work if we mix patterns. Alternate the pink floral plates with the white ones trimmed in gold. Those are Pickard, I think, and rather nice."

"What a great idea," Ava said. "Make it kind of a crazy quilt."

"Just like this house."

Once the table was set, with a large turtle-shaped soup tureen placed as a centerpiece for added effect, it was time to put out the candles.

Carmela grabbed four tall tapers. "Let's place these on the dining table, and then — let's see — maybe some of the pillar candles on the sideboard?"

"Got it," Ava said. She pulled a box of wooden matches out of her pocket. "Think we should light 'em up?"

"What time is it?"

"A little past one thirty."

"The tour kicks off at two, so let's do it," Carmela said. When they finished in the dining room, Carmela headed into the library. She arranged candles on a table, placed a couple candles on a shelf, and tucked two more candles on a small side table. As soon as she struck a match to light them, Carmela's thoughts slipped back to her conversation with the owner of Primo Candles and Torches. He'd mentioned a car dealership–pyrotechnics connection, and that strange bit of news was still making the neurons in her brain buzz with curiosity.

Carmela moved to the center hall, more candles in hand, and heard a knock at the front door. Oh no, already? People were that anxious to schlep through a house and view a few spiffed-up rooms bathed in candle-light?

Apparently they were very anxious, because just then a more insistent knock sounded.

Placing two lit candles on the side table, Carmela unlocked the front door and swept it open.

And glory be, at least a dozen people were waiting to come in, standing all crunched together on the front veranda. They all stared at her for a split second, then a gray-haired woman waved her program under Carmela's nose and said, "Tell me, dearie, with the Civil War raging and all, how did Buford Wolper manage to build such a fancy house?"

"Well, I . . ."

Two men pushed past the old woman. "You're blocking the way," one groused. "If you're going to have a conversation, kindly move out of the doorway."

"Ava, I need you." Carmela tried to put as much sugar as possible in her voice as she beckoned all the tour-goers into the front hallway.

"I can't get this stupid candle to stay lit," Ava's voice wafted back to her.

"Our guests have begun to arrive," Carmela said, adding a note of urgency to her voice.

"Oh!" Ava said, suddenly popping out. "They *are* here. And a little early at that." She swallowed hard, pasted a gregarious smile on her face, and said, "Welcome, y'all, to the Wilkes home, one of the major stops on the Grand Candlelight Tour. If you'll just follow me, I'll guide you into the front parlor, which is the first room on our tour. Then we'll be visiting the dining room and the library." After her first misstep, Ava began to sound like a blasé tour guide who'd perfected her patter nicely. "But please," she continued, "do observe the velvet ropes and don't stray away from the tour."

Carmela continued to shoo more guests in when a teenaged girl suddenly thrust a sheet of paper into her hands. "Could you answer these questions for us?" The girl circled her hand to include a couple more giggling girls wearing crop tops and ripped jeans.

Carmela scanned the paper and read aloud. " 'When was the house built? What architectural style is it? How many families have lived in the house since it was built? Are there any secret passages?' " Carmela was getting the gist. She handed the paper back to the girl and said, "School assignment?"

The girl and her friends all nodded enthusiastically. "History class. Can you help us out?"

"Maybe you should take the tour," Carmela suggested. "Then you might learn something. Like the answers to all those questions."

"We were hoping to ditch early and go to a movie," one of them said.

Carmela gave a wan smile. "Take me with you."

Then Ava popped her head in. "*Cher,* could you please go into the library and stop people from taking books off the shelves? Remind them this is not a public library?"

Carmela hurried into the library, where one of the men (the grouchy one) was sitting in a leather chair, thumbing through the loose pages of an ancient hardcover. He'd stacked a pile of books on an end table and was chewing the stem of an unlit pipe.

"Sir, I am sorry," Carmela said. "There's no smoking in here, and these books are not to be removed from the shelves. This is an open house, not a college seminar."

The man stared at Carmela over the edge of his glasses. "If you don't want people to look at the books, why do you have the library on the tour?" He turned another page.

Carmela reached out and gently pried the book from his hands. "I am sorry, sir. I'm going to have to put this back."

The man pulled the pipe from his mouth and pointed the stem directly at Carmela. "You really will be sorry, miss. Kitty Burell happens to be my next-door neighbor, and I intend to report you for insubordination. Just see if I don't."

"Knock yourself out," Carmela muttered as she reshelved the books.

Out in the parlor, another problem had boiled up.

"Can you take that painting off the wall so I can get a better look at it?" a woman asked.

"I'm afraid not," Carmela said. "The paintings have to stay where they are so everyone can enjoy them."

"But that's a painting of the Battle of New Orleans, and I'm quite sure my great-uncle Ezra is depicted in it."

"Perhaps you could come back another time," Carmela suggested. "When the Wilkeses are actually at home. They might be happy to honor your request."

The woman blinked at her. "You're not one of the Wilkeses?"

Carmela shook her head. "No, ma'am, I'm not. I'm just helping out today."

"You sure look like Leona Wilkes. Yes, you do, I'd know you anywhere."

Before Carmela could answer, another woman accosted her. "Are refreshments being served?"

"No, ma'am."

"Not even a measly chocolate chip cookie?" a male voice asked in a jesting tone.

Carmela spun around to find Jake Bond staring at her. He had a droll smile on his face and a notebook in one hand. It looked like he'd already made a few scribbles in it.

Taken by surprise, Carmela blurted out, "What are *you* doing here?"

Bond held up his notebook. "I'm doing a story on the Grand Candlelight Tour."

Not convinced, Carmela decided to challenge him. "I thought you said no broadcast or print outlet wanted to hire you — except for the *NOLA Vindicator.*"

"I'm doing this on my own. Freelance. Writing a buzzy little story that I hope to sell to the Historic Homes Society for their monthly magazine." He shrugged. "A guy's got to get by one way or another." He smiled at her, then sauntered off toward the library.

Carmela pulled Ava away from a group of

tour-goers and said, "Jake Bond just showed up."

Ava glanced around. "Where is he?"

"He just went into the library."

"You think he's going to try and steal books?"

"I think that's the least of our problems," Carmela said. "Right now I'm worried that he may have been the one driving the SUV from hell last night."

"You just made the hair on the back of my neck stand up," Ava said. "Do you really think Bond was the one who chased us?"

"I don't know," Carmela said. "But it's strange that he suddenly turned up. I'm going to keep an eye on him. When he leaves, I'll try to see what sort of car he drives."

"Do that," Ava said.

But when Carmela went into the library, there was no sign of Jake Bond. *So where did he go? Unless . . . . unless he made a sharp left turn in the hallway and went upstairs?*

Before Carmela had time to react and check on Bond, there was a loud kerfuffle happening in the dining room. Voices were raised in anger. Arguing. She flew into the dining room to find two women waving their arms at each other and engaged in a heated battle.

"It's Wedgwood," a woman in a purple hat

screamed.

"You are so wrong," a woman in a green dress sneered. "That particular rose pattern is Rosenthal. I'm positive of it."

"You're both wrong," Carmela said as she tried to get in between them, before any dishes were actually broken. "This particular floral pattern is Haviland Limoges."

"Then the white dinnerware is Royal Crown Derby, right?" said Green Dress.

"I believe it's Pickard." Carmela picked up one of the white plates, turned it over, and showed the maker's mark to the woman. "Yes, it's Pickard."

"Carmela!"

Carmela recognized Ava's cry and hurried out of the room. She caught her foot on the corner of an Oriental carpet that had been dislodged and stumbled into the parlor. "What?" she said when she saw Ava.

Ava hurried over and pulled Carmela into a corner. "You know that art dealer guy you were talking to at the funeral luncheon?"

Carmela nodded. "Tom Ratcliff?"

"That's the one. I only saw him that one time, but I'd swear he just walked through here."

"That's totally weird," Carmela said.

"Isn't it?" Ava glanced around. "So where did Jake Bond run off to? Did you tail him?"

Carmela threw up her hands. "No. I don't know where he is. I can't keep tabs on any of these people. Between Bond and now Ratcliff . . . and all our crazy guests . . ."

"We need to call out the National Guard," Ava said.

"Something like that." Carmela thought for a few seconds. "Okay, here's the deal. I'll try to locate Bond, and you keep an eye on Ratcliff, okay?"

"Deal."

Carmela found Jake Bond lurking in the front hallway.

"Can I help you with something?" she asked. She hoped he hadn't just tiptoed down from upstairs. Was he that much of a creeper? Maybe he was.

"Oh," Bond said, sounding innocent. "I was just having a look at this oil painting."

Carmela tilted her head back and peered at the painting. "Ah, it's by George David Coulon. A cityscape of the French Quarter painted, no doubt, at the turn of the century. Not this century, the one before it."

"You know something about art?" Bond asked.

"Not really." *It isn't any of your business what I know or don't know.*

"I did hear that you're a rather skillful graphic designer."

"Where did you hear that?"

Bond offered a smug smile. "I have my sources."

"How lovely for you." Carmela reached for the front door and yanked it open. "Well, it's been grand having you here."

"You're kicking me out?"

"Not at all, but I'm sure you have to move along if you want to visit some of the other homes on the Grand Candlelight Tour. Since you're writing a . . . what did you call it?" She gave a mocking chuckle. " 'A buzzy little story.' "

Bond brushed past Carmela and stepped out onto the veranda. "I'll stay in touch," he said.

Carmela closed the door and hurried back to the parlor. Ava was there, doing her spiel, shuffling guests to and fro. When she spotted Carmela, she mouthed, *Help.*

Carmela was at Ava's side instantly. "Now what?"

"I don't know where that art dealer ran off to."

"Were you keeping an eye on him?"

Ava's arms flailed. "Trying to."

"Maybe Ratcliff left." *Hopefully he left.*

"This whole ordeal is like dealing with first graders," Ava said. "With a few snooty socialites tossed in for good measure."

"Take heart, it'll be over soon."

They welcomed more guests, answered questions, and tried to remain upbeat and helpful. And, finally, it really began nearing the end. The crowd thinned out, the questions stopped coming, and the tour-goers seemed better behaved. Carmela and Ava did their civic duty for another half hour, until it was time to call it quits.

"Let's start in the dining room and gently usher everyone toward the front door," Ava suggested.

"I like it," Carmela said.

And Ava's plan worked fairly well. Sure, there were a few stragglers, but, all in all, everyone was well behaved.

When the last of the guests shuffled out, Ava heaved a big sigh of relief. "I feel like I've been through a hurricane without a shelter. Just kind of clinging on with my fingernails."

"I hear you," Carmela said. "I'm about ready to drop in my tracks."

"Or start drinking."

"No, no, girlfriend, no partying for you. This is going to be a quiet night."

"So now that the tour is over, how do we wrap things up?" Ava asked.

"I'll start snuffing out candles," Carmela said, "while you lock the front door. We don't want to have a Johnny-come-lately wander in on us."

"Got it."

Carmela blew out the candles in the dining room. Then, amidst a cloud of lingering smoke, started on the candles in the library.

"Hey," Ava called, her voice echoing down the hallway. "Come and look at this."

"What?" Carmela said. She was still busy with the candles, her face felt half frozen from smiling, and her feet were aching. *Should have known better and worn flats. Or slippers.*

"Come take a look."

"What's she worrying about now?" Carmela mumbled to herself as she practically limped toward the front door. She found it standing ajar and Ava grinning happily. "What's got you so happy?" Carmela asked. "Somebody leave a fifty in the tip jar?" *Hmm, maybe we should have put out a tip jar.*

Ava opened the front door even wider to reveal a white cardboard box sitting on the front porch. It was about the size of a shoe box.

"Look at this," Ava said. "Some nice person left us a gift."

Carmela gave the box a cursory glance, then turned to straighten one of the hall paintings that had been knocked askew.

Probably by one of their clumsy departing guests.

"Probably from one of the tour organizers," said Ava, "thanking us for all our hard work."

"What's that?" Carmela still wasn't focused on what Ava was saying. "Oh. You mean somebody left us candy? Or flowers?"

"I don't know," Ava said. "It's just a box on the front steps."

A box.

Carmela froze for a second as a terrible thought streaked through her brain like a rogue meteor falling to earth. *It couldn't be. It wouldn't be . . .*

Carmela darted outside, shoved Ava aside, and snatched up the box. Mustering every bit of strength, she wound up like a major-league pitcher and hurled the box out into the middle of the street.

Ava was stunned beyond belief as she watched the box sail through the air.

"Crap on a cracker, Carmela, what do you think you're doing! That was probably a really nice . . ."

KA-BOOM!

An explosion loud enough to be heard in Baton Rouge rocked them back on their heels and rattled windows in nearby houses. Yellow and orange flames shot fifteen feet into the air. Hunks of cardboard, now reduced to confetti, fluttered in the sky. Dust and bits of leaves blew back, coating Carmela and Ava in a fine layer of grit. A dozen car alarms started bleeping wildly.

"Oh my Lord," Ava said. She sat down hard on the front steps and dropped her head into her hands. "Oh my Lord."

CHAPTER 23

Carmela and Ava's frantic 911 call brought a rush of first responders. Namely the bomb squad, a K-9 unit, four police cruisers, and a shaken-up Detective Babcock. One glance at Carmela and Ava — at the terrified, forlorn looks on their faces — and Babcock choked back his *holy hell* and the various admonishments he was about to rain down upon them. Instead, he gently urged them back inside the house.

When Carmela and Ava were settled on an ugly maroon sofa in the parlor, Babcock sat on a chair directly across from them and said, "Okay, give me the poop. Tell me exactly what happened."

"We thought somebody left us a thank-you gift," Ava said, wiping away tears. "But then the box blew up with, like, the biggest kaboom you ever heard. My poor ears are still ringing."

"Mine, too," Carmela said. "Like a million doorbells are bonging away."

"No, no, before that," Babcock said. "While the Grand Candlelight Tour was still happening. Tell me exactly what you were doing. Who showed up here for the tour? What strange incident might have possibly led to the explosion? Don't leave a single thing out. Even if it seems unimportant to you, I want to hear it."

"Maybe we should tell him about the two guys who ghosted through here today," Ava said.

Babcock was suddenly on high alert. "A couple of strange people showed up here today? Who were they?"

"Everybody was strange," Carmela said. "It was kind of a bad scene all around."

"No," Babcock said patiently. "Ava specifically said two guys. Who were they? Did you know them?"

Carmela let loose a harsh laugh. "Of course I know them. I've been warning you about them all along."

"Carmela . . ." Babcock was half angry, half coaxing.

"Jake Bond and Tom Ratcliff stopped by," Carmela said.

Babcock gave a slightly encouraging nod. "The reporter . . ."

"Ex-reporter," Ava said.

"And the guy who's an art dealer," Babcock finished. "They both took the tour?"

"Not exactly," Carmela said.

"Then what did they do that aroused your suspicions?" Babcock asked. "Were they threatening you or acting strangely?"

"What's strange is that they both showed up and kind of wandered around," Carmela said. She proceeded to tell Babcock about Jake Bond taking notes for his supposed article for the Historic Homes Society. And about Tom Ratcliff, who only Ava had laid eyes on, hustling through the house rather quickly.

"So no confrontations, no threats," Babcock said. "You just found it unusual that they both showed up here today."

Ava nudged Carmela with an elbow. "You'd better tell him about last night."

Babcock leaned forward. "Something happened to you last night? When? You mean at Baby's party?"

"Afterward," Carmela said.

"When we were walking home," Ava said.

"What was it?" Babcock asked. "You saw something? Overheard someone talking?"

"I'm afraid it was much more dramatic than that," Carmela said. "We were chased."

"What!"

"I said we —"

Babcock held up a hand. "I heard you. Okay, explain, please." He was trying to remain calm. "Who chased you? Did you get a look at his face?"

"He was driving a car," Ava said. "Well, actually more like one of those macho-type SUVs, like a Jeep or a Land Rover. With a shiny grill on front and big knobby tires."

Babcock's eyes bugged out. "You're saying someone actually tried to run you down?"

So Carmela had to tell him that part of the story, too. About walking down the alley. The SUV coming after them. Their wild and crazy escape through someone's backyard.

"And you say the SUV had big tires," Babcock said. "Like the suspension was jacked way up?"

"No, it just had big tires," Ava said.

"Trouble follows you ladies around, do you know that?" Babcock said.

"But not because of anything we *did*," Carmela protested. "We didn't bring this on ourselves."

Babcock's mouth dropped wide open. "Of course you did," he finally managed to sputter. "You've been poking around all over town, spoofing people, asking leading questions — trying to investigate Hughes Wilder's murder. Yes, you made a couple leaps of faith and found a tentative clue here and there, but now you've made a complete and utter mess out of things."

Carmela lifted a shoulder. "I wouldn't call it a *complete* mess."

"Then it's a fine imitation of one," Babcock snapped back.

"Don't yell at me," Carmela said. "I feel bad enough as it is. Because I pulled Ava into this stupid investigation, too."

Ava flung an arm around Carmela's shoulder. "I don't mind, *cher*. I really don't. We all know you're a little crazy."

"Right," Carmela said. "And you're the sensible one."

"If the shoe fits . . ."

"Except you *lost* your shoe," Carmela said. For some reason, her comment made both of them start to giggle. And clutch each other even tighter.

"Okay." Babcock said, slapping both hands against his knees. "Is there anything else you need to tell me? Any other random threats, car chases, or explosions?"

"You make it sound like a Bruce Willis movie," Ava said.

"There's nothing more to tell at this exact moment," Carmela hedged. There was plenty more to tell Babcock. She just didn't think this was the optimal time, since Babcock seemed pretty . . . well, freaked-out.

"What's going on outside?" Ava asked. "Did the explosion blow the front off the house? Singe the columns? I never got a good look at the damage. And the thing is, Harrison's folks would *kill* me if something terrible happened to their precious house."

"They can stand in line," Babcock said. "Somebody else is trying to kill you first."

Carmela, Ava, and Babcock walked out onto the front porch to see what was going on. From the look of things, it was a cross between a three-ring circus and a political convention.

More law enforcement had arrived, which meant that squad cars and shiny black vans were parked everywhere. Black and yellow crime scene tape had been strung around the front lawn, and the street was blocked off at both ends. Nosy neighbors had spilled out onto their lawns to gawk in surprise. There was even a small bomb-detecting robot — something that looked like a silver bread box with a claw arm — scooting around and making an annoying buzzing sound.

"Now what?" Carmela asked. She couldn't

believe that she and Ava were at the hub of all this activity. It was embarrassing. She just wanted it all to go away.

"Wait one," Babcock said. He ambled down the steps and walked over to talk with two of the bomb guys, who still wore their padded bomb-proof uniforms. He talked to them for five or six minutes, then must have said something about Carmela and Ava because the bomb guys turned and looked over at them. Ava saw them looking and gave a brave smile and a little finger-wave.

Finally, Babcock came back over to where Carmela and Ava were waiting.

Carmela was anxious and still hopped up on adrenaline. "Did you send a squad car to Tom Ratcliff's house to see if he's at home?" she asked.

"Yes, we did," Babcock said.

"And Jake Bond's place, too?"

Babcock nodded.

"So . . . were they both home?" Carmela asked.

"No," Babcock said. "No answers, no more investigating. You touched a nerve somewhere, rattled the killer . . . brought him out of hiding."

"That's good, huh?" Ava asked.

"It's terrible," Babcock said. "Especially since you were both almost blown to bits.

From here on, there'll be no more sharing of information. Carmela . . ." He stared at her, his brow furrowed, his eyes pinpricks of intensity. "This means you. I should have *never* given you any of the bare basics. This, today, is my fault. I brought on this trouble by silently encouraging you. Now the killer has you and Ava directly in his sights, and I'm to blame."

Carmela put a hand on Babcock's arm. "Of course you're not. I'm the one who's been snooping around, asking all sorts of questions."

"Yeah, me too," Ava said, wanting to get in on the action. Or maybe deflect the blame game from Carmela. "We're just a couple of wacky amateur sleuths. You know, à la Nancy Drew."

"Whatever you pretend to be or aspire to be, it ends here and now," Babcock said.

"Please don't say that," Carmela protested. "You can't just legislate our actions. We're free to . . ."

"Free to be you and me," Ava said.

"Take your sob story somewhere else," Babcock said. "Because I'm not listening. I don't want to hear word one about any more investigating, your thoughts on the Neptune Bomber, or who you think might be a prime suspect." He grimaced as though he were biting back more harsh words. "You got that? Stay out of it. Just *please* let me do my job."

Carmela had been about to mention the possibility of a pyrotechnics buff who owned a car dealership. But in that moment she decided not to. Babcock would surely have a brain embolism if she shared that tasty nugget of information. He'd put Danny Labat under strict surveillance — and put the kibosh on her driving in the road rally tomorrow. And she didn't want that to happen.

Ava had already surveyed the house. Now she turned her attention to the front yard, with its singed plants and banged-up magnolia trees. "I suppose we should start cleaning up. If the coast is clear."

"What I'd like you both to do is go back to your own apartments," Babcock said. "I don't think you'll be safe if you stay here."

"But I promised Harrison's parents that I'd keep watch over the place," Ava said.

"And you have," Babcock said. "But this . . . this explosion changes things dramatically."

"Look at it this way," Carmela said to Ava. "At least the house didn't get blown off the face of the earth. As it stands now, just a couple of magnolia trees and a few palmettos got dinged."

"You think I'll have to pay for the damage?" Ava asked.

"I bet we could judiciously trim those bushes and nobody would be the wiser," Carmela said.

"What about that big burned spot in the street?" Ava asked. "And the singed grass?"

"Make something up," Carmela said. "Tell them there was a freak lightning strike. Or a UFO crash-landed."

"Gas leak?" Babcock said.

Ava nodded slowly. "Yeah, that all sounds plausible." Then her lower lip quivered. "But I promised . . ."

"Tell you what," Babcock said. "Why don't you let me worry about this place? I'll park a squad car outside. Have the officers keep an eye on the Wilkes house."

"How long can you do that?" Carmela asked.

Babcock looked grim. "As long as it takes to keep the both of you safe. As long as it takes to catch this . . . this maniac."

So Carmela, Ava, and Ava's cat went back to Carmela's place. While Ava rattled around in the kitchen and dug out a bottle of wine along with some cheese and crackers, Carmela went around the corner and fetched Boo and Poobah from her neighbor's apartment.

"This is kind of fun," Ava declared, once they were lounging around in the living room. "All of us together, having a sleepover."

"If the critters get along, that is," Carmela said. Every time Poobah walked past Ava's cat, the cat made a playful swipe with its paw.

"Aw, they're just having fun."

"I hope so. I truly do."

Ava poured a finger of wine into her glass. "You said we weren't going to party tonight. And now we're drinking wine."

"This isn't partying. This is purely medicinal. I'm still having heart palpitations from that stupid bomb."

"Thanks to your smart thinking, we didn't get blown to kingdom come," Ava said. "Thank you for that. Thank you for always being the nosy, suspicious one."

"You're welcome." Carmela took a sip of her wine. "I know Babcock warned us — well, mostly me — about investigating, but I can't help thinking about what that candle guy told us."

"About the car dealer guy who also specialized in pyrotechnics? Yeah, I've been thinking about that, too. I wondered why you didn't bring it up to Babcock. Seems to me you had the perfect entrée. I mean . . . the entire New Orleans bomb squad was there, after all."

"If I'd have brought it up then, Babcock would have totally flipped out," Carmela said. "Shipped us off to someplace super-safe. Iowa or some far-off, exotic locale where they probably don't have homicidal killers who are also experts in explosives."

"*Cher,* I hate to tell you this, but I think every place has its share of homicidal maniacs."

"Yeah. Probably." Carmela helped herself to another cracker. "This isn't going to do it for me. Want to order out for pizza?"

"I was hoping you'd say that," Ava said.

They sent out for a pizza topped with fennel sausage and sweet marinated peppers. When their pie arrived — extra large, of course — they dug into it.

"I don't understand people who say things like, 'I forgot to eat,' " Ava said. "What planet are they from? For me, eating is everything. It's all I ever think about."

"Me, too," Carmela said. She reached for a third slice of pizza, pulling it away from the pie, stretching a huge hunk of molten mozzarella cheese. "Look at me, I've even combined eating with stretching. It's practically a workout."

"It is a workout," Ava laughed.

They finished the evening by watching a couple hours of TV, and then went to bed early. Ava stayed over with Carmela, the two of them snuggling under the down comforter and talking quietly. Wondering if this would all be over soon — wondering if the killer might come after them again.

Finally, with the cat on the bed and the dogs on their own beds, they drifted off to sleep. But for Carmela it was an uneasy slumber.

CHAPTER 24

Carmela had read somewhere that most heart attacks occur on Monday mornings. Well, it was Monday morning, and she was definitely feeling the stress. In fact, the first thing she did when she got to Memory Mine — even before she made a pot of strong, hot coffee — was warn Gabby not to accept any deliveries.

"Why on earth not?" Gabby asked. Gabby looked like a perfectly perky candidate for the Mrs. Louisiana pageant this morning, dressed as she was in a rose-colored twinset, kitten heels, and a double strand of pearls.

"Oh . . ." Carmela drew a deep breath. She supposed she had to tell Gabby about the explosion. She probably *owed* it to her to give full disclosure. "We had a little incident yesterday. At the Garden District house where Ava is house-sitting."

"You're talking about the one that was on

the Grand Candlelight Tour?"

"That's the one," Carmela said.

Gabby was half listening as she sorted through the morning mail. "What happened? One of the tour guests get a little out of hand? Or did Ava see a cute guy and get frisky?"

"Actually, there was a bomb."

Envelopes and a couple of local tabloids fluttered out of Gabby's hands. "That's fu-funny," she said. "I thought you said *bomb*."

"I did."

"You mean *bomb* like the one that blew up the King Neptune float?"

"It was a much smaller bomb." Carmela made a shaping motion with her hands to indicate the explosion was more like a firecracker than a nuclear warhead that would blow everyone halfway to Mars. "So you can see why we should probably be wary of deliveries?"

"But we've got a shipment of tag board and rubber stamps coming in. We get deliveries every day." Gabby leaned down and gathered up the mail that she'd dropped.

"I still think we should ask the FedEx and UPS guys to hold everything for a couple of days."

Gabby gazed at her, a tiny frown crinkling

her brows. "We've already had a delivery."

"What are you talking about? From who?"

Gabby sifted through her stack of recovered mail and handed an envelope to Carmela. "This arrived this morning. Well, I'm *assuming* it was hand delivered, because I found it slipped under the front door when I came in."

Carmela studied the plain white envelope. Her full name was printed on it, but nothing else. There was no store address, return address, or stamp. The only thing that was clear was that the envelope had come off a laser printer.

There was a sudden knock on the door, and Carmela glanced up. It was Jill and her daughter, Kristen, two of her scrapbooking regulars.

"Knock knock," Jill said. "Are you guys open for business?"

"We sure are," Gabby said. "Come on in."

Carmela tucked the envelope into her pocket. "What can we help you ladies with today?"

"Handmade paper?" Jill said.

Carmela started for the paper files. "Got some lovely paper right over here."

For the next few minutes, Carmela pulled out sheets of mulberry paper, Japanese Moriki paper, and flax paper. "And this is amate bark paper that's handmade in Mexico," Carmela said. "Made from the fibers of downed fig and mulberry trees. What would you be using this paper for? Bookbinding?"

"We're making collages," Kristen said.

"With five different colors to choose from, the amate bark would be perfect."

Then two more women wandered into Memory Mine, and Carmela found herself busy as could be.

"I have a rubber stamp that I'd like to use with white ink," one of the women said. "Is that possible?"

"It's easy if you've got the right ink," Carmela said, reaching for a stamp pad. "This particular ink, in frost white, goes on very opaque. So it works extremely well, even if you're stamping on black cardstock."

"Another question," the woman said. "I have a rather large rubber stamp of some grapes and wine bottles — maybe three-by-four-inches in size. But when I stamp with it, the ink coverage ends up being very sparse in the middle and some of the details are lost."

"Here's a tip," Carmela said. "Remove the handle from the rubber stamp, then ink it up and do your stamping. I think you'll find that the image turns out a whole lot better."

It wasn't until a good forty-five minutes later that Carmela remembered the envelope she'd tucked in her pocket. She went into her office, tore open the envelope, and pulled out the note.

It was a single page, also typed, also printed off a laser printer. The contents of the note were grammatically correct but written in slightly stilted English. And they stunned her.

Miss Bertrand,
I hold some critical information concerning the demise of Hughes Wilder, but under no circumstances do I want to get involved with the police. Would it be possible for you to meet me at 1218 Barracks Street, apartment 2-G, at 10:30 this morning? I will wait for you there for exactly thirty minutes.

A Friend

Carmela glanced at her watch. It was ten twenty. And the address was just a few blocks away. But . . . should she go? Did she *dare* go? Or was this some sort of elaborate trap?

The note was intriguing, to be sure. Had she touched an outer strand of a spider's web and set something in motion? Had someone peripherally involved in the case discovered that she was investigating? And if this outside person really existed, did they truly not want to get involved with the police?

Carmela wanted to believe the note, but she was also a skeptic by nature.

Critical information.

The writer of the note claimed to have critical information about the demise of Hughes Wilder. Was it about his finances? His wife? His murder?

This could most definitely be a trap. On the other hand, it could be an innocent bystander with information to share. Information that could genuinely lead somewhere. It could solve the mystery of Wilder's bizarre death, it could settle a lot of questions in her own mind, and it could help get Babcock off the hook.

Against her better judgment, Carmela decided to go.

As Carmela moved along the sidewalk, the French Quarter seemed even more crowded and alive. Music plinkety-plinked out of saloon doors as she passed by. T-shirt and souvenir shops were selling massive amounts of purple and green beads. Even the guys selling fake designer handbags and scarves were racking up big sales.

Carmela passed by Dulcimer Antiques and saw the owner, Devon Dowling, standing in the front window. He waved at her, so she stopped and waited. Seconds later, Devon hurried outside carrying his dog, Mimi the pug. He was wearing his self-selected uniform of black shirt and cream-colored slacks. Winter or summer, rain or shine, cotton or silk, that's what Devon always wore. Black shirt, cream slacks.

"Miss Carmela," Devon said. "How are you doing, dawlin'?"

"Hanging in there," Carmela said. She chucked Mimi under the chin and wasn't surprised when the dog just yawned.

"I saw your *inamorato* on television the other day," Devon said. "It sounds like he's the head honcho on the investigation of that terrible Neptune float mishap." His eyes bugged out. "Although it wasn't so much a mishap as *murder,* I suppose. Since that awful night, the Quarter's been crawling with homicide detectives. They're questioning everyone."

"Questioning you?" Carmela asked.

"No, but they talked to my dear friend Charles Chittendon, who owns Victoriana Antiques on Royal Street." Devon patted Mimi's chunky backside. "But Charles didn't know anything either."

"Babcock says they've put everyone on the case," Carmela said. "Detectives, uniformed cops, even some guys from vice. I guess the mayor is really breathing down their necks."

"I would imagine he is," Devon said. "And can you believe it? Fat Tuesday is tomorrow. The big day when millions of people crowd into the French Quarter. I'm just *praying* nothing horrible happens."

"So are we all," Carmela said as she hurried off, still questioning whether she should even try to meet up with her mysterious note-writer.

When Carmela arrived at 1218 Barracks Street, she found an apartment building she was completely unfamiliar with. She'd probably walked by it a million times, but had never been inside. The façade of the building was painted light brown, with a high, narrow blue door and windows covered with decorative metal grates on each side. She lifted the hasp on the door and pushed it open. The rusty hinges creaked out a faint warning as she entered a small cobblestone courtyard. There was a fountain, masses of unkempt greenery, and a brick wall that rose up on two sides. A narrow stairway led up to an open-air balcony and a long row of apartments.

Carmela glanced around. Except for a fat tabby cat snoozing in the sun, there was no other living thing around. Even the noise from the street seemed dampened.

Okay, decision time. Should I stay or should I go?

Well, she was here. So . . . Carmela walked over to the rickety wrought-iron stairs, grasped the railing, and began to climb. The stairs were old, which caused them to clang and shake the higher she went. When she hit the second floor, she breathed a sigh of relief. Here the decking seemed a lot sturdier. A wood-plank balcony led along the front of the various apartments. The curtains were drawn in every unit she passed, and the outer windows were all covered with bars. Finally, Carmela found herself standing in front of 2-G, the very last apartment in the complex — she was a little shocked that she was actually there.

Was this the stupidest thing she'd done since she'd given herself a home perm and her hair turned green and sprouted like an artichoke? Yeah, maybe.

She bit down, worrying her lower lip with her teeth. And then she knocked on the door.

Her knock sounded loud and impetuous, and seemed to echo in the courtyard below. She glanced over the balcony and saw the cat looking up at her. She knocked again, and waited.

Nobody's going to answer the door. Deep in my heart I kind of knew that. So now what?

Feeling a slight emotional letdown, Carmela held her breath and knocked again. Harder this time. Still, nobody came to answer the door. No mystery man or mystery woman suddenly appeared to beckon her inside and have a whispered conversation about the murder.

Seriously? There's really nobody here? Then who sent the note? And why?

Now a feeling of annoyance crept in. Carmela's watch said ten forty-five, and the note writer had said they would wait for half an hour. Technically, she still had a grace period of fifteen minutes.

Carmela put her hand on the doorknob, was about to turn it, and then hesitated. Remembered the bomb from yesterday. Instead, she went to a dusty window and peered in.

But no — it was way too dirty to see anything at all.

She dug in her bag, found a hanky, and swiped at the window. Which only smeared the dirt and made things worse. She scrubbed harder and was finally able to clean a small space so that she could look through.

Moving a step closer, Carmela put an eye to the window and looked in.

The apartment was sparsely furnished. There was a low wooden table covered with a good half inch of dust and two wooden chairs. Against a brick wall was some kind of bookcase, which held a couple of ratty cardboard boxes. The place was grubby, dusty, and looked as if it had been abandoned. As if it hadn't been inhabited for several years.

Carmela wondered if this apartment could have possibly been empty since Hurricane Katrina. Could an apartment be abandoned for that long? Would the building owners forego rent and let that happen? She didn't know.

Carmela squared her shoulders and bent forward to look inside again. Just as she did, she caught the briefest flicker of movement.

Were her eyes playing tricks on her? Was the sun that streamed in from the southwest simply hitting a twirl of dust motes?

Carmela looked again, her eyes moving from the dusty table, past the bookcases, to a darkened interior room.

Yes! There it was again: a slight movement, and then a shadow. And it wasn't twirling dust.

"Hello?" Carmela called out. She moved to the door and rapped on it again. "Hello? Anybody in there? Open the door, please."

Her hand grasped the doorknob, ready to turn it . . . and then she stopped. Her inner warning system was blipping out a loud message, telling her not to be so hasty, not to make any foolish mistakes.

Instead, Carmela walked back the full length of the balcony and around the side of the building, where she found an even narrower back balcony.

Hmm.

She stopped, turned slowly, and suddenly decided to leave things well enough alone. Coming here had been a foolish venture on her part. Who knew what was in that apartment? Maribel with a gun? Crazy Jake Bond? Some other bomb-setting maniac?

As Carmela was slowly descending the shaky front steps, she heard footsteps moving fast along the back balcony. Someone running.

What?

Carmela spun back around, grasped the hand railings, and climbed back up, taking the steps two at a time. She sprinted down the side of the building, ready for a come-to-meetin' confrontation with whoever was there. But when she rounded the corner, she saw no one and heard only faint footsteps descending the opposite stairway. Stunned, she stood there listening as the footsteps completely died out.

Whoever had been creeping around . . . she'd just missed them!

CHAPTER 25

Carmela returned to Memory Mine, feeling more than a little shaken up. But she had a surprise guest waiting for her. Sam Spears was leaning up against the front counter, looking friendly and relaxed as he chatted with Gabby.

Gabby saw Carmela and immediately blurted out, "Look what we got!" She hoisted up a green-and-white-striped box for Carmela to see. "Beignets. From Café du Monde."

Sam grinned at Carmela as she joined them at the counter. "I figured these little gut bombs might be your drug of choice."

It took both Sam and Gabby a few seconds to notice the look of concern that still lingered on Carmela's face.

"Carmela, what's wrong?" Gabby asked. "Did something . . . ?"

Sam jumped in, equally sympathetic. "Are you okay?"

Carmela tried to wave them off. "I'm fine, I'm fine. I just ran into a strange . . . um, something problematic. I'm over it now, okay?"

But Sam seemed genuinely concerned. "If this is a bad time for you, I can come back later."

"No no, I'm fine," Carmela assured him.

"Sam was wondering if we could help him design a corporate brochure," Gabby said. She loved it when they were able to step out of their comfort zone of scrapbooking and crafting and work on actual graphic design. Carmela was an experienced designer, having worked at several small design firms, while Gabby was still honing her skills. But she was clever and a fast, astute learner. So far she'd designed a table topper for Bread and Chocolate Café and a brochure for Cara Lee's Florals.

"It's not a big deal," Sam said to Carmela. "I was just on my way to a Silicon Bayou luncheon over at the Marriott and thought of you. Decided to pop in."

"Silicon Bayou," Carmela said. "What is that?"

"It's a bunch of tech firms who get together every other month or so. We talk marketing, the pros and cons of IPOs, that sort of stuff. But, really, if this is inconvenient for you, I can stop by another time. There's no rush on this."

"A brochure," Carmela said. "For a tech company. It sounds like fun." She'd never designed anything for a tech company before. It could be a feather in her cap. And a welcome addition to her portfolio.

"You have an idea of what you want?" Carmela asked.

Sam seesawed a hand back and forth. "Kind of."

Carmela led Sam back to her office.

"So this is where the magic happens?" he said, looking around.

"More like trial and error," Carmela said. "But we usually manage to come up with a few designs that meet our clients' approval."

"And I do like what I see." Sam studied the various sketches that were pinned on Carmela's wall and then sat down in one of the director's chairs. He pulled out a business card. "You remember this?" He twiddled the card between his thumb and forefinger and handed it to her.

"Your velociraptor." Carmela sat down behind her desk.

"The Velocitech logo."

"All in all, I'd have to say it's a pretty memorable image. Which is half the battle right there when it comes to marketing.

Remind me, what is it your company does?"

"Project and asset management of IT services."

Carmela raised a hand and made a whooshing motion over her head. "You want to run that by me again?"

"Asset management is just a fancy way of saying we're consultants," Sam explained.

"Okay. But what do you consult on?"

"Mostly helping companies develop their IT system — the correct system — and then creating a good strong fire wall. Network security is a huge issue these days."

"I guess I can understand all that," Carmela said.

"Sure, but that's because you have a basic grasp of technology. A lot of our clients have a terrible time understanding our capabilities — or even realizing they have a need for them. If we're dealing with CEOs, or company presidents, or even a general manager instead of an IT guy, we really have to dumb our message down."

"And that's where I come in," Carmela said. "Layman's terms and easily digestible explanations instead of technical gibberish."

"Something like that," Sam said. "What we need right now is your basic all-purpose corporate brochure. Something we can give to potential clients as well as investors."

"Do you have anything sketched out yet?"

"Not really."

"Do you have a writer on staff?"

"I was hoping you could help with that," Sam said. He laughed. "As you can see, we require a bit of hand-holding."

"That's what I'm here for. So give me the CliffsNotes version on Velocitech."

Sam told her about how he and two partners went out on a limb, quit their jobs, cashed in their 401(k)s, and started the company. He talked about Velocitech's strengths, and outlined what he saw as business opportunities.

"Of course," Sam said, "as we grow, we're going to need additional financing. Possibly do an IPO or look for outside investors."

"Obviously you were familiar with Hughes Wilder's firm, Pontchartrain Capital Management," Carmela said. "Did you ever consider talking to him?"

"No, but only because we weren't at that point yet." Sam drew a deep breath and said, "Of course now it feels like they've pretty much tanked."

But Carmela was curious. "Are you familiar with any of the tech firms that Pontchartrain Capital Management invested in?"

"A few, yes. Some are located in the I-10 Tech Corridor near Slidell, where Pontchartrain Capital Management is located."

"Did Wilder know much about technology?"

"I don't think so. At least it would appear that way in hindsight."

"Yet he invested in it heavily," Carmela said. "Strange."

Sam shrugged. "He was a good guy, at least in my opinion. Now I guess we'll have to wait and see if the company is able to regain its footing."

Carmela picked up a sketch pad and made a few notes. She was already thinking ahead. "For your brochure, I'm thinking you probably need eight pages. That would mean a front and back cover, plus three inside spreads. That should give you enough space to tell your story."

"That sounds perfect. What about visuals?"

"Well, your raptor image should be on the cover for sure."

"Yup. But how do we convey the technology part? I don't want to look like an ad for Jurassic Park."

"What about making your raptor look a little more fierce? And adding some text?"

"Such as?"

"What's the most important service you deliver to your customers?"

"Oh, that's easy," Sam said. "We help them drill down through their files to obtain critical data."

"So what if we had this fierce-looking raptor with the headline, 'I want my data and I want it now!' "

"I love it!" Sam said. "Wait, really? You just came up with that idea this exact minute?"

Carmela nodded.

"This is gonna be great. How soon can I get my team together for a brainstorming session?"

"Probably next week."

Sam's cell phone rang and he took a quick call. He listened for a few moments and then laughed. "Twenty-one plus three extreme? Why not?" When he hung up he said, "Sorry about that. Tech talk."

"No problem," Carmela said.

Sam smiled as he looked around Carmela's office again, obviously impressed by her designs. He spotted a zoo brochure on her desk and picked it up. Studied the front cover and flipped it open.

"Did you design this?"

Carmela nodded. "Guilty as charged."

"Pro bono?"

"I'm afraid so. I had to twist a few arms to get the printing done. But the event is such a worthwhile cause."

"Well, blessings on your head, my dear, because I'm a cheerleader for the zoo as well. In fact, my company even donated money to help build Alligator Alley, that new gator pond."

"That's wonderful," Carmela said.

"Don't mind me," Sam said as he reached for a ceramic mug that was sitting on Carmela's desk. "I'm quite fascinated by all the intriguing stuff you have in here." He held up the mug and chuckled. "This is very cool." It was a white mug with a photo transfer of a skull on it. The mug was one of several Carmela had made for a client for a Halloween promotion.

"It's just a photo transfer," Carmela explained. "A fairly easy process."

"Maybe for you." Sam turned the mug over and studied it. "How much would four dozen of these cost?"

"With your logo on them?"

He glanced at her. "You think it would work?"

"Oh sure," Carmela said. "I think it would look great. Tell you what, I'll do a sample mug and you can see for yourself."

"You can do that right here?"

"Well, not right now. But in a few days, when I have a little more time."

"That'd be great. A mug like this is the kind of thing we could give to prospective customers as well as existing ones. They'd use it and keep it on their desk, so we'd stay top of mind." He grinned at Carmela. "You know, Shamus thinks the world of you."

Carmela shook her head. "I don't think so. Shamus must have me confused with somebody else."

"No no," Sam countered. "We were at the Pluvius den just the other night, and all Shamus did was brag about how smart you are, what a great little detective you are."

"He's dead wrong about that. Because I'm not exactly getting anywhere with this Hughes Wilder thing."

"Even though you promised him you'd help?" Sam said. He sounded almost disappointed.

Carmela shrugged. "Shamus and I promised each other lots of things. But . . . not everything works out."

"Even so," Sam said, looking serious. "If you could figure out *anything* concerning Hughes Wilder's death, any kind of tiny thread that the police could follow up on, it would mean the world to us. Wilder was our krewe captain, after all. We loved the guy. Which means that, come next election, there are going to be awfully big shoes to fill."

Just as the delivery guy from Pirate's Alley Deli was handing Carmela two spicy shrimp salads, the phone rang. Gabby snatched it up, listened for a couple seconds, then practically flung it at Carmela.

"Babcock," Gabby said. "And, holy catfish, is he ever steamed."

Carmela grabbed the phone. "What's wrong?" she asked, without bothering to say hello.

"Have you seen this crappy little rag called the *NOLA Vindicator*?" Babcock shouted at her.

"Um, yes," Carmela said. She moved the phone a little farther away from her ear and glanced over at Gabby. Gabby was, at that precise moment, reading a copy of the *NOLA Vindicator* and had her pert little nose buried in what must have been a very tantalizing story. Probably the one that Babcock was so up in arms about.

Gabby looked up. "Is Babcock freaking out over this article?" she whispered.

Carmela nodded. Was he ever.

"Have you read it? Have you read it?" Babcock screamed.

"I haven't seen it yet," Carmela said.

"What exactly —"

"I'll tell you what exactly. Your buddy, Jake Bond, has accused the police of mishandling the Hughes Wilder case!"

"He's not my buddy," Carmela said quietly. "And I'm the one who warned you about Bond, remember?"

Undeterred, Babcock continued his rant. "Bond claims that we've screwed up completely. Can you believe it? What a skeezy little snake that guy is. You know, this is the kind of fake, unfounded article that makes the public lose faith in their police department."

"I don't think anyone's lost faith in you," Carmela said.

"This just burns me up, it makes me crazy. We're working 'round the clock to solve the Wilder case and Bond makes these sweeping statements so it looks as if we don't give a crap." Babcock paused to gulp a much-needed breath. "I don't know, I just don't know."

"Maybe you should —"

"I gotta go, Carmela. Sorry to call and dump on you like this. Bye-bye, sweetheart, take care." And he was gone. Just like that.

Carmela hung up the phone. Babcock had been so infuriated that he'd completely forgotten that she was driving in the road rally today. No admonishments, no lectures, no nothing. Maybe that was a good thing?

"Babcock's pretty upset, huh?" Gabby had placed her takeout salad on top of the *NOLA Vindicator* so she could spear a fat pink shrimp.

"He completely flipped out. You heard his rant?"

"How could I not?" Gabby said. "The thing is, if Bond is trying to take the moral high ground on this investigation — if he's chastising the police and making accusations against them — then he can't be the Neptune Bomber, can he? So doesn't that pretty much eliminate him as one of your suspects?"

"Possibly. But there's always the chance that Bond's carefully crafted article is really an elaborate smoke screen," Carmela said. "A total misdirection."

"Ah," Gabby said as the phone rang once again. She snatched it up and practically threw it at Carmela, expecting it to be Babcock again.

"Yes?" Carmela quavered. She dreaded what Babcock would have to say this time.

But the caller turned out to be Ava, bubbling over with excitement.

"Hey, girlfriend," Ava sang out. "I got Miguel watching the store. So it's time we get our cute little chassis in gear and hit that racetrack!"

CHAPTER 26

The racetrack, formally known as NOLA Motorsports Park, smelled like motor oil, fried spark plugs, and burned rubber. Probably because it was jam-packed with people and cars. In fact, Carmela had never seen so many sports cars, muscle cars, and classic cars together in one place.

"What kind of road rally is this, anyway?" Ava asked as they threaded their way through an enormous blacktop area. Colored pennants fluttered overhead, sponsor booths and tire displays were jammed one after another, and cars were parked bumper to bumper. "Are all these cars gonna race at once? Is it gonna be like the Minneapolis 500?"

"*Indian* apolis 500," Carmela said. "And no, they won't be racing together. There are different groups. Cars and drivers are classed in divisions."

"Sounds like fun," Ava said. "Where are

you supposed to pick up your car?"

"Good question. I suppose I'll have to find Danny Labat and ask him."

"While you're wandering around, I'll keep an eye on all these studly-looking guys. I bet men outnumber women fifty to one here. We'll have to keep this place in mind."

"Don't you think you should break up with H before you find his replacement?" Carmela asked.

"That's a done deal," Ava said. "It'll take me all of two minutes. Hey, there's a couple guys over there with clipboards and official-looking armbands. Maybe they can point us in the right direction."

Carmela flagged down one of the race monitors, who did in fact point her in the direction of a large, white, open-sided tent.

"This way," Carmela said to Ava.

With exotic cars parked everywhere, Carmela was fantasizing about the kind of car she'd be driving. Maybe a Koenigsegg CCR or a McLaren F1?

Carmela and Ava waded into a throng of people who were clustered around a half-dozen hot-looking sports cars. They found Danny Labat there, looking a little frantic. He was wearing a white nylon windbreaker with the word *PENNZOIL* down the left sleeve.

When Labat caught sight of Carmela, he raced up to her and threw an arm around her shoulders. "You made it, great! I've got a terrific car for you to drive."

He led her over to an apple red Alfa Romeo. "I took you at your word when you said you were good with an Alfa."

Ava snapped her fingers. "Carmela can drive anything with four wheels. Just wait until you see her flying around the track."

Labat laughed. "I'm looking forward to it. In fact, if you girls want to place a small wager on any of these races, I might even know a guy."

"No thanks," Carmela said. "So . . . keys are in the car?"

Labat nodded. "You're all set."

"Where do I go from here?"

Labat pointed toward the track. "Just drive over to the pits, try not to run anybody down, and look for the big orange banner. That'll be our crew. They'll get you all suited up."

"When does she drive?" Ava asked.

"Third race," Labat said.

"What is that exactly?" Ava asked. "Like a Formula One race? With all the hotshot drivers from Italy and France?"

"It actually used to be our powder puff race," Labat said. "Only we can't call it that anymore. Lots of women complained."

"I can't imagine why," Carmela said in icy tones.

"Anyway," Labat continued, "now we just call it the Pro-Am."

"That sounds exciting, too," Ava said. "Pros and amateurs racing together."

"I said we *called* it that," Labat chuckled. "I didn't say it was. In actuality, all our racers today are amateurs."

Carmela glanced around. Drivers were jumping into cars, engines were roaring, and lights were flashing. She decided to take a chance and see if she could mousetrap Labat. "This is all so exciting," she said. "Do you ever add pyrotechnics to the mix?"

Labat looked at her as if she'd lost her mind. "What are you talking about?"

"You know . . . fireworks, Roman candles, that sort of stuff?"

"Are you kidding? With all this fuel around? We'd have to be insane to shoot off something like that. We don't even allow smoking in the pit area."

"But you're an amateur pyrotechnics guy, aren't you?"

Labat gave her a withering look. "Who told you that?"

"I guess I just heard it somewhere."

Shaking his head, Labat turned away from

Carmela. "Lotsa luck," he mumbled.

"Now what?" Ava asked.

"Now we go get ready," Carmela said. "Hop in and we'll drive this beauty over to the pit."

"Hop in? Into that tin can of a car? I'll squish my road rally outfit." Ava had worn a red leather miniskirt and a checkered T-shirt.

"I'm sure it's been wrinkled before," Carmela chuckled.

"Ooh . . ." Ava gingerly folded herself in.

Carmela turned the key, revved the engine, and grinned. "This is very cool."

"The pit, girl. Drive us over to the pit."

Carmela put the car in first gear, and she and Ava rolled over toward the pit, the feisty little car rumbling and backfiring the whole way.

"There's the orange banner," Ava shouted.

Carmela pulled into the pit. "Did you hear the power in this engine? This baby is raring to go."

Ava glanced around at the all-male pit crew. "So am I, dawlin'. And look over to your left, there's a TV crew here, too."

"It's Zoe," Carmela said, bumping to a stop. Zoe Carmichael was a young reporter with KBEZ-TV. It looked as if she and her cameraman, Raleigh, were doing a few interviews, getting some glamour shots for the evening news.

Carmela waved at her. "Zoe!"

Zoe saw Carmela and Ava and came walking over. "Are you two racing today?" she asked. Motioning to Raleigh, she said, "Get a few shots of Carmela and Ava sitting in that car."

"I'm happy to pose," Ava said. "But I'm no motor head. I don't know a carburetor from a carbuncle. Carmela's the one who's racing today."

"That's great," Zoe said. "Which race?"

"Third one," Carmela said. "Sports car division. The Pro-Am."

"Well, good luck to you."

"Thanks." Carmela climbed out of her car and stepped closer to Zoe. "Do you have a minute? I need to ask you about someone who used to work at KBEZ-TV."

"Sure," Zoe said. "Who is it?"

"Jake Bond."

Zoe wrinkled her nose. "Oh, him."

"Was there a problem with Bond?" Carmela asked.

Zoe hesitated. "Well, he was fired from his job."

"I heard that. Do you know why exactly?"

"Bond always claimed that he was canned for doing a hatchet job on Hughes Wilder.

365

You know, the guy who was killed on that exploding float last week."

"Yup, I was there. Front and center."

"Poor you," Zoe said. "Anyway, if you ask me, I think it was because Bond just didn't fit in. He was always kind of a strange duck, a loner type."

"He didn't get along with the TV crew?"

"It wasn't so much that, as he was always pestering them. When he was supposed to be in a meeting or working on a story, he'd be in the control room fooling around. Drove the engineers crazy."

"I can understand that."

"Bond didn't really belong in front of the camera. He was a real electronics nut. Always hanging around, fussing over the latest widget or gadget."

Electronics, Carmela thought. Wouldn't someone who was into electronics know how to rig explosives to a detonator? Weren't those the kind of instructions you could pick up on the Internet? Or that an electronics nut could figure out?

The thought unsettled her. She wondered once again if Bond could be the Neptune Bomber.

Ava tapped Carmela on the shoulder. "Sorry to interrupt . . ."

"No problem," Zoe said. "I gotta get back

to work anyway. See you guys. Good luck. Film at eleven."

"Guess who's here?" Ava said in a low voice.

"I'm afraid to guess," Carmela said. "Wait, is it Maribel?"

"Girl, you are downright psychic. Lady Macbeth just floated past us."

"Did she have a guilty look on her face?"

"More like she didn't have a care in the world." Ava shook her head and frowned. "Maribel should be wearing widow's black and crying tears into her Ramos gin fizz. Instead she shows up at every social event in town."

"I hear you."

"Carmela? Carmela Bertrand?" a man called out.

Carmela threw up a hand. "Right here."

"Hey there," said a short, stocky man in an orange and white jumpsuit. "I'm Mike, the pit crew boss. It's time to get you suited up. Third race, right?"

"Right," Carmela said.

"Awright then." Mike handed Carmela a white jumpsuit, gloves, and a helmet.

"Is there a changing —"

"No, ma'am," Mike said. "Just pull your gear on over your street clothes."

Carmela stepped into the jumpsuit,

shrugged it up over her shoulders, and zipped up. Then she put on the helmet to make sure it fit, and pulled on her gloves.

"Oh my Lord," Ava said, bent over with laughter. "You should see yourself, *cher,* it's hysterical, you look like the Michelin Man."

"There are times when safety trumps fashion," Carmela said.

Ava was still laughing. "Not for me, but I guess you can't be too careful when you're hurtling down a racetrack at ninety miles an hour. You sure don't want to crash and end up as aerial footage from a TV news helicopter."

"Thanks for that cheery note," Carmela said as she climbed into the Alfa Romeo and pulled her harness across her. She studied the gauges and dials for a moment, feeling the adrenaline beginning to pump.

Good, it'll keep me chill, but on my toes.

Everything sounded like an echo inside her helmet, but Carmela heard the voice on the loudspeaker announcing the Pro-Am race. Her race. She slid into first gear and drove out onto the track. Suddenly, it all felt very real to her — she was going to race a sports car on an actual speedway!

There were six cars in Carmela's division, and they lined up two abreast. She was in the second pair of cars, right behind a

Porsche 911 and a Mercedes SL. Then the starter car, a blue Mustang plastered with sponsor logos, began to roll. The six of them followed behind. As she heard the Mustang's engine roar, Carmela looked ahead at the flagman. Suddenly, the starter car blew down the track and the green flag dipped, rose up, and dipped again.

Without a second's hesitation, Carmela double-clutched the Alfa into third gear, tromped down on the gas, and popped it into fourth gear. She was able to maintain her pace until she had to back off slightly at the first turn, where a Chevy Corvette passed her.

Once Carmela was safely past the first turn and getting accustomed to how the Alfa handled, she picked up speed and finessed her way past the Corvette. Now she just had the Porsche and the Mercedes ahead of her.

Carmela was loving the speed, delighting at how well her car handled. And she was beginning to think she might have a shot at winning. She kept her eyes firmly on the shiny black Porsche directly ahead of her. She moved up, nipping at his back bumper, determined to get around him.

But no, another turn was coming, and she had to ease back on her speed. Now a

Dodge Viper was coming up on her left. She built her speed up again, but the Viper just hung there. They completed two laps, maintaining their same positions, then the Viper dropped back on the third lap and was replaced by a Jaguar.

No way is a Jag gonna take me.

Carmela eased to her right, effectively blocking the Jaguar. They flew around laps four and five that way. She roared into another turn, feeling infinitely more confident, and slid through it, figuring her oversized tires would hug the track and do their job. They did indeed.

Every few seconds, Carmela pulled closer to the Porsche, but the driver just wouldn't let her pass. She tried to zigzag her way around it, moving left, then right, then left again, but it was as if the driver anticipated her every move.

Finally, on the next-to-last lap, Carmela moved up next to the Porsche.

Gonna run this dude down.

But when she turned her head for a split-second glance, she recognized Tom Ratcliff as the driver.

Ratcliff? Seriously?

Carmela poured on the speed, determined to beat his brains out. He was a skillful driver, for sure, but now she was determined to take him, even though he'd nosed ahead of her again. She pressed the gas pedal to the floor, anticipating that she'd fly by him. But just as she pulled almost even, the Porsche jigged right. She saw him coming, trying to cut her off. Then there was a loud grating sound, metal on metal, because he'd bumped her.

A split second later, Carmela spun out!

Whoosh! Carmela was spinning around on the track, watching the wall rush by, then the grassy green infield, then the wall again. As she headed for a safety barrier — basically a wall of tires — she grasped the hand brake and pulled it back with all her might. She uttered a silent prayer that the brake would slow her down, and, at the very last second, it did.

The Alfa Romeo bounced off the crash wall and rocked to a stop.

Am I okay? Yes, I'm okay, but that doggone Tom Ratcliff . . .

The announcer on the PA system was instructing all drivers to hold their positions. And then, not fifteen seconds later, a pit crew car pulled up beside her. Mike jumped out and pulled open her door.

"Are you okay?" Mike asked.

Carmela clambered out of the Alfa and pulled off her helmet. "I'm fine," she said.

But she wasn't really. Her mind was in turmoil. Had Ratcliff's move been deliberate? Did he hit her on purpose because he knew she was investigating, or did he just want to win at any cost?

If it was a calculated move, had Ratcliff been trying to cause a serious crash? Had he hoped to kill her?

Carmela and Mike waited as the tow truck came out onto the track and took the Alfa away. Then Carmela climbed into Mike's car, and they drove back to the pit.

Ava came running toward her as fast as her high heels could carry her. "*Cher,* are you okay? What happened? You were doing so well and then, bam, you spun out!"

Carmela shook her head. "I'm fine. But I didn't just spin out on my own. I was pushed. Did you see who was driving that black Porsche? It was Tom Ratcliff."

Ava looked shocked. "The art dealer guy? He banged into you? Why?"

"My guess is Ratcliff found out I was doing some investigating."

"My Lord, Carmela, do you think he could be the killer?"

"I don't know," Carmela said. "But if he is, I'd like to see Babcock stuff him in a cell the size of one of those porta-potties over there."

Ava glanced over at a row of green porta-potties and wrinkled her nose. "Nasty."

CHAPTER 27

It was the night of the Nepthys parade, the
evening right before Fat Tuesday — and like
a dangerous hurricane, Mardi Gras fever
had swept through New Orleans.

"This is a great spot," Ava exclaimed as
she gripped a wrought-iron post in front of
the Cat Key Club. "We'll catch all the action."

Carmela, who was still smarting from her
loss in the race, was glad they'd arrived a
little early and staked out a place on the
curb. Of course, a geaux cup full of St. Tam-
many Vineyard Chardonnay helped alleviate
some of her pain. She'd almost managed to
forget about Tom Ratcliff. Almost.

"Here it comes, here it comes," Ava
hooted as the first float came into view.
"And is it ever gorgeous."

An enormous purple skull — eyes blink-
ing with red lights, head moving back and
forth — rode like a prow on an old sailing

ship. Lights twirled, the skull's mouth dropped open, and a musical blast boomed out.

"You can always count on Jekyl for some kind of crazy," Carmela said.

"But look at the rest of the float," Ava sang out. "It's covered with musical instruments."

"A tribute to New Orleans's musical heritage."

Gigantic shiny tubas, saxophones, and trombones covered the triple-decker float. Nepthys krewe members, dressed in sparkly purple tailcoats, gold top hats, and purple masks, hung off simulated wrought-iron balconies, tossing beads and toy drums into the crowd. Every thirty seconds, the skull let loose another musical blast, and thousands of purple and white lights flashed.

"I'm loving this," Ava called out. She stuck a hand up, snagged a string of purple beads, and blew a kiss to the krewe member who'd thrown it to her.

"Get a load of this second float," Carmela said.

The float was an enormous, thirty-foot-long green alligator. But the pièce de résistance was when the gator opened his mouth to reveal teeth that were really piano keys. A pianist was sitting inside those jaws, bouncing around, rocking out a jazz tune. Strobe lights flashed up and down the gator's tail.

"Can you believe this?" Ava said. "I've never seen this much whiz-bang electronics on Mardi Gras floats before."

Electronics. That was the word that made Carmela sit up like an eager prairie dog and take notice. She'd become more and more convinced that electronics — the kind that triggered an explosive — might be the key to Hughes Wilder's murder. And here in the Nepthys krewe, there was definitely someone who was fairly expert in electronics. It surely wasn't Jekyl — he was an artistic designer, not an electronics nerd. But someone had helped rig these floats. Who could it have been? And did a knowledge of electronics mean that someone from this krewe, possibly even Tom Ratcliff, had blown the Pluvius krewe's float to smithereens? And murdered Hughes Wilder?

Carmela went back to sipping wine, high-fiving with Ava, and cheering the parade. But Tom Ratcliff remained firmly in the back of her mind.

Finally, when the last float rolled by, and the last beads were flung, Ava said, "Where to now, *cher*? Where's the best party? Or should we drop into Mumbo Gumbo and go facedown in some hot and spicy crab gumbo?"

"You know, there's going to be a huge party at the Nepthys float den," Carmela said. "The floats will be heading back there, the krewe and volunteer float-builders will all be there . . ."

"Ah," Ava said, "that would mean *crashing* their party."

"Nothing we haven't done before."

No one was checking memberships at the door, so Carmela and Ava slipped right into the chaos of the enormous float den. A few floats were already parked around the outer walls, and a four-sided bar had been set up in the middle. Ground zero. A five-piece band — spiffed up in cowboy shirts, boots, and jeans — was wailing "Railroad Drag," and a few partiers were struggling to dance in the crush of the crowd.

"We may as well hit the bar first," Ava said. They elbowed their way to the bar, grabbed a couple of Abita longnecks, and looked around.

People were still pouring into the party. And floats continued to glide in as well.

"See anybody you know?" Ava asked.

"Recognize, yes," Carmela said. "But I don't see anybody I'm bosom buddies with."

"That's good, huh?"

"Maybe. We'll have to see how this plays out."

They strolled casually through the crowd, Carmela keeping one eye out for Tom Ratcliff. When they came upon the float with the enormous skull, two men were busy covering it with a giant tarp.

"Did you guys build that?" Ava asked.

One of the guys looked down from his perch on the float. "We helped."

"Did you do the electronics?" Carmela asked. "Because they really were something special."

"Naw," the guy said. "You'd have to talk to Leveret-Earl about that."

"That's his name? Leveret Earl?"

"That's his first name. His full name is Leveret-Earl Suggs."

"Is he here tonight?" Ava asked.

The man laughed. "Lady, everybody's here tonight."

Ava pulled Carmela away from the float. "Maybe we should try to find this Leveret-Earl Suggs dude."

Carmela nodded. "What I thought we'd —"

"What are you two doing here?" a loud voice boomed out.

Ava's head spun around. "Say what?" It

378

was Jake Bond, staring down his nose at them, a quizzical look on his face.

Carmela recovered first. "What are *you* doing here, Bond? Last I looked, you hadn't been invited to join the Nepthys krewe."

"So what?" Bond said.

"And while we're talking about your shortcomings," Carmela said, "that was some poison-pen article you wrote for the *NOLA Vindicator.*"

"Every word of it was true," Bond said.

"Au contraire," Carmela said. "It was fiction, and not even good fiction at that."

"You're just sore because your boyfriend is heading the investigation. You're worried sick about his reputation being damaged."

"Babcock is doing a fine job," Carmela said. "Making lots of inroads. If I were the guilty party, I'd be running scared right about now."

"What a joke. If your boyfriend is such a hotshot, then how come nobody's been arrested yet?" Bond asked.

"Babcock is right on the killer's heels." Carmela planted her hands on her hips and glared at him. Ava followed suit. "Better take care," Carmela continued. "You could be the one who gets arrested."

"Then I'd have to be guilty," Bond said. "And I know I'm not."

"Don't forget about Napoleonic law — guilty until proven innocent!" Ava said. "This is Louisiana, after all." She lifted her chin. "We've been French for a long, long time."

"Excuse me, what's going on over here?"

The three of them turned to find Tom Ratcliff glowering at them. He tilted his head and stared at Carmela. "Seriously?" he said. "You turned up *here*, too?"

"Hard to get rid of me, isn't it?" Carmela said.

"Not really," Ratcliff said. "Since this is a private party for krewe members only, I'm going to politely ask you to leave."

"I really don't want to belong to any club that doesn't want me as a member," Ava giggled. Then she pulled out a tube of bright red lipstick and applied it to her lush lips.

"You're very cute," Ratcliff said. "But you still have to leave."

"We're going, we're going," Carmela said as they turned and headed for the exit.

"You, too," Ratcliff said to Bond.

Carmela and Ava hurried ahead so they wouldn't have to talk to Bond again.

"You really think we should leave?" Ava asked. "We could just melt into the crowd all sneaky-like."

"No, it's time," Carmela said.

But as they were exiting the float den, who should appear but Maribel Wilder — driving a brand-new silver Bentley convertible!

"Would you look at that," Ava said. "Like she's rolling in cash."

"She must have gotten that car from Labat." Carmela made a rude noise. "Something tells me the two of them deserve each other."

Maribel pulled into a reserved spot and climbed out of the car. She was wearing a brown leather jacket with a mink shrug casually tossed over it.

"Get a load of Maribel's eye shadow," Ava said. "She looks like she fell face-first into a box of sidewalk chalk."

"It's the car and the outfit that kill me. She's spending her dead husband's money for sure."

"Which still makes her a murder suspect, huh?"

"Only we've got no proof," Carmela said. "Which has been our problem all along."

Carmela unlocked her front door and stepped inside. And hesitated. Something felt wrong. For one thing, Boo and Poobah hadn't come bounding over to greet her.

Slowly, carefully, she grabbed an umbrella from the stand by the door and crept into her apartment, the point of the umbrella thrust forward like a lance.

Her place was as dark as a coal chute, but halfway in, she recognized a familiar profile.

Babcock was sitting there in the dark. Boo and Poobah were sitting on either side of him like silent guardian sphinxes.

"Holy crap, Edgar, you scared me half to death." Carmela wasn't angry, just a little discombobulated.

"Sorry. Didn't mean to." His long legs shifted in the chair.

"What's up?"

"I hope you're happy now."

"Why? What's wrong?" Carmela asked. Had she screwed something up? Did Babcock already know that she'd been kicked out of the Nepthys den? Did he have spies everywhere? Infrared cameras? Satellite images?

"The mayor heavily suggested to me that I hold another press conference. And by suggested, I mean . . ."

"He ordered you to." Carmela knew Babcock detested making nice with a yammering press corps. "But why?" she asked. "Did something happen? Was there a break in the Wilder case?"

Babcock shrugged. "I wish. No, the powers that be wanted me to throw a bone to the press. Make it look like the NOPD is really onto something."

"Are you?"

A delicate snort. "No. If I was, I wouldn't have to play nice with the media."

"So what bone did you throw them?" Carmela climbed into Babcock's lap and settled in. She was relieved that her head wasn't on the chopping block, and happy that he might be in the mood to get cozy.

"We made a sacrificial offering and gave them the VP at Pontchartrain Capital Management," Babcock said. "A guy named Roger Colton."

The guy who gave the eulogy. "Is Colton a legitimate suspect?"

"I suppose he's as legit as everyone else we've been looking at."

"But you don't think Colton did it? Killed Wilder?" Carmela asked.

"Probably not." Babcock sighed deeply and said, "There's still not much to go on as far as material evidence. The crime scene guys recovered what appeared to be a mangled, half-burned plastic credit card, but so far we haven't been able to identify it. They're still checking with Amex, Mastercard . . . you know how that goes."

Carmela touched a hand to his cheek, wishing she could be of some help, feeling that she'd somehow let him down.

They sat there in the dark for a few minutes, snuggled together but lost in their own thoughts.

"How'd you do in the road rally?" Babcock finally asked.

Carmela lifted a shoulder. "Lost."

"*You* lost?" Babcock wrapped his arms around her and pulled her closer. "The way you drive?"

"I got run off the road," Carmela said. She laid her head against his chest, listening to the steadiness and strength of his heartbeat. "I guess I'm just an also-ran."

"No, Carmela." Babcock's lips closed on hers. "That could never be."

CHAPTER 28

Fat Tuesday kicked off early in New Orleans. Sometimes it even started the night before, with revelers partying all night long. And this particular Fat Tuesday morning, as Carmela scurried down Governor Nicholls Street, heading for her shop, she figured that most bars and restaurants had thrown open their doors around six o'clock.

For one thing, the streets were jammed with people, happy people, who were lumbering and lurching all over the place. Which meant they'd definitely started early. Too early, in her estimation. You start partying hard at six o'clock, and you were gonna wear yourself out. By the time the Zulu, Rex, and Crescent City parades got under way, that champagne and sugar-high just wouldn't be enough to sustain you. Then you had a long afternoon to fill until the big Atropos parade kicked off in the evening.

Carmela stuck her key in the lock and let

herself into Memory Mine. She turned on the lights and smiled to herself. Blessed quiet. The shop was officially closed today, but she had a few things she wanted to take care of. There were her classes next week to plan — she was doing an altered-book class and a polymer clay class. And the Mardi Gras rush had pretty much cleaned them out of supplies.

No problem. Carmela settled in at her desk and got to work. She sketched out a few ideas for the classes, ticked off a list of needed supplies, and made her way through a stack of invoices. She was just writing out a check to RapidPrint when a tremendously loud *thump* sounded against her back door.

What on earth?

Carmela rarely used her back door. Hardly ever opened it unless a truck showed up with a major delivery involving multiple cartons. But when a second loud *thud* sounded, she tiptoed over to the large metal door, threw the latch, and slid it open a couple of inches. And was shocked to see . . . nothing. Their small wooden dock was deserted; the alley was deserted. Nobody home. No crazies in costumes, no delivery trucks, nothing.

She opened the door a few more inches and leaned out. The cobblestone alley was still bathed in shadows, but now she could definitely hear someone walking. Walking away from her shop.

Okay. Probably just a false alarm. Or was it?

Hustling back inside, Carmela slid the large metal door closed and locked it. Checked a second time to make sure it was locked. Then she sat down at her desk again.

But now she felt a little rattled. And irritated, too. It had been a trying week since the Pluvius float had exploded right before her eyes. She'd been chased, chastised, harassed, harried, bombed, and run off the road. Too much bad stuff had happened, and she still didn't have any concrete answers.

Shaking her head to try to clear out the negative thoughts, Carmela's eyes fell upon her white mug with the skull on it. She'd promised Sam Spears that she'd design a mug with a photo transfer of his velociraptor logo on it. Maybe now was as good a time as any. Maybe a craft project would take her mind off the jumble of thoughts that flitted through her head like so many restless spirits.

There were lots of ways to do an image transfer — transparency transfer, cold laminate transfer, GlueFoil transfer, and so on. But for demonstration purposes, to show Sam a single sample mug, Carmela decided to do a basic down-and-dirty decal transfer. She went to Velocitech's website, found a good, clean image of their logo, and printed it out on special transfer paper. Then she cut the image so that it would fit neatly on the mug, and soaked the image in a shallow pan of warm water. Some ten minutes later, the velociraptor image slid right off its backing and Carmela was able to press it gently onto a plain, white ceramic mug.

"Sam's going to love this," she said, gazing at her handiwork. Yes, he was. In fact, she might even take it with her to the zoo party tonight and show it to him. It wouldn't hurt to get his order lined up. What had he asked for? Maybe four dozen mugs? Maybe Sam would like the mug so much he'd order eight dozen. That would certainly help to fluff this month's bottom line.

That done, Carmela went out into the main part of her shop and began tidying up. For some reason, the albums were scattered and the paper bins weren't particularly orderly. Which was unusual, because Gabby was generally a confirmed neatnik. As Carmela worked, mindful of the quiet in the shop, her mind wandered back to the weird note that had been slipped under the door yesterday morning. And about how she'd been lured to that empty apartment.

Even though nothing had really happened — no harm had come to her — the more she thought about it, the angrier she got.

Had she been lured there as part of a crazy prank? Was this something Jekyl had dreamed up? Or Shamus? Had cameras been filming her?

No, she thought, the whole thing had seemed way too elaborate. Way too sneaky.

So why was I lured there?

Carmela stood stock-still in the middle of her quiet-as-a-graveyard store.

Because someone wanted to kill me?

The notion made her practically reel with fear, until she reached out and gripped a sturdy shelf for support.

Was it because she'd stumbled across a trip wire somewhere along the line? Because she'd somehow rubbed shoulders with the killer, come in direct contact with him, and caused him to worry big-time?

Maybe. But wouldn't that point to one of her so-called suspects being the killer?

Or maybe she just didn't have enough clues yet.

Okay then, so what *did* she have? Well, she knew the address of the apartment. If she could find out who owned it, maybe she could backtrack and figure out who'd been so almighty interested in her.

Carmela went to the front counter, looked up the number for Miranda Jackson — her Realtor — and called. Miranda's phone rang five times. Carmela was just about to hang up when Miranda finally answered.

After a quick hello, Carmela said, "If I gave you a street address, do you have some magical way of looking it up and finding out who owns that property?"

"Carmela, my love," Miranda crooned, "you're calling me on Fat Tuesday! I'm in the middle of lacing myself into a hot pink corset and I want to tell you, it isn't easy. I seem to have gained . . . well, I guess there's a reason they call it Fat Tuesday."

"I know it's the big day and I'm sorry to interrupt your corsetry," Carmela said. "But . . . could you do this one little thing for me? It's really, really important. Practically life or death."

"Carmela, after the commission I made selling that white elephant of a house Shamus gave you in your divorce settlement, I'm happy to help. So to answer your question, yes, I can look up an address. I just don't know *when* I can get to it. I'm not at my office and my —"

"No no, that's okay. I'm just grateful you're able to do this for me." Carmela quickly gave Miranda the address and then repeated it.

"Okay," Miranda said, "I'll call you. I don't know *when* that will be, but I'll call you."

Carmela had just said good-bye to Miranda and hung up the phone when it rang again. But this time it was Shamus, calling from a restaurant. Carmela could hear the telltale clink of silverware and the tinkle of glassware in the background. Fairly loud music, too.

"Where are you?" Carmela asked.

"Where else would I be on Fat Tuesday?" Shamus said. "I'm enjoying a fantastic lunch at Antoine's." Antoine's was the legendary French Quarter restaurant where oysters Rockefeller had been invented.

"You're with a bunch of men? Krewe members?"

"Men, women, whatever," Shamus said. "Hey, just to let you know, that guy Bobby Gallant was on my ass again."

"He shouldn't have been."

"*You* know that and *I* know that, but the NOPD apparently doesn't give a flip. So can you please do something? Intercede for me with that hotshot boyfriend of yours and

391

call off the wolves?"

"Just stop worrying about it, Shamus, okay? You're off the hook, I guarantee it. I mean, what do you want from me? You asked me to investigate and I did. I poked my nose where I shouldn't have and basically got nothing for my efforts." Carmela hesitated. "Actually, that's wrong. I got all sorts of blowback!" She was going to tell him about the explosion yesterday, then figured, *Why bother?*

"You're a tough cookie, Carmela, you can take it. And I'm *positive* you've made some serious forward progress."

"I'm not so sure about that."

"Come on, you ferreted out all sorts of suspects. Came up with a darned good list. Your problem is, you just haven't narrowed it down yet."

"Maybe I never will." Carmela stared out her front window — a marching band was going by. She could hear the tinny coronets and feel the drumbeats deep within her stomach. "Are you planning to party all day?"

"Yeah, probably," Shamus said in that lazy, disinterested way he had. Then he seemed to reconsider. "No, I have to put in a quick appearance at that zoo thing tonight. Crescent City Bank is one of the sponsors."

"They are?"

Carmela flipped open one of the zoo brochures that was lying on the front counter. Sure enough, she'd dropped the Crescent City Bank logo onto the back page without even thinking about it. Maybe that was a positive sign that she was moving on with her life. Or maybe not.

"Are you by any chance bringing Glory along?" Carmela decided that if Glory was going to be there, she would stay home. Eat Cheetos and paint her toenails a flaming red color. Even if Ava threw a horrific fit and cried herself to sleep because she wanted to attend the party so badly.

"Naw," Shamus said. "Glory hates stuff like that. Hates animals, really."

Yet another good reason for me to despise Glory.

"Then you'll probably be bringing one of your barely legal girlfriends?" Carmela said.

Shamus yawned loudly. And Carmela could picture him at lunch, legs crossed, sipping a bourbon on the rocks.

"It'll probably just be me and Sam. We'll pop in for the requisite five minutes, make nice with the director, and then head over to a couple of the Rex krewe's parties. They're a lot more fun and tend to go all night."

"Whatever."

After Carmela hung up, she realized that she'd talked to Shamus more this week than she had to Babcock.

Gotta fix that. Like, real fast.

Ten minutes later, Carmela dropped the finished mug in her handbag, locked the front door, and headed for home. Since the Zulu parade was just winding up and the Rex parade was about to begin, the French Quarter was absolute bedlam.

Carmela pushed her way through the crowds, trying not to be a curmudgeon — trying to savor the music and the carnival-like atmosphere. A costumed crowd ebbed and flowed at the doorway of every bar and club, while from wrought-iron balconies overhead, colored beads rained down on everyone's heads. There were small, loosely organized neighborhood parades, too, which streamed past her in the streets. Some of the parades were all vampires, some all Venetian lords and ladies. One small contingent even had a float with cats and dogs.

As Carmela moseyed along, her cell phone rang. "Hello?" she said, sticking a finger in her opposite ear to block the noise.

Her caller was Bobby Gallant, Babcock's second-in-command.

"Is he with you?" Gallant asked. Carmela knew that *he* meant Babcock.

"No, I haven't talked to him today. What? He's not answering his phone?"

"Ah, his mailbox is probably full," Gallant said. "You're going to see him later?"

"That's the plan. Babcock promised to meet me at the big zoo party tonight." *I hope he actually will.*

"If I e-mail something to your phone, will you make sure he sees it?"

"Sure. No problem."

"Thanks, Carmela. Later."

Carmela hung up, waited while a contingent of colorfully costumed African drummers went by, and then crossed Ursulines Avenue. Halfway down, Danny Labat staggered out of a bar, wearing a bright red clown costume and grinning like a monkey that was high on crack.

"Carmela!" Labat cried when he spotted her. "Hey, girl." It was obvious that Labat was half in the bag because he was acting happy in that drunky, foolish, shambling way that guys get when they've had a few too many.

Carmela tried to hurry past him, but Labat grabbed her arm.

"Come and have a drink with me," Labat slurred.

"No thank you," Carmela said. Having a drink with a very inebriated Danny Labat was the absolute last thing Carmela wanted to do. For all she knew, Labat was the one who'd lured her to that apartment yesterday. He could be Hughes Wilder's killer.

"Say now," Labat said, unwilling to let Carmela go. "You were terrific in that race. You really put that Alfa through its paces."

"Sure, until Tom Ratcliff ran me off the track." She stared at him. The clown costume, with its ruffles and pompons, was freaking her out.

Labat chuckled. "Yeah, that was a hell of a thing. But, I gotta say, the crowd loved it."

"That's what it's all about, isn't it?" Carmela said. "Putting on a great show. Hearkens back to the Christians versus the lions."

Labat poked a finger at her. "No, it's the *Saints* versus the Lions. Or maybe Green Bay."

"Whatever."

"You're a good sport, Carmela," Labat said, practically slobbering all over her. "A damn fine driver, too. Come on, you gotta join me for a drink. I got some friends waiting for me in Sassy's Tavern that I want you to meet. You'll like 'em."

"No thanks." Carmela couldn't wait to get away from this creep.

"Maybe later." Labat staggered backward, then flailed his arms to steady himself. "Hey, you going to that big zoo party tonight?"

Carmela shrugged. "Could be."

"Ah, I'll bet you are," Labat said. "Social butterfly like you. Maybe I'll see you there."

"Will you be there with Maribel?" Carmela couldn't resist. But her words, intended to sting, didn't seem to faze him.

Labat gave her a drunken wink. "Could be. Then again, you never know. Maribel ain't the only starfish in the sea."

CHAPTER 29

Night fell and so did Ava's neckline. She exploded into Carmela's apartment wearing the teeny-tiniest black cocktail dress with the most incredible plunging neckline Carmela had ever laid eyes on.

"That's a daredevil of a dress," Carmela blurted out. "I mean, it doesn't quite, uh, cover you up." If your friends won't speak the truth, who will?

"I know," Ava said. "Ain't it great? It's so tight because it's three sizes too small."

"Then why would you pour yourself into it?" Carmela hated anything that was uncomfortable or tight-fitting.

"Because it shows off my kibbles and bits to perfection, and I got it on sale. I mean a slide-that-decimal-point-to-the-far-left kind of sale."

"You thought it was a great deal when you bought that froufrou wedding gown last summer. And now it's just hanging in your closet."

"That's because I was young and foolish," Ava said. "Thinking I *might* be getting married. And that a peach-colored gown would be fashion forward and trendy. I've since learned my lesson."

"Have you?" Carmela asked.

"And by the way, girlfriend, is that *really* what you're wearing?" Ava pointed a finger at Carmela, barely stifling a giggle.

Carmela put a hand on her hip. "What's wrong with this dress?" Her cocktail dress was sleeveless, nipped at the waist, and had a sweetheart neckline. It looked good — at least she thought it did.

"Nothing's wrong with the dress. It's a gorgeous dress, but you've covered it up with a weird, fringed piano shawl."

"This happens to be my evening wrap. And it's vintage."

"It's so vintage it looks like it came off my aunt Badelia's piano," Ava said. "Seventy-five years ago. Back in the olden days."

"What do you suggest I do?"

"Nothing."

"You have nothing to say?" Carmela asked. "That's a first."

"No, I suggest you wear the dress and nothing else."

"What if I get cold?"

"Snuggle up to Babcock."

"If he even shows up," Carmela said.

Ava sighed. "Okay, wear the piano shawl. But don't blame me if somebody tries to tickle your ivories."

"I think we might be a little late," Carmela said as they made their way through an ultrachic crowd of people buzzing with excitement and already well into their third and fourth drinks. Strings of colored lights lit the zoo's main plaza, where white-coated waiters served flutes of champagne and tasty appetizers.

"Better to arrive late than to arrive ugly," Ava said.

"Are you still razzing me about my shawl?" Carmela asked. She had it folded over one arm as a slight capitulation to Ava.

"Actually, I'm referring to my stellar makeup and hairdo. I did a cat eye and pinned in three hairpieces tonight because I'm hoping to meet the man of my dreams."

"You think it's going to happen just like that?"

"Call me an eternal optimist." Ava gave a little shiver of anticipation as she glanced around at the throng of elegantly dressed guests. "Ooh, don't you just love a man in black-tie? Like you could pop him on top of a wedding cake."

"Down, girl."

"What's this zoo boo thing called again?"

"The headline we came up with for the invitation was 'Monkey Around for Mardi Gras.'"

"This party looks awfully fancy for a fundraiser," Ava said.

"Well . . . it's really more of a private party and thank-you event for all the zoo's high-ticket patrons — what they call their Platinum Patrons. So there are a lot of influential leaders here representing business, government, media, and philanthropy."

"In other words, the Lexus-Rolex crowd. People dripping with money."

"You could say that," Carmela said.

"No wonder everything is so glammed up."

And the zoo did look fabulous. Besides the colored lights and champagne and food, there were animals on display in a petting corral. The nearby botanical gardens were lit with flaming torches, an orchestra played dance tunes, and there was a large, roped-off casino area. All this in the zoo's magnificent setting of gardens, winding paths, waterfalls, and animal exhibits.

Carmela saw Cynthia Ronson, the zoo's

development director, and waved at her. Cynthia saw Carmela waving and ran over to give her a big hug.

"Isn't this marvelous?" Cynthia gushed. "This is going to be the highlight of our social calendar. Look at the crowd we were able to attract! And everyone loves your delightful programs!"

Always shy about receiving praise, Carmela responded with, "Everything looks so gorgeous."

Never one to be shy, Ava stuck out her hand, introduced herself to Cynthia, and decided to toot Carmela's horn. "Carmela always does a whiz-bang job," she said. "Did you know she's one of New Orleans's top graphic designers?"

"I'm not," Carmela said, but Ava and Cynthia weren't even listening. Ava was jabbering excitedly about the casino area, and Cynthia was promising to get her a hundred dollars' worth of free chips.

"Oh." Cynthia put a hand to her mouth as if she'd just remembered something, and turned to Carmela. "I ran into your ex-husband, Shamus, a few minutes ago. He asked me to be sure to introduce you to one of our guests." She hesitated, glanced around the crowd, and finally said, "There he is. Come with me, Carmela."

Cynthia towed Carmela over to a dapper-looking man with slicked-back hair and a clipped mustache. He was sipping a martini and gazing into a pen where llamas in gold harnesses were being petted by some of the guests.

"Carmela," Cynthia said, "this is Roger Colton, the vice president at Pontchartrain Capital Management." She smiled and drew a sharp breath. "Now please excuse me while I dash off to take care of about a million other things." And she was gone.

Carmela stared at Colton, who looked somewhat baffled. "Do we know each other?" he asked. "Or are we supposed to?"

"Not really," Carmela said, though she recognized him from the memorial service. "This is just a stupid pet trick my ex-husband dreamed up." She was aware of Ava hovering at her elbow, listening in.

Colton furrowed his brow. "And your ex would be . . . ?"

"Shamus Meechum from Crescent City Bank," Carmela said.

"One of our investors."

Carmela decided to give Colton a jab to see how he reacted. "One of your unhappy investors."

Colton looked stunned for a moment. Then he gathered himself into a nice, tight ball of indignation and said, "I don't know why people are so down on us." He shook his head as sadness and regret practically oozed from his pores. "The company's not going bankrupt, we're not in free fall. Yes, we tragically lost our founder and president last week. But we're determined to weather this tragedy. We will get back on our feet again and serve our investors."

"That's if you don't get arrested first," Carmela said. She spun on her heel and left him standing there.

"Jeez," Ava said as she tagged along after Carmela. "Why'd you have to be so mean to him? Why were you pushing him so hard?"

"I wanted to see how he'd react," Carmela said.

"I thought he seemed kind of sad."

"More like unhappy. I'm guessing he feels like a pariah."

"Yeah," Ava said. "I noticed nobody was talking to him."

"Probably because Babcock tossed Colton's name out to the press as a possible suspect."

"Babcock did that? Why?"

"To call off the media jackals, and as a kind of litmus test. To see how hotheaded Colton might be."

"Don't you have to be coldhearted to commit murder?"

"Jeez, Ava, I don't know."

They flagged down a passing waiter, and each of them grabbed a flute of champagne.

"Mmn," Ava said. "Love the fizzy stuff."

"But it doesn't love you in the morning."

"I'll be careful. After all, I don't want to be tipsy when I meet the man of my dreams."

On their way to the casino area, they ran into Shamus.

"You did show up, you rat," Carmela said.

"Yeah, yeah," Shamus said. "Same old Carmela, always so sweet."

"Thanks for setting me up," Carmela said.

"Hmm?" This was Shamus acting innocent.

"You know what I'm talking about," Carmela said. "Phonying up that introduction to Roger Colton. That was a rotten thing to do."

"I thought you should meet him face-to-face. Seeing as he's a murder suspect."

"He's not," Carmela said. "The police just threw his name out as a ploy. They thought they needed to give the media something to chew on."

Shamus shifted nervously from one foot to the other. "Yeah, well, if it was in the press, then it's not my fault, is it?" He started backing away into the crowd. "I gotta go find Sam. We're gonna hang around for fifteen minutes, wave the flag as zoo patrons, and then ditch this thing."

"Nothing is ever your fault, is it, Shamus?" Ava asked.

"Not hardly," he mumbled.

Carmela turned to Ava. "How do you like the evening so far? Do you see anybody else I can insult and pick a fight with?"

"I think you should take a deep breath and chill out, *cher.* Go pet a llama or ride a pony. And for gosh sakes, don't act all wigged out when Babcock finally gets here."

"*If* he gets here."

Carmela was genuinely wondering if Babcock was going to make it tonight. Would this be another pop-in-hello/good-bye scenario, like he'd managed at Baby's party? She fervently hoped not.

As Carmela wondered about Babcock, she remembered the e-mail that Bobby Gallant was going to send her. Did he send it? She hurriedly checked her phone.

Yes, Gallant had sent an image of what looked like a very badly damaged credit card. Like it had been mangled and then melted. He'd also attached a short note to pass on to Babcock — a note that said there was a slim chance this wasn't a credit card at all, but rather a player's club card from one of the local casinos. Crime scene analysts were still checking it out.

How strange, Carmela thought. *And how interesting.*

"Hey," Ava said. "There's Cynthia again. I'm gonna go grab our free chips."

Just as a waiter was offering Carmela a miniature crab puff, her phone rang. It turned out to be Miranda, her Realtor.

"Yes, Miranda," Carmela said. "Thanks so much for getting back to me. Did you find out who owns that particular apartment building?"

"The provenance is a little tricky," Miranda said. "The entire building was owned by a company called Arcadia Holdings. Then, six months ago, it was transferred to a parent company by the name of Aces High."

"Do you know who they are?" Carmela asked.

"I've never heard of them before. But remember, I deal mainly in residential real estate, not commercial."

"So you don't know anything about them?" Carmela asked.

"Well, let me . . . give me a minute here . . . um, I see Aces High is located in

Slidell. But there's no address listed, only a post office box number."

"Okay thanks," Carmela said. "Wait, did you say Slidell?"

"That's right."

"Thanks, Miranda. I owe you one." She clicked off the call, set her phone to vibrate, and stuck it in her velvet hobo bag.

As Carmela was pondering the Slidell reference, Maribel Wilder walked by on the arm of Danny Labat. Maribel noticed Carmela and curled her upper lip into a snide smile, as if she had some wonderful secret.

Which made Carmela wonder again if Maribel had a hand in her husband's death. Then her mind was drawn back to the Slidell reference. There were dozens of tech companies located in Slidell, as well as Pontchartrain Capital Management. Was that the connection? Was Roger Colton the killer, no matter how sad and bereft he looked? And what about the casino player's club card that had been found? How did it fit in? Had it belonged to Hughes Wilder, or did the killer drop it?

Carmela reached for her phone and called Babcock. But he still wasn't answering. So she dialed the duty officer in the Homicide Division and left a detailed message asking

Babcock to please hurry over to the zoo.

Carmela looked around for Ava, started across the plaza, then had to wait while a line of exotic-looking Bactrian camels clip-clopped their way through the crowd. The camels were followed by two zebras and three zookeepers carrying a koala bear, a marmot, and a large yellow snake.

By the time Carmela got to the casino area, she was shocked to see that Ava had struck up a sort of conversation with Tom Ratcliff at one of the blackjack tables. Ava was peering over his shoulder, watching him play. As fast as Ratcliff pushed his chips in, the dealer slapped down cards. Interestingly, Ratcliff appeared to be winning.

Carmela approached the blackjack table and gave Ava a little *What are you doing here?* frown.

"This is a fascinating game," Ava said. "Just fascinating." She was clutching a stack of chips and looked as if she wanted to toss a few on the table and play a hand.

Ratcliff, who was smoking a cigar and looking fairly chipper, turned in his seat and saw Carmela. "You again," he said.

"Looks like you're having some luck," Carmela said. Ratcliff had at least five hundred chips stacked up in front of him.

"I'm a lucky guy."

"You're not worrying about your luck running out?" Carmela asked.

Ratcliff shook his head as he laid down his cards. He chuckled, and the dealer pushed more chips his way. "Never. Luck always comes my way." He glanced back at Carmela again. "You gonna sit down and play, or are you just going to hang out?"

"Excuse me," Ava said. "Are we bothering you? Do you intend to kick us out again?"

"Nope," Ratcliff said. "It's cool." He was obviously mellowed out by a few drinks.

Carmela looked at the next blackjack table over and noticed that Roger Colton was seated there. He, too, had a large stack of blue chips piled up in front of him.

"You're not the only one blessed with good luck tonight," Carmela said. She nodded in the direction of Colton. "Too bad he's more skilled at gambling than his company is at investing."

"Mmn," Ratcliff grunted unhappily.

Carmela thought about the melted player's club card that had been found at the scene of Hughes Wilder's murder. Ratcliff and Colton appeared to be well versed in gambling. Could that mean one of them was the killer? The thought terrified her and tantalized her at the same time.

"Do you ever play blackjack at the local

casinos?" Carmela asked Ratcliff.

He shrugged. "Sometimes."

"Do you ever see Roger Colton at the various casinos?"

"I see a lot of people."

Carmela glanced at Ava and shook her head. This was like pulling teeth. She wasn't getting anywhere.

Ava tucked her shoulders back and leaned in close. "That appears to be a different kind of blackjack they're playing over there," Ava said in a throaty purr. "What is it, anyway? European style? Caribbean? Turks and Caicos?"

Ratcliff took a peek at his cards, then glanced over at Colton's table. "Ah, they're playing twenty-one plus three extreme. It's just a variation."

Carmela moved closer. Had she heard him correctly? Twenty-one plus three extreme was . . . a game?

Her mind was churning overtime now. She knew she'd heard that term before. But where? Oh sure, Sam Spears had mentioned it. Could it be that Sam knew something about Roger Colton's involvement in the murder, but he just hadn't put it together? Maybe if she talked to Sam, tried to jog his memory, the two of them could figure something out.

"Ava, let's go!" Carmela said.

"What? Now?" Ava was itching to sit down and play, but Carmela pulled her away from the table.

"What's wrong?" Ava asked. "I was starting to feel lucky."

"I just had this thought, Ava, and . . . oh dear Lord, I think we need to talk to Babcock right away. Hopefully he's on his way over here."

"What's wrong? What's going on? Better yet, where are we going?" Ava was bravely trying to keep her strapless dress from sliding down as she scampered after Carmela on five-inch stilettos.

Carmela pulled her aside from the boisterous crowd. "It's about that guy Roger Colton. I think he might be the killer."

"Huh?"

Carmela hastily explained to Ava about the apartment she'd been lured to and how it was owned by a shell corporation located in Slidell. And about the player's club card found at the scene of the murder. And about the twenty-one plus three extreme.

"Wait, you're telling me we've been running around, investigating all these different people, and that mild-mannered little card-player sitting over there could be the real killer?"

"He could be."

"Holy crap! If that's true, Carmela, you just solved a murder!"

CHAPTER 30

But the answer wasn't quite that cut-and-dried.

Ava was all whipped up, ready to grab Roger Colton and drag him into the bushes — or throw him in the lion's den — to beat a confession out of him.

"You've been binge-watching too many crazy revenge shows," Carmela said. "I think we have to stay put until Babcock arrives. Colton is dangerous. Much more dangerous than he looks."

"Wait a minute, did I hear you correctly? *You* don't want to rush in where angels fear to tread? Are you sure I'm talking to the real Carmela and not her avatar?"

"What I'd really like to do is find Sam Spears and talk to him. I'm guessing that he knows something big about Colton, but he just hasn't connected the dots."

"Okay, then let's go find Sam."

There was no more cocktailing for Carmela and Ava, now that they were on a serious mission.

"Let's check the monkey house first," Ava suggested. "I saw a whole bunch of people go in there."

But when they went in, they were met by the interested faces of tamarin, spider, and saki monkeys, as well as party guests. But there was no sign of Sam.

"Since that didn't pan out, how about we look in that greenhouse over there?" Ava suggested.

"I think that's an aviary," Carmela said.

"Birds of a feather, then."

When they looked inside, there was lots of tweeting and squawking going on, and lots of people — but Sam Spears wasn't one of them.

"Yipes," Ava said. "Kinda noisy in here."

Then Carmela remembered Sam telling her that Velocitech had helped to fund Alligator Alley. Could he be there?

"I've got an idea," Carmela told Ava.

Together they wandered down a winding flagstone pathway illuminated by pagoda-style garden lights. When they came to a T, there was a large wooden directory. Seals and otters were off to the right; the alligator pool was off to the left.

"This way," Carmela said.

"I feel like I'm following the yellow brick road through a jungle," Ava worried. And she was half right. Palm trees, banana trees, and willow oaks rose up to create a virtual tunnel. Spooky rustlings on both sides of the pathway told them that they were walking very close to animal pens.

"We're kind of straying away from the party, *cher*," Ava said. "We're getting nothing out of this but aerobic exercise."

"I think we're almost there," Carmela said. "Looks like a clearing up ahead."

The pathway widened considerably to reveal a large enclosure.

"What is it?" Ava asked. "You see any critters?"

They peered through the bars and saw two large gray wolves pacing back and forth.

"*Loup-garous*," Ava murmured. "And they look tough. Let's go back to the party." Her nerves were definitely starting to jangle.

"Those are not werewolves, if that's what you're worried about," Carmela said. "They're ordinary, garden-variety wolves. Besides, I'm positive the gator pond is just up ahead. Once we check it out, we'll head back. Then I promise you can play blackjack to your heart's content — win, lose, or draw. I'll even give you my chips."

"Deal!"

Ten steps beyond, they came to a small pond. It looked cool and dark, dappled with moonlight, and they could see ripples — something was swimming in there.

"What's in that pond?" Ava asked. "Friendlies, I hope. Ducks."

"Something like that."

Carmela suddenly froze in her tracks, overcome by a strange sense of déjà vu, which had descended on her like a damp cloud. Then she realized that this scene was exactly the same as her tarot card reading! Two wolves, the moon shining down upon a pond.

"What's wrong?" Ava whispered.

"I just realized . . ." Carmela's mouth snapped shut. In that instant, she'd heard something. Voices. They drifted toward her in the dark, fading in and out, like a signal from a faulty radio.

Was it Sam Spears? Carmela wondered. Had they finally tracked him down? There was only one way to find out.

"What's that noise?" Ava asked. She was nervous and hyperalert. "Crickets?"

"Frogs," Carmela said. "Croakers."

"What's that other noise?"

Carmela and Ava continued down the pathway. With each tiptoed step they took, the voices got louder and more pronounced.

Two men were having a hellacious argument with each other, and it sounded as if they were about to start throwing punches.

"What's going on?" Ava whispered.

"Shh." Carmela held up a finger, trying to tune in. Something was very wrong. She felt it . . . like a sonar ping.

A man's voice, a voice she didn't recognize, suddenly erupted. "I'm gonna need more money." He was clearly angry and upset.

Then a second voice, one Carmela recognized as belonging to Sam Spears, said, "There isn't any more!"

"Isn't that your friend Sam?" Ava asked in a low voice.

"I think . . ." Carmela's phone suddenly vibrated, scaring her half to death.

"What?" Ava asked as Carmela jerked like a puppet whose strings had been yanked.

Carmela dug deep in her bag, fumbling to grab her phone and turn it on. "Is that you?" Carmela whispered into her phone.

Babcock's voice came back to her. "Why are you whispering?"

"Because . . . oh jeez, Edgar, are you here? At the zoo?"

"Just walking in the front gate, staring at the back end of a giraffe."

"I think something big is going down,"

Carmela said. "Just keep quiet and listen for a minute."

Carmela held up the phone so Babcock could hear exactly what was being said. And though every nerve ending fizzed with fear, she tiptoed ever closer with her phone.

"Listen," the unknown man snarled, "you were the one who wanted me to wire that float. I didn't know you packed in enough explosives to blow that poor sod sky-high. If I'm going to disappear for a while, I'll need more money."

"I already paid you," Sam shot back. "We had a deal, Suggs."

"Sorry, pal, blowing up a float is one thing, murder is a whole 'nother problem."

"Listen," Ava whispered. "They're all but confessing!"

Carmela nodded silently. Sam and his cohort Suggs. She hoped Babcock was getting all this.

"You've got twenty-four hours to get the cash."

There was a low, angry exchange, and then the scraping of shoes against cement as one person walked away.

Carmela moved in closer, put a hand out, and gingerly parted the bushes.

Sam Spears was there, all right. Shaking his head, looking both furious and frustrated as he paced in front of the new Alligator Alley pond.

Carmela turned toward Ava and made a pointing gesture. Ava nodded — she got it. Carmela wanted them both to retreat as silently as possible.

But as they both turned at the same moment, anxious to get away, Ava brushed up against Carmela. The phone Carmela had been balancing bobbled for a second and then tumbled out of her hand.

No!

Carmela gasped as she fumbled blindly to grab the phone, but she was too late. The phone landed facedown on the pavement, and the rifle crack of the screen shattering gave them away!

"Who's there?" Sam Spears shouted.

Before they could make a move, Sam was right there, cutting them off, blocking their escape.

"Sam," Carmela said, hating that her voice suddenly sounded so shaken.

"Carmela," Sam said in a voice that was calm and perfectly in control. His smile was cold, too, as he pointed a gun at her.

CHAPTER 31

At that instant, Carmela knew their only hope was Babcock! But would he get to them in time? Would he even know where to find them? And what should she do right now, in this critical moment? Her mind was whirling like a centrifuge.

"Sam," Carmela said again, deciding she would try to bluff her way out. "I know all about you and Suggs. So does Detective Babcock. We know you killed Hughes Wilder."

Sam basically sneered at her. "So what if we did? Wilder was a fool anyway. I had the old man buffaloed into investing all his money into my company."

"Only you never used the money for your company, did you?" Carmela was playing a hunch, making a wild guess.

Spears looked suddenly thoughtful. "I'm afraid gambling debts did seem to intervene."

421

"I can relate," Ava said, finally speaking up. "This one time up in Biloxi I was playing a Slots O' Fun machine and I —"

"Shut up!" Sam screamed at her. "Just shut up."

"You shut up," Carmela shouted back at him. "Do you really think you can get away with this? Of course not. There are police officers crawling all over these grounds, ready to close in at any minute. They've probably arrested your partner Suggs already." She snorted. "The mad bomber, your hired help."

Sam favored Carmela with a tolerant smile. "Nice try, but you and I both know you're grasping at straws."

"No," Ava said. "Carmela really did talk to —"

"Shut up!" Sam screamed again. "Do you think this is a game? You're in deep shit, and I —"

"Drop it!" Babcock shouted as he rushed out of the darkness. His gun was drawn and he looked about as intense as Carmela had ever seen him. "Weapon down, hands on your head!"

Quick as a rattlesnake, Sam reached out and grabbed Carmela. He spun her like a top and smashed her hard up against his body, using her as a shield. Carmela was so stunned she could barely react.

But Babcock remained calm and focused, keeping his gun leveled at Sam Spears.

"It's no good, Spears," Babcock said. "Put down the gun."

Sam slid his arm around Carmela's neck and cranked it hard, cutting off her breathing.

"Let her go!" Ava screamed.

Sam lifted his gun and aimed it at Babcock.

"Noooo!" came Carmela's strangled cry as she fought to twist her way loose from Spears's grasp.

Spears fired his gun anyway. There was a shattering *BOOM* right next to Carmela's ear, and she felt the hot kick of the gun.

"Ahh!" Babcock yelped in pain. The gun spun out of his hand and clattered on the pavement. The only saving grace was that Carmela's last-ditch, heroic effort had knocked Sam slightly off balance. Instead of hitting Babcock squarely in the chest, at center mass, Sam had shot him in the hand.

"You see what you made me do?" Sam said to Carmela through clenched teeth. "Now I have to shoot him again."

Carmela twisted harder, her vision going dark from lack of oxygen. "Please . . . no."

Sam shot a murderous glance at Ava.

"You. Go pick up the detective's gun and throw it in the alligator pond. Don't get cute. Don't try to use it on me. If you do, I'll shoot your friend in the head and then I'll kill you."

Reluctantly, Ava picked up the gun and tossed it in the alligator pond. It landed with a loud *plop.* "Asshole," she muttered.

Carmela hadn't taken her eyes off Babcock, who was grimacing with pain. Sam loosened his grip slightly, and she gasped out, "He's bleeding. Losing blood. At least let him wrap something around his hand."

Sam waggled the gun at Babcock again. "Yeah, whatever," he said. He knew he had the clear upper hand. "It's not going to make a difference in the long run."

"Have you got a hanky?" Carmela cried out to Babcock.

Babcock nodded as he reached into his pants pocket. He unfurled a white hanky, seemed to struggle with it, then wrapped it clumsily around his hand. The white cloth immediately bloomed bright red. He was bleeding badly.

Carmela jerked her head around toward Sam. "I'm going to kill you," she seethed. At that moment she felt pure, cold hate running through her veins.

"Wrong," Sam whispered harshly in her

ear. His breath felt hot and loathsome to Carmela. "I'm going to kill you. You're all going to die."

"You can't . . ." Ava began.

"I want all three of you to march into that alligator pond," Sam said.

"You're crazy," Babcock said.

"Your deaths will simply look like a terrible, unfortunate accident," Sam said. "A tragedy. But accidents happen at zoos with some frequency. People take stupid chances and fall into the tiger pit or get mauled by a gorilla.

"Now . . ." Sam Spears waggled his gun. "Get over there and line up." He released his hold from around Carmela's neck and gave her a hard shove, which sent her coughing and staggering.

Reluctantly, Carmela, Ava, and Babcock shuffled over to the edge of the alligator pond.

"Keep going," Spears ordered. "Climb over the wall."

They climbed over the four-foot-high cement safety wall onto a narrow ledge. They were now inside the alligator pond, with dark water lapping at their ankles.

Carmela gazed out across the pond. It was filled with at least a dozen alligators, maybe more. And the reptiles were curious. They were swimming toward them, tails moving slowly, their eyes and rough, humpy backs protruding above the water.

Spears stepped up onto the cement wall and looked down at his prisoners. Watched with a smirk as the alligators continued to swim dangerously close. "Time to go swimming," he said. His voice was low and threatening.

Carmela and Ava watched in horror as the alligators drew closer and closer.

"No . . . ." Ava sobbed. "I don't want to get ripped apart."

Just as Spears leaned forward to get a better look, Babcock whipped a bloody hunk of leather out from behind his bloody hanky and tossed it sideways. It landed directly at Spears's feet.

In a split second, the alligators changed direction and charged at Spears. One enormous alligator lunged up out of the water, jaws gaping, jagged teeth flashing.

Sam's high-pitched scream rent the night air as he lost his balance. Arms akimbo, his gun forgotten, Spears tumbled down into the alligator pond with a loud splash.

Carmela's mouth dropped open in shock while Ava let loose a bloodcurdling scream.

CHAPTER 32

In that same split second, Babcock scrambled back over the barrier. His arm shot out, and he grabbed Spears by the collar. Using his good hand, he bent the man back sharply, dragging him awkwardly, arduously, over the wall. When Spears was finally safe, Babcock let out a groan and dropped Spears on the cement. Spears's head bounced twice, and he gave a low moan.

Carmela, who had clambered back over the embankment with Ava when the alligators rushed at Spears, reached down and slammed Spears in the back of the head with the Velocitech mug she'd been carrying in her bag. The mug shattered as Spears groaned a second time, and then he collapsed in a motionless heap.

"You saved him!" Ava shouted at Babcock. She was shocked by his heroics.

"Saved him for a judge and jury," Babcock said. He was cradling his wounded hand, struggling to catch his breath. "What the hell did you hit him with?" he asked Carmela.

"Mug," Carmela said. She held up the handle — the only piece that was left intact.

"She mugged him," Ava said.

While Carmela and Ava stood watch over Sam Spears, ready to conk him again if need be, Babcock pulled out his phone and called for help.

Two minutes later, a half-dozen off-duty policemen — most of whom had been working as zoo security — came rushing in.

"Jeez," a short, stocky officer said as he skidded to a stop. "Babcock? Detective Babcock, is that you?"

"Hey, Dillworth," Babcock said, a half grin on his face. "How you doin'?"

Dillworth glanced at Babcock's wounded hand. "Better 'n you, Detective. You better get that looked at."

Spears, still groggy, was pulled to his feet and unceremoniously hauled away. Babcock gave hasty orders to search for the second man, Suggs, then called for even more backup.

"When did you know it was Sam Spears?" Carmela asked Babcock.

"Not until an hour ago," Babcock said. "It was a process of elimination. Both Maribel and Labat checked out financially. No sudden influx of cash to their bank accounts. Same with Ratcliff. Truth be told, his gallery is struggling."

"And you didn't think the killer was Jake Bond?" Ava asked.

"He was never a serious suspect," Babcock said. "Maybe for you two he was, but not for me."

"And that Colton guy you threw to the press?" Ava asked.

"Seems like a stand-up guy," Babcock said. "Maybe he can even turn his company around."

Carmela didn't care about the cleared suspects — she was anxious about having an EMT tend to Babcock's injured hand.

"It's not so bad," Babcock said. "Spears wasn't a very good shot."

"But you're bleeding like crazy!" Carmela cried.

"I got creased," Babcock said. "It's a flesh wound at best."

"But what exactly did you do?" Carmela asked. "What did you throw at Spears's feet that made the alligators change course and rush at him?"

"It looked like you tossed some kind of leather pouch," Ava said.

"It *was* a leather pouch," Babcock said. "I

soaked it with blood. My blood."

"You squeezed your own blood out so it soaked the leather?" Carmela said. She'd never heard of anything quite so cunning. Or so brave.

"Dear Lord," Ava said. "The gators smelled your blood and figured it was something good to eat."

Carmela gazed at Babcock, a question on her face. Why was he carrying a leather pouch in his pocket? "What was in the pouch, Edgar?" she asked.

Babcock ducked his head.

"Edgar?"

The serious look on his face gradually faded to a sheepish smile. "I kind of hate to admit this, Carmela, but it was your engagement ring."

"What!" Carmela said.

Ava placed both hands on top of her head as if she feared her brains would explode. "Tell me you didn't!"

"I had to do *something*," Babcock said. "Spears would've killed us. The leather, the blood, I figured it would create a tantalizing lure."

"I have to admit, it was a slick diversion," Ava said. "Sure saved our skin."

"Detective," one of the officers said to

Babcock, "do you want me to bandage your hand?"

"Wait one," Babcock said.

Carmela just stood there in the moonlight, gazing at Babcock, the man who'd thought fast and saved their lives. Tears rolled down her cheeks; her heart swelled with love.

"How many carats did you sacrifice to that big old gator-monster?" Ava asked.

Babcock shrugged. "Three."

"Three carats?" Ava said. "That's a serious diamond." She turned to Carmela. "You're a lucky girl."

"Don't I know it," Carmela said. She couldn't pull her gaze from Babcock, knowing she'd almost lost him. That they'd almost lost each other.

"Of course, now that ring is gone forever," Ava said. She turned to Babcock, a sad look on her face. "Tell me, Detective, what was the cut? What'd the ring look like?"

"It was an antique old mine-cut diamond from the late 1800s," Babcock said.

Ava clapped a hand to her chest. "Lord have mercy. To think a gorgeous rock like that got gobbled up by a nasty gator."

"That's the old boy right over there," Babcock said.

Carmela and Ava turned in unison to gaze at the enormous alligator that was staring straight at them. Its bumpy eyes held a malevolent gleam. Its row of crooked, jagged teeth seemed to glow in the moonlight. The critter looked as if it had just crawled out from the depths of the Barataria bayou, where it had reigned supreme for five decades.

"Bad alligator," Ava said. "Bad, bad alligator."

Babcock choked back a chuckle, even as he cradled his wounded hand. "It's not a dog, Ava."

"But he swallowed Carmela's ring," Ava said tearfully.

My ring, Carmela thought. *Babcock went out and bought me a beautiful antique engagement ring.* She was thrilled by such a romantic gesture, but terribly sad that it had been lost. That she never got a chance to see the ring, to slip it on her finger and bask in its sparkle.

Babcock reached out and took Carmela's left hand, then pressed it to his lips. "I love you, Carmela. You're wonderful, adorable, and the most important person in the world to me."

"I love you, too," Carmela murmured back.

Ava clasped her hands together across her chest. "Young love. Well, sort of young." She turned her attention to one of the police officers and batted her eyes. "Excuse me, officer . . ."

A shadow fell across Babcock's face. "Sweetheart," he said, "I am so sorry about your ring . . ."

"Never mind the ring," Carmela said. "All I care about is you. And getting you to a doctor." She was suddenly flustered. "Where are the EMTs? Should we walk back to the party? *Can* you walk back?"

As if to answer her, Babcock put both arms around Carmela and pulled her close. As he nuzzled the top of her head, Carmela felt his warm breath on her, making her feel all tingly inside.

"You know," Babcock whispered, "there might be a way to get your ring back."

Carmela looked up at him, a ray of hope lighting her face. "You really think so?"

"How would you feel," Babcock asked, "about a pair of alligator shoes?"

SCRAPBOOK, STAMPING, AND CRAFT TIPS FROM LAURA CHILDS

Long on Sentiment, Easy on Effort

If you're often pressed for time — or don't want to deal with a lot of embellishments — choose a smaller album for your scrapbooking efforts.

A 5-by-7-inch or a 6-by-8-inch album will allow you just enough space for one or two photos as well as a line or two of text.

Title Pages

If you're undecided about the theme of your scrapbook, leave the first page — the title page — blank. Fill your scrapbook with photos, memorabilia, jottings, etc., and *then* go back to your title page. Once your album is completed, you'll have a much better handle on what type of headline or introduction you want on that all-important first page.

Creating a NonTraditional Album

Remember, your scrapbook doesn't always have to take the form of a traditional album with a fancy cover and inside pages. You can scrapbook on smaller 4-by-6-inch cards and create a kind of "flipbook," holding it all together with one or two loose-leaf binder rings, or stitching it with yarn. This type of casual album is also the perfect way to incorporate postcards, scraps of fabric, recipe cards, and greeting cards.

Wedding Scrapbooks

The bride and groom certainly take center stage when it comes to wedding photography, but don't forget to take photos of all the wonderful aspects that make a wedding so memorable. These might include the venue (garden, poolside, old barn), tabletop décor, food and wine, candles and lanterns, limos or horse-drawn carriages, flowers and corsages, etc. And when designing your wedding album, be sure to put the invitation on the very first page. It will serve as the perfect introduction to this special day!

Travel Scrapbooks

Taking a trip? Besides keepsake photos, be sure to save airline tickets, maps, concert programs, napkins with restaurant logos, and hotel postcards and brochures. If you hear a fun fact while traveling, jot it down and add it to your scrapbook when you get home — it will help make your trip remembrance extra special.

Create Your Own Stationery

You can use rubber stamps for more than just embellishing scrapbook pages. Select stamps you've been using for borders — leaves, flowers, swooshes, butterflies, teacups, etc. — and stamp them on your stationery or note cards. If you're using light-colored ink, you can create overall background patterns. If the ink is dark, just do the top and bottom of the pages. Initial stamps also look terrific as headings and give your stationery a personalized touch.

FAVORITE NEW ORLEANS RECIPES

EASY OVEN CHICKEN JAMBALAYA

1 chicken, cut into 8 pieces
oil for frying
1 large onion, chopped
4 tomatoes, chopped
1 green pepper, chopped
2 stalks celery, chopped
8 oz. uncooked rice
1 1/2 pints chicken stock
8 oz. ham or sausage, cut into pieces

Preheat oven to 350 degrees. Fry chicken in oil until golden brown. Place in a large casserole dish. Fry onion and tomatoes, then stir in green pepper and celery and fry for 3 to 4 minutes. Add fried vegetables to casserole dish. Fry rice until golden, adding a little more oil, if necessary. Add rice to casserole dish and stir everything together. Pour in chicken stock and simmer in oven for 11/2 hours. Ten minutes before serving, add ham or sausage and return to oven to heat through. Serves 4 to 5.

BAYOU CRAB CHOWDER

4 spring onions, diced
1 stalk celery, diced
6 Tbsp. butter
3 potatoes, diced
1 Tbsp. salt
1 quart water
1 1/2 to 2 lb. shrimp, crabmeat, or scallops, in any combination
1 pint heavy whipping cream

Using a large saucepan, sauté spring onions and celery in butter until translucent. Add potatoes, salt, and water and bring to a boil. Simmer for 30 minutes. Add seafood. When seafood is heated through (be careful not to overcook), add in whipping cream, making sure not to let mixture boil. Serve immediately. Serves 4 to 6.

CRAWFISH BEIGNETS

cooking oil
1 egg, beaten
1 lb. chopped crawfish meat (or shrimp)
1 1/2 tsp. butter, melted
salt and pepper to taste
1/3 cup flour

Sauce

3/4 cup mayonnaise
1/2 cup ketchup
1/4 tsp. hot sauce

In an electric skillet or deep-fat fryer, heat oil to 375 degrees. Combine egg, crawfish (or shrimp), butter, salt, and pepper. Stir in flour until well blended. Drop spoonfuls of batter, a few at a time, into hot oil. Fry until golden brown on all sides. Drain on paper towels. Mix mayonnaise, ketchup, and hot sauce together and serve as an accompaniment. Yields 10–12 beignets.

MANGO SHRIMP IN ENDIVE LEAVES

1/2 lb. shrimp, cooked, peeled, deveined, and chopped
1/2 mango, finely diced (about 1 cup)
2 Tbsp. fresh cilantro, chopped
2 Tbsp. olive oil
1 Tbsp. fresh lime juice
2 tsp. fresh ginger, grated
kosher salt and black pepper
24 endive leaves (from about 3 heads)

In a large mixing bowl, combine the shrimp, mango, cilantro, olive oil, lime juice, and ginger. Add salt and pepper to taste. When thoroughly combined, spoon the shrimp mixture into the endive leaves. Yields 4 entrée servings or 24 small appetizers.

SURPRISE BISCUITS

4 Tbsp. mayonnaise
2 cups whole milk
2 cups self-rising flour

Preheat oven to 450 degrees. Combine all ingredients in bowl and toss with fork until batter is moist and hangs together. Drop by spoon onto a greased cookie sheet, making 24 small biscuits. Bake for 7 to 8 minutes. Serve with butter and jam. (Tip: Can also be gently rolled out and cut with biscuit cutter.)

LAZY GIRL PEACH PIE

1 stick butter
1 cup flour
1 cup sugar
1 cup milk
1 (15-oz.) can peaches
1/2 tsp. cinnamon
1/2 tsp. nutmeg
1 Tbsp. brown sugar

Preheat oven to 350 degrees. Melt butter in 8-inch glass or Pyrex pan. Combine flour, sugar, and milk and pour this mixture over butter. Reserving juice, spread peaches over batter. Now pour juice over mixture. Combine cinnamon, nutmeg, and brown sugar and sprinkle evenly over the top. Bake for 30 to 40 minutes or until brown. Serves 4. (Tip: Wonderful with ice cream!)

SOUTHERN SPOON BREAD

1 cup cornmeal
1 tsp. salt
1 Tbsp. butter
1 cup boiling water
2 cups buttermilk
2 eggs, separated

Preheat oven to 400 degrees. Add cornmeal, salt, and butter to boiling water. Cool. Add buttermilk. Fold in well-beaten yolks and mix. Then fold in stiffly beaten egg whites. Pour mixture in a greased baking dish and bake in oven for 30 to 35 minutes. Serve as a side dish, scooping mixture out with a spoon. Serves 4.

NEW ORLEANS FRENCH DRESSING

1/2 tsp. salt
1/2 tsp. sugar
1/4 tsp. pepper
1/2 tsp. paprika
1/4 tsp. prepared mustard
2 Tbsp. vinegar

1/2 tsp. Worcestershire sauce
1/2 cup salad oil

Combine all ingredients in bowl and beat with a wire whisk until well blended. Makes about 3/4 cup.

TANDY'S MICROWAVE FUDGE
4 cups confectioners' sugar
1/2 cup unsweetened cocoa powder
1/4 cup milk
1/2 cup butter
1 tsp. vanilla extract
1/2 cup chopped nuts

Grease a 9-by-9-inch dish. In a microwave-able bowl, stir together confectioners' sugar and cocoa. Pour in milk and add butter, but do not mix. Heat bowl in microwave until butter is melted, about two minutes. Stir in vanilla extract and chopped nuts until mixture is smooth. Pour mixture into greased dish and chill in freezer for 10 minutes. Cut into squares and enjoy. Yields about 9 squares.

CARMELA'S DOG TREATS
2 small jars strained beef baby food
1/4 cup nonfat dry milk
1/2 cup wheat germ

Preheat oven to 325 degrees. Mix all ingredients together and shape into small balls. Arrange on cookie sheet and flatten with fork. Bake for 15 to 20 minutes. Store in refrigerator when cool. Yields 12 to 20 treats, depending on size. (The size of the cookies, not the size of your dog!)

ABOUT THE AUTHOR

Laura Childs is the *New York Times* best-selling author of the Scrapbooking Mysteries, the Tea Shop Mysteries, and the Cackleberry Club Mysteries. In her previous life she was CEO of her own marketing firm, authored several screenplays, and produced a reality TV show.